Bound to the Bear

ALSO BY KATHY LYONS

The Bear Who Loved Me
License to Shift
For the Bear's Eyes Only
Alpha Unleashed

Bound to the Bear

Book Five of Grizzlies Gone Wild

KATHY LYONS

New York Boston

Copyright © 2018 by Kathy Lyons
Excerpt from *Taming Her Mate* copyright © 2018 by Kathy Lyons
Cover design by Brian Lemus
Cover copyright © 2018 by Hachette Book Group, Inc.

Forever Yours
Hachette Book Group
1290 Avenue of the Americas
New York, NY 10104
forever-romance.com
twitter.com/foreverromance

First published as an ebook and print on demand edition: September 2018

Forever Yours is an imprint of Grand Central Publishing. The Forever Yours name and logo are trademarks of Hachette Book Group, Inc.

The publisher is not responsible for websites (or their content) that are not owned by the publisher.

The Hachette Speakers Bureau provides a wide range of authors for speaking events. To find out more, go to www.hachettespeakersbureau.com or call (866) 376-6591.

ISBNs: 978-1-5387-6213-4 (ebook), 978-1-5387-6214-1 (print on demand)

Bound to the Bear

Chapter 1

I need a clue."

Cecilia Lu stared across her microscope at her coworker. He was snoring quietly on the couch. His entire body looked like a scarecrow with the stuffing pulled out, and no wonder. They'd both been logging twenty-hour days and were no closer to solving the mystery of the Detroit Flu than when they'd first showed up a week ago.

"No, really," she continued. "You know, like a place to look. Because right now, as far as I can tell, the answer could be in the neurotransmitters. Or the blood. It could be the phases of the moon because I sure as hell don't know."

She stared at the monitor where it was trained on their latest patient. The image on the screen was just too unbelievable to credit. But when she blinked her eyes and looked again, there was Brittany still looking like something out of a horror film. Brittany was a sweet girl. A gymnast with a B+ average at school and a laugh that made Cecilia think of unicorns snorting. It was both earthy and magical at the same time. But instead of the perky strawberry-blond girl who appeared in her social media profile, Brittany now had reddish black fur on her face, slit-shaped yellow eyes, and nails that extended in sharp, curved points like claws. Even her ears had changed into tufted points.

Impossible.

The girl had come in hysterical and bloody; she'd tried to claw out her own eyes. They'd knocked her out in the ER and sent her straight up here to the Weird Ward as it was now called. Yes, the CDC had jurisdiction of all the strange cases because—the theory went—the CDC had all the answers.

Not.

And now Brittany lay slack-jawed and restrained, but all Cecilia could see was the dark hair against white hospital sheets.

For most people, the illness put them in bed with congestion and a killer headache. Others threw up for a couple days, which was how the disease had gotten its "flu" name. This last outbreak had added hallucinations to the list of symptoms, and now half the city was in bed seeing elephants wearing tutus on their ceiling. Clinics and hospitals quickly became overwhelmed by society's most vulnerable members—the elderly and the very young. Add in crazy people seeing things, and the ERs had gotten many times the normal cases of gunshots and car crashes.

And then there were Cecilia's cases. People like Brittany who came in deformed. Some arrived crazy. Others went insane afterward. Every one so far had died and their autopsies showed deformities in their brains. Something happened to their nerves causing them to warp. And the brain had a whole lot of nerves to warp.

"Maybe I should get something to eat." Her stomach rumbled at the thought, but that might just be a reaction to the sludge they called coffee in this hospital. She'd been drinking it nonstop since the day she arrived. "Some kind of brain food." She leaned back in her chair and stretched her spine. How long had she been slumped over that microscope? "Bet I'd know the best foods if I were a brain surgeon. And I'd know if the answer is in the neurotransmitters, too. If only I'd studied neurology, then maybe I'd have a clue."

Or maybe not. Dennis on the couch—the one who had collapsed in exhaustion—was one of the top neurologists in the world, and he was as confused as she was.

Cecilia hopped off her stool and stretched her aching back. She thought about ditching her lab coat as she went in search of brain food, but it had deep pockets that held her many different colored pens, her Detroit Flu dedicated notepad, and her phone. No sense in—

"Dr. Hayes? Are you Dr. Hayes?"

Cecilia spun around on her toe, pretending for a moment that she was Brittany doing a gymnastic move. Such are the things her brain did when it was exhausted.

"Sorry," she said as she finished her spin, smiling as she…

Whoa.

Big guy. Big black guy with the broadest shoulders she'd ever seen and a jagged scar that cut across his jaw. It was an old one, probably happened years ago and had never been stitched properly. Poor guy. A good plastic surgeon could have made it nearly invisible. Instead, it was one of the first things anyone saw when they looked at his face. But even with the scar, she had to admit he looked pretty sexy. It wasn't just his muscles and cut body, but also because his expression seemed warm and open. Like he was a big, soft place for her whole being to rest.

She blinked, startled by her own thoughts. Must be the exhaustion. Meanwhile, she smiled as she dropped down onto her heels and walked toward him. "Dr. Hayes isn't here. He had to go back to DC." Or more accurately, he'd fled when he realized he was as clueless as the rest of them. She hadn't thought the man was a coward, but two hours before the quarantine, he declared he had "important business" in DC and hopped on the last flight out of Detroit.

Cowardly wuss.

"Can I help you?"

The man gave her a weary smile as he gestured to her name on the lab coat. "Dr. Lu? Are you with the CDC?"

"Yup. Started with them right out of school." Then she abruptly jumped to his side. "You're bleeding!" His forearm had dark red spots in the shape of an animal bite. Most of it had sealed over, but some of the punctures were jagged and still bleeding sluggishly.

She grabbed his wrist with her right hand, turning the wound toward the light. Wow. He had big hands and it was impossible not to notice the strength in his wrist and forearm. Attraction stirred inside her, and she covered her embarrassment by yanking gloves out of a nearby box.

"Let's get you down to the ER. Did you know the animal that bit you?" There had been scores of reports of pets going crazy. Docile lapdogs suddenly becoming vicious terrors. Old cats that barely moved from their spot in the sun abruptly tearing around and howling. The CDC didn't have reliable statistics on it, not with the human problem their main focus. But Cecilia had heard enough stories just from the hospital staff to guess that the two were related.

She wanted to see if she could isolate the same bizarre enzyme in afflicted pets as she'd discovered in her patients, but she wasn't a veterinarian. She'd already sent the request up the chain of command, but it would take some time. Plus asking the police to bring in any "crazy pets" that they found was like asking guys in a war zone to stop fighting for their lives to play with the wildlife. It was frustrating because she could take the samples herself. You didn't need to be a veterinarian to pull blood and saliva, but she didn't have the credentials or the resources to get the pets in the first place.

"Um, yeah," the man answered. "It's okay. I was an army medic. Already treated it."

She rolled his wrist to look at the underside of the bite. "That's a really big bite. Was this dog a pet?" She looked up, her mind scrambling with hope. Was this her clue? "Was it unusual for him to react like this? I mean, if he was a pet, did he suddenly get wild? Do you know where he is? Can you take me to him?"

Her questions came out rapid fire, her mind already sorting through research possibilities. She steadfastly ignored the fact that the last thing she should do is wander off after dog saliva samples. But it wasn't like she was making progress here.

"Yeah, I can," the man said. "And this was definitely weird."

She snorted. "That's what they call us. The Weird Ward." Then she sobered as she realized that was probably an inappropriate comment. They were the CDC, after all. They were supposed to inspire confidence and scientific know-how. "I mean…um…" She flushed. "Look, let's get you down to the ER to get those wounds cleaned up." She wanted to take samples of his blood and swab the wounds even though he'd already doused it with antiseptic. You never knew what interesting stuff could survive an alcohol swipe. And she wanted to stay with him. He was the first warm, comfortable person she'd been around in a very long time. Everyone else was either a patient, panicked family, or another uptight scientist like herself, completely absorbed in fighting a possible pandemic. "Give me the address of the dog. I'll have the cops pick it up."

"Cops are spread too thin, and nobody gets close to my dog without me."

She pounced on his words. "So this was your dog? Your pet? He doesn't bite people normally, does he?"

"Of course not." He turned and used his free hand to grab her elbow and started leading her out of the lab. "I can take you to him, no problem."

She laughed as she fell in step with him. "I'm not equipped to handle a dog. Certainly not an angry one."

"It'll be fine. He's my—"

"First things first. Let's get you to the ER. What's your name? I'm Dr. Lu, but you can call me Cecilia."

"Hank Coleman," he said, extending his good hand to shake hers. His palm was huge, easily dwarfing hers, but it surrounded her in a pleasing warmth. As did his eyes. Light brown in a dark face. The edges crinkled when he smiled at her, and though everything about him felt sexy, what she most noticed was how he felt calm. As if everything inside him was quiet when every part of her was edgy, ragged, and way too caffeinated. She liked that about him, and she felt herself settle into his rhythms as they walked.

"Nice to meet you, Hank," she said, her words coming out a little breathless. "Tell me more about your dog. What breed? How old is he? How long have you had him?"

They walked together to the elevator as she peppered him with questions. He answered easily, frowning when he couldn't remember the creature's exact age and had no clue about the breed.

The dog was a mutt, he said, with the sweetest temperament until this morning.

They stepped into the elevator and she waited for him to continue. He was just talking about his dog, but she loved the cadence of his deep voice. She could stand there listening to it for hours just to hear the rich timber of it. But he'd apparently run out of words and stood there, looking awkward.

"Tell me more about when he bit you. Did you notice anything different? Like was he foaming at the mouth or barking strangely?"

"Um, nothing like that. He was angry. Wouldn't stop barking." His words stumbled to a halt and she frowned. Most patients couldn't stop talking about their attack. They usually rambled in a disorganized way, often focusing on all the wrong details. But Hank, here, seemed to be a man of very few words. That made him intriguing to her—and sexy as hell—so she focused even more on the details of his face, his body, and his words.

"What did you do that made him attack?" she pressed.

He rubbed his face, and she began to think something was off. As if he felt uncomfortable and that made her uneasy. But before she could ask him for more details, the elevator doors opened. They were on the main floor, but instead of heading to the ER, he steered her toward the outside door.

"This way," she said as she tugged away from his grip. Or she tried to. He held her fast. "The ER—"

"I don't need the ER. My car's in the parking lot."

She dug in her heels. She wasn't one to judge based on size, color, or even an ugly scar, but she also wasn't stupid. "I'm not going with you to get your dog."

"He's in my car. I brought him in because he's not right." Hank gave her an aw-shucks kind of shrug that was downright adorable. "That's why I went to the CDC. He's not okay. Thought you guys would know something about that."

She wished.

"You've got him in a cage? In your car?"

He nodded. "Look, I can keep him quiet. I just want you to look at him."

"Let me get security to help." Safety had been drilled into her from her first days at the CDC. Protocol stated that she not walk outside with him even if it was just across the street into a well-lit parking lot. Except when she looked around, security was nowhere to be seen. Probably all in the ER dealing with a full house of hallucinations. All the hospitals had been overrun since the first appearance of the Detroit Flu. But once the quarantine went into effect, it had been wall-to-wall patients in every ER in the city. And the clinics. And even a dental surgery center.

Hank turned and looked her in the eye. His demeanor was quiet, his entire body language gentle. "Look," he said softly. "I know I look scary, but I really am not here to hurt you. I served honorably as an army medic. I save people. Here, I'll show you." He pulled out his wallet and showed her his military ID.

She flushed, feeling stupid for doubting him. He didn't seem scary. In truth, she was really attracted to him. His car was right across the street. But most important of all, she really wanted to look at his dog. She'd seen too many of the Flu victims at their worst. She needed to know if Hank's dog was acting just like that. If there were physical changes like with the humans. Plus, dogs didn't get hysterical like humans did. At least not in the same way. If this was finally the big clue she'd been waiting for, then she was really anxious to get on with it. It seemed silly to wait for security when the dog was just across the street.

"Okay," she finally said. "Let's go."

His body softened then with a smile that came from deep inside. She could see the relief as it flowed through him, but it didn't quite meet his eyes. What she saw there was more of an apology. As if he was sorry for the trouble he was causing. Which was silly because this had to be the clue she'd been praying for. And how nice of the universe to deliver it in such a sexy package.

So she kept him talking, asking him questions as fast as they came to her, and they came really fast. He answered in frustrating monosyllables or something worse like "I don't know. You'll just have to see." Talk about nonspecific.

They made it to a beat-up Chrysler 300, and he unlocked the back door and swung it wide with a see-for-yourself gesture. She started to duck to look inside when he caught her arm.

"Dr. Lu?"

She paused in a semi-crouch. "Yes?"

"I've been ordered to do this by my alpha. I disagree, but only an idiot disobeys in a crisis. And I don't see another way."

She didn't know what to think. His words didn't make any sense, but when she started to react, he added two more words.

"I'm sorry."

And then it was too late.

Chapter 2

The attack came startlingly quick. So fast, Cecelia wasn't even sure it was happening at first. She suddenly felt his large hands on her back and she was shoved down, hard.

Even then she was more confused than alarmed. She'd face-planted straight into the seat. There was no dog, no cage, nothing but an empty back seat. Her nose smashed flat and her breath was cut off as she tried to inhale leather.

Her mind started to catch up then. She needed to breathe, and her nose hurt. She cried out and reared backward, but he was damned fast, gripping her arms and wrenching them behind her. She felt hard thin plastic drawing her wrists tight together. A zip tie? And while she was still processing that, he wrapped one meaty arm around her knees and restrained her ankles.

What the hell? One second she was looking for a dog, and the next, she was hog-tied and he was shoving her legs into the backseat of his car.

Damn it, fight!

She screamed.

She screamed like her life depended on it. And she wrenched her body every which way, but it was too late. She was crunched with her knees at her nose as he shut the car door.

Oh shit! Oh shitshitshit!

She kicked back as hard as she could, but the door was solid. She tried to scramble upright while her shoulders screamed, and she tried to wriggle her hands free.

It was useless. And then he was in the front seat, turning the ignition, and slamming the car into gear as he pulled out of the parking lot. Didn't anyone hear her? She was lying sideways on the seat and screaming with every breath.

"Help! Help! Help!"

He didn't even flinch. Damn it, why hadn't she noticed he was right by the far exit? It was late at night. No one heard her bellowing except him.

Fine. She'd bring her feet around and kick the back of his seat. Anything to disrupt him. And maybe she could get her hands on the door handle.

"Help!" Her words were a constant scream. Damn it! She kicked hard against the back of his seat.

He grunted, but that was it. He just kept driving. No time to waste. They were traveling farther and farther from the hospital.

"Help! Help! Help!"

It was awkward as hell, but she twisted on the seat. Pushed with her knees and…there! She fingered the car door handle and pulled. And pulled again. And pulled.

Nothing.

And now she was out of breath, gasping as she pulled in air.

"I'm not going to hurt you." His voice was calm and filled with an apology that might have touched her if she weren't being abducted.

She hauled on the door handle again. Hell. The child protection lock was on. No way was she getting out from the backseat. Fine, she'd just climb into the front. Or maybe she'd head-butt him hard enough to knock him unconscious. Something. Anything.

She fell backward as he accelerated onto the freeway.

"I've got information on the Detroit Flu."

She saw the headlights of another car. She was flat on her back on the seat, but at the sight of the headlights, she put extra force into screaming. If she could just get her feet around, maybe she could break the passenger window.

"I'm not going to hurt you," he said, his voice cutting in whenever she had to draw breath. "I've got data. Information."

"Help! Help!"

"You have to calm down."

Her wrists were slick and painful. Blood? Sweat? She didn't know and didn't care. She drew back and shoved her feet outward as hard as she could against the window.

Like hitting a brick wall.

She did it again. Nothing.

"We're trying to do the right thing," he said. "You're the CDC. You need this data."

She kicked her feet again. WTF? Why wouldn't the window break?

"I just want to give you the data. Then I'll take you back to the hospital."

She wasn't screaming anymore. All her concentration was on

slamming her feet into the window, which would not break. Her heart was pounding, and she couldn't catch her breath. Why the hell wouldn't the damn window break?

"What's your email? I'll email you the data."

She didn't want to listen to him. She didn't want to hear his world-weary tone or his false promises that he wouldn't hurt her. Except, of course she did. She wasn't escaping. And head-butting him while they were on the freeway going sixty was a quick way to suicide. But most of all, he kept saying weird things. Stuff that she didn't expect to come from an abductor. Who kidnapped a woman then asked to send data to her email?

She stared at him, her breath coming in short, gasping pants through her burning throat. She couldn't possibly have heard him correctly. But when she stared at him, he was holding up his phone.

"Your email address, Dr. Lu. Spell it for Siri, please."

She frowned. He had a message app open with the microphone turned on.

"You want my email address?"

"I'll text it to my boss. He'll email you the data. They sent it to me, but I can't email and drive."

"Abduction is a felony. It carries the death penalty."

"No, it doesn't. And Michigan abolished the death penalty in 1846. One of the few good things about this state."

Great. Her abductor had a wry sense of humor.

"Life in prison sucks, too," she said. "Most people say it's worse."

"Nah. Death is always worse." His gaze met hers in the rearview mirror. "At least it is for me. I can survive just about anything."

She believed it. Something about the flatness in his expression had her believing he'd seen a lot worse things than she could even imagine. And while she was processing that, he set his phone down.

"I'm not going to hurt you, Dr. Lu. I swear. But we're not exactly normal people here, so we didn't know how to get you this information. People are dying. We're trying to help."

"So you abduct the nearest doctor?"

He huffed out his breath. "I went to the CDC. I was looking for Dr. Hayes."

"He bailed. To DC."

He snorted. "Figures. So yeah, I grabbed you. You were awake and right there. But only to make you believe and to give you the data. Now will you please spell your email address for Siri?"

God, he seemed so reasonable. But why the hell hadn't he just asked for her email address at the hospital? "You didn't have to throw me into your car for my email address."

"You have to see the truth before you believe the data. Please?" He tilted the phone at her. And damn it, it wasn't like she could kick out his car window and leap out. She'd tried. And that's when she realized why.

"Bulletproof windows?"

"Yes."

Hell. Who ran around Detroit with bulletproof windows? Gangsters, drug lords, anyone who lived near 8 Mile assuming they could afford it. She swallowed. Just whom was she dealing with?

"We're trying to help, Dr. Lu."

She nodded and pitched her voice to his phone, spelling out her email address so that it appeared in full on the screen.

"Thank you," he said as he hit send. "They'll send you all the data they've got."

She blew out a breath. "Okay. So take me back—"

"Well, here's the thing. You're not going to believe any of it until you see for yourself. Like really see."

She sighed, reluctantly starting to believe his tale. Obviously, he was involved in crime of some sort. He'd zip tied her with professional speed and had bulletproof windows. And since the CDC had already figured out that whatever was causing the Detroit Flu was most likely man-made, it stood to reason that a criminal element might have information they didn't.

"Data is data," she said. "We don't have to see anything but the numbers. If it's repeatable then we don't care where it came from."

She watched his mouth tighten. He didn't say anything, just waited her out. In fact, it was the exact expression she used when her aunts started talking to her about how to catch a husband. She pressed her lips together, assumed a fake expression of interest, and waited until they finished with their nonsense.

"Do you even know how real science works? If it's a real lead, you just have to send it to us. We'll look at it."

"Because you always open files from strange email addresses."

Okay, so he had a point. "Fine. You have my email address. Take me back to the hospital and I'll look at it."

"You have to see first. Otherwise, you won't believe."

She snorted. "Let me guess. Weird body changes. Hair. Claws, even dental. Look, we've seen the disfigurements—"

"Shape-shifters, Dr. Lu. The Detroit Flu activates shifter DNA. Full shifters go adrenaline-rush crazy. Normal people just feel sick and hallucinate for a bit. But those with only some shifter DNA? They become different. Hybrids, if they don't die from the stress."

Ah hell, she'd been kidnapped by a crazy person. Then she snorted. Of course, he was crazy. He was a kidnapper!

"Werewolves. Bear-shifters. Cat-shifters. All of them exist. And yeah, I know you don't believe me, which is why you have to see. But I can't shift while driving my car so I'm taking you somewhere safe to show you."

No sense arguing. She needed to focus only on the true details in his crazy reality. "Where? Where is safe?"

"The Griz have a central—"

His words were cut off as his phone vibrated. He grunted under his breath, then frowned. She saw it distinctly as he cut her a hard look.

"Make a sound—any sound—and I'll knock you unconscious. Got it?"

His expression was fierce, and she immediately nodded. Let the crazy person think that she was cooperating, but was she really going to be quiet? When the person on the other end of the line might be able to save her?

She was still undecided because, honestly, she absolutely believed he could knock her out. Quickly, quietly, and probably while driving at sixty miles an hour. But maybe that was a chance she was willing to take. Until his very first word as he pressed the phone to his ear.

"Mother?"

Damn it. Any woman who had raised a crazy kidnapper was not going to help the kidnappee. She grimaced and adjusted her position on the seat. He was just pulling off the freeway. Maybe she could use his distraction—and his slower speed—to engineer some kind of escape. Though one look at the neighborhood had her gut tightening in fear. This did not look like a neighborhood where she should be wandering around alone after dark. Or in full daylight.

Meanwhile, Hank—if that was his real name—growled low and deep in his throat. It was a dark animal sound, and it made goose bumps rise on her skin.

"Get out. Get out now!"

Cecilia's gaze shot to him. He wasn't looking at her but at the road as he abruptly spun the car around in a hard U-turn. She saw his hand grip the steering wheel and his jaw clenched in his large, square face. It was the side with the scar on it, and she watched the jagged edge of it pulse under the sporadic streetlights.

"Fine. Then bar the door." Pause. "With a table! Anything. Hell, get everything! I'm coming."

And he was coming. He ran straight through the stop sign and back up onto the freeway. Before he'd been going a respectable sixty miles per hour, heading toward seventy. Now he blew past that and she watched in horror as he topped eighty. She was sure he'd have gone faster, but he was already taking the off ramp. She was up now and braced against the car door so she could read the signs.

She wasn't a native of the city, but even she knew this was not a good area. And yet, he was torpedoing down the streets like it was safe. Or perhaps like he was the baddest person around. And then he started talking. It took her a moment to realize he was speaking to her because his tone was so casual. And even then, she had to replay his words in her head just to make sure she'd heard him correctly.

"So you're going to get that demonstration differently, Dr. Lu. I've got a situation here, and it's dangerous. We're going to Mother's house. Not my mother, but a woman who takes in shifter strays. We all look out for her because being a shifter kid is hard, and she's been there for us no matter the breed." He sighed. "I know you don't believe any of this, but one of her kids is in trouble and I'm going to help. I'll undo your restraints, but I promise you, if you run, you'll find a whole lot worse trouble outside."

Cecilia nodded and tried to smile with genuine warmth. It probably came out more like humor-the-crazy-person because he rolled his eyes. Weird that, given he was speeding down the street straight through red lights and everything.

"I'm not crazy. This is real."

"I believe you," she lied.

"And it's dangerous."

"Right." Her gaze cut to the apocalyptic neighborhood. "Dangerous."

"Yeah. And it has werewolves, too."

Of course, it did. Which is why she resolved to run as far and as fast as she could the second he stopped the car.

Chapter 3

Hank glared at the woman zip-tied in his backseat. She didn't believe him. And she was planning to run the minute he parked.

Damn it, why had Simon ordered him to do this? No non-shifter doctor would listen. She might as well have pulled her white lab coat right over her eyes. She'd labeled him a lunatic the minute he'd mentioned shifters, which was apparently even worse than kidnapper because at least she'd been willing to talk when he was just a criminal. After the screaming, that is. Damn, what a set of lungs she had.

Didn't matter. Mother was having a crisis and he was two blocks away.

"Don't fight me on this, Cecilia. It's too dangerous." He used her first name to see if that made a difference. He'd gone with "Dr. Lu" when he was trying to be deferential. Educated people tended to like that, but he could already tell she wasn't susceptible to flattery. So he was trying to be friendly.

No go. She just smiled that false smile and was clearly counting the seconds until she could run. Which meant he had two seconds to come up with a new plan because he was arriving at Mother's right now.

He pulled into the driveway, slamming the car to a stop. They were in werewolf territory and who knew how many of the dogs had drunk the tainted water. Simon had put out the word as soon as he could, but bears and dogs in Detroit did not get along. Hadn't for generations. Knowing these wolves, they probably liked the aggression rush the tainted tap gave to full-blooded shifters.

He glanced at the night sky. Nearly a full moon. Just what they needed…not. Though the wolves claimed they didn't react to the phase of the moon, Mother had called bullshit on that years ago. And she lived in the thick of it, so she would know.

He hit the send button on his phone. No words in the text but Mother would know he was outside and pull open her door. Which meant it was time to run. But first, he popped open the big blade on his Swiss army knife.

He heard Cecilia gasp and he shot her a hard look. "Extend your feet to the door. Be ready to run."

Her eyes widened and once again, he regretted the fear he'd put on her face. Damn it, he was not a man to terrorize innocent scientists. He popped open his car door, took a deep whiff of Detroit air as it mixed with wet dog, and rushed to her door.

She was ready; her legs were extended and she had a fixed smile on her face. He could feel her tension in the air and see the twitch of her gaze as she looked past him to where she meant to run. It would be a bad choice. There wasn't a cop around for miles and plenty of regular human trouble she could get into on the way. Even worse, he smelled werewolf thick in the air. Damn it, they were too close.

He grabbed her ankles and slit the plastic in one quick move.

Then he grabbed her by the waist and helped her scramble out of the car. The minute her feet touched pavement, she took off.

Or at least she tried. He still had a hand around her waist and when she surged forward, it was just the momentum he needed to throw her over his shoulder. She screamed and kicked as he moved—double time—to Mother's front door, all the while keeping his eye out for werewolves. Given the way she was wailing, she was going to attract the whole damn pack.

He hit the front porch and Mother swung open the door. Her eyes were huge in her weathered face, but she stepped out of the way while he barreled through. Then she slammed and bolted the door with a speed one wouldn't expect given her age.

"Help! Help!"

"Shut up, you damn fool!" Mother snapped as Hank set Cecilia down on her feet. He wasn't too gentle about it because she'd just nailed him in the center of his sternum. Her knees buckled enough that she tumbled backward onto the couch. She was going to leap up again but he kept a hand in the center of her chest. And—damn it—he was human enough to feel the soft mounds of her breasts. It was a damn shame that this was the first time he'd touched a woman's breasts in nearly two years, but he also felt the way her pulse beat like a frightened rabbit. She took a deep breath, obviously prepared to scream again, but he shoved her hard enough to cut it off.

"Stop it or I'll gag you," he said.

He didn't think she would listen, but then Mother racked her shotgun and aimed it straight at Cecilia.

"Why would you bring a damned fool here?" Mother demanded.

"Jesus, Mother, aim that outside." Hank stretched his hand back, knocking the shotgun toward the window.

"I'll aim that where I want in my house," she said pulling it right back to Cecilia's pale face. "And if she don't shut up—"

"She's a doctor. She's going to help fix things."

"She can't help if she gets us all kill—"

Roar.

It's hard to describe a grizzly roar up close. To someone who's never heard it, it's like putting your face right next to a locomotive as it speeds by. But even that is just a machine. Loud and overwhelming, but still impersonal. A grizzly roar is damned personal. It contains threat and fury headed straight at you. It can be felt in the vibration against your ribs and in every hair on your body.

And that's what all three of them felt. A roar coming straight from the door behind the couch. Obviously, Mother had slid the couch in front of the basement door to block it. And now that he took a second to look around, he saw that she'd shoved the kitchen table and a couple chairs against the far end of the couch, too. Not that any of that would stop a mature grizzly from getting through. Fortunately, this particular bear-shifter was very young. First shift, to be exact. And that made the creature a little smaller and a lot more unpredictable.

Meanwhile, Cecilia scrambled off the couch. He let her, though it was only to pin her against the wall.

"What was that?" she gasped.

"The reason we're here," he snapped as they heard claws scratching at the basement door. Then he looked to Mother. "How long has that been going on?"

"Just quieted down until she started screeching." Mother slowly tilted her shotgun to the floor.

"And the wolves?" he asked, his gaze cutting to the window. It was dark as far as he could see, but that could change at any moment.

"They been howling all night, but none real close." She shot Cecilia a hard look. "Unless they heard her. Then we're going to have werewolves up our ass thanks to you. And right now, ain't none of them being too reasonable."

They watched as Cecilia's expression shifted into a bleak realization that they were both crazy. Her eyes grew dull and her mouth pulled into a tight frown. Her gaze darted to the front door, obviously gauging the distance and wondering if she could make it out before he tackled her or Mother shot her. Her odds weren't looking too good.

Meanwhile, Mother obviously read the expression right off Cecilia's face.

"Ah hell. Why'd you bring a blind person into this fight? She can't fix anything she won't see." "Blind" was Mother's word for people who weren't in on the shifter secret. People who were too set in their own way of thinking to even consider anything supernatural.

"We have to convince her. I figured Sam might as well help with that."

Mother gaped at him. "Sam? Sam?" She waved the shotgun wildly at the barred basement door. "Sam is trying to tear out of here to get—"

"To the river. I know. We've got to stop that. It's not safe yet."

All shifters in their first change had an irrational need to get back to the place of their clan birth. For much of the Michigan grizzlies, that meant Gladwin state park. A whole grizzly pack protected the area just for that reason. But for the Detroit bears, wolves, and some of the cats, it was the River Rouge. Different spots, but all pretty close to one another. For the most part, this happened in the spring and every shifter helped watch for the young. There were even special cabins set up for kids who were expected to pop.

This was summer, though, and if it weren't for the Detroit Flu, Sammy would likely have had another year before going grizzly.

"I told you not to drink the water," Hank grumbled.

"Didn't. But the stupid kid forgot coffee was made with water. Had one of those damned expensive coffees as a birthday treat and bam: fur, snout, and me blocking the basement door. Thought I could handle it but then the howling started." She jerked her head outside. "Howling and roaring. Finally quieted down and then you brought—"

Another roar cut through the room, and the hair on Hank's arms shot straight up. He was well versed in grizzly howls, and this youngling was on the verge of wild panic.

"I've got to go in there," he said. He motioned with one hand for Mother to move the kitchen table aside.

"Are you crazy?" Cecilia gasped. He still had her pinned against the wall, but he would need to release her soon. He turned to look at her, wondering just how the hell he was supposed to deal with a panicked doctor on the run while safely taking down a young shifter.

There was only one way, and damn it, he just didn't see how it could possibly turn out well. But he really had no choice. So with a quick glance at Mother silently telling her to keep her head, he hauled Cecilia over to the bannister. Good thing he had a full stock of zip ties. He lifted her bound wrists and used another zip tie to latch her to the bannister.

"Please don't do this," she begged.

He wanted to believe that she meant *Please don't risk your life by facing down an angry grizzly*, but he knew better. She was begging him not to restrain her.

"Please, I'll listen. I'll do whatever you say." She looked over at Mother. "My name is Dr. Cecilia Lu. He's abducted me from the CDC—"

"Save your breath," Mother interrupted. "You're stupid and blind. Sit there with your eyes open and learn."

He sincerely doubted that anyone had ever called Dr. Cecilia Lu stupid. Certainly not an old black lady living near the projects, but he had to give Dr. Lu credit. She didn't turn huffy or pompous. Instead, she buttoned her lip and waited for another opportunity to escape.

One problem down. Now he turned to Mother. "Please don't shoot her. She's blind right now, but—"

"Yeah, yeah. What you gonna do about Sammy?"

He grimaced. "The only thing I can do. Talk bear to bear to calm things down. But once things are quiet, you gotta do the rest. Talk like a person—"

"I know what to do. You just…" She gestured vaguely with the tip of her shotgun. "Just be careful. We got a brand-new TV down there."

And right there was why he liked Mother. Angry wolves outside, kidnapped doc inside, and him about to face down a new grizzly. And what did she care about? Her new TV. He knew she was really saying, *Don't get killed*, but sentiment had never been her way, and that's what made him smile.

"Got the cable hooked up and everything?"

She grinned at him. "Looking forward to next year's Super Bowl."

Then she set the shotgun down. "You can come to the party if you don't break it."

He nodded at her once, accepting the invitation. Then he leaned down and hauled the kitchen table out of the way. Next came the couch, but the noise set Sammy to growling. And the scratches on the door were getting louder. He doubted the thing would hold out much longer even though the door was solid oak. He knew because he had bought and installed it himself in anticipation of this moment.

Mother looked worriedly at the door, her expression tight. "I'll open it. Better hurry."

He nodded and pulled off his shirt. He'd learned how to strip out of his clothes in under three seconds and he didn't take much longer this time. Shirt, shoes, pants, underwear. Everything off and set neatly on the couch. Then he turned full frontal to Dr. Cecilia Lu.

Her eyes were wide, her expression shocked. Then he said slowly and clearly for her benefit. "I'm a shifter. I turn into a black bear. I'm going to do it now."

Mother cut in. "So pay attention, girl. Open your eyes."

Chapter 4

List of possible explanations for what she was seeing:

1. She was asleep on the lab table and was having one hell of a bad dream.
2. She was so exhausted, she was hallucinating.
3. She'd caught the Detroit Flu and was hallucinating.
4. She'd hit her head, and this is what happened when one had brain damage.

A zillion other explanations burst through Cecilia's brain, all of them equally plausible and way more likely than a man being able to turn into a big black bear. That just wasn't possible, and 100 percent of her brain rejected it out of hand.

And that's what finally convinced her to really look at what she was seeing. Because as a scientist she prided herself on exploring all the possibilities. Had aliens abducted the deli guy at her local grocery store? Absolutely possible until she saw evidence of a different explanation. Nessie lived in Loch Ness and came up occasionally to help boost tourism? Unlikely but possible. Big Foot, fairies, even ghosts and all other paranormal activity? She'd consider them along with a dozen more likely explanations.

But suddenly shifters were 100 percent impossible? Even though she watched a man thick with bulging muscles and zero body fat face her straight on and start to sprout fur. There might have been a golden glow. She didn't know. It was too fast for her brain to process. But she absolutely saw sleek black fur, a lengthening muzzle, and bright brown eyes flow wider on an expanding face. She watched as he dropped to all fours. As hair—er, fur—rippled down his back into a short, rather cute little tail. And those narrow hips and his tight, manly ass thickened and spread until she saw the rounded back end of a bear.

But even as she was looking—and maybe screaming a little—his sweet brown eyes remained the same. Sure, they'd flowed outward on a bone structure vastly different than a man's, but they had the same calm expression, the same color, and the same steady resignation that had been on the man. As if he was doing his best by her but sincerely doubted it would work.

And then she was looking at a big black bear with liquid eyes and a long pink tongue.

And yet she was 100 percent sure that she was hallucinating? That was bullshit because nothing was ever 100 percent certain in science. Nothing.

Which meant…

Oh hell. Shifters existed.

She blinked and looked at her environment with a new perspective. Everything appeared the same as it had a second ago. Big black bear in front of her. Wiry black woman with a shotgun to the left. A wolf's howl that came from outside, echoed over and over by at least six other voices. Had she been hearing that for a while and just now noticed? How could she *not* have heard that?

Mother stepped to the basement door and whipped it open.

The bear was ready, but so was whatever was on the other side. With a sudden roar, out leapt a grizzly bear. It had light brown fur, sharp white teeth, and a powerful paw that shoved the door into Mother. Or at least it would have if the woman hadn't leapt onto the couch and out of the way.

The creature started barreling toward the front door, which is when the black bear—Hank?—caught it on the side. He rammed it with his head, and the grizzly went tumbling. Unfortunately, it went tumbling straight at her. Or maybe not *straight* at her because it rolled into the wall about four feet away. But damn it, in this tiny house, four feet was too close. Plus, it was pissed as hell as it scrambled back onto all fours and roared.

The sound cut straight through Cecilia and had her climbing up the bannister as far as her tied hands could go. The black bear looked at her, and she would swear she saw concern in his eyes. Concern. From a bear. But then he focused on the grizzly as he opened up a mouth as big as a truck and roared right back.

Think logically!

Her brain tried to tell her that. Her brain tried to tell her that this entire situation was illogical and therefore impossible. She gave her brain the finger and kept her gaze on the fight. But she did allow it to tell her that the black bear's mouth was in no way the size of a truck. It would, however, feel like a truck had dropped on her if that mouth ever managed to clamp its massive jaws on her.

Strangely enough, the black bear's roar was more impressive than the grizzly's. It was deeper, more sustained, and it didn't hold that same note of *I'm going to eat you* in it. Maybe because Hank wasn't facing her but was squaring off with the grizzly. Or perhaps because it sounded more like a parent telling a child to chill out. Hadn't she heard her father growl that way at her and her brothers more than once? It was the grumble of a parent who was about to bring punishment. And Cecilia straightened up out of reflex, as much as she could while wrapped around the top of the bannister.

The grizzly—Sammy?—snapped back. A loud *click* of its jaws followed by another roar, but it wasn't as ferocious as before. And it held a note of confusion. And was she really interpreting bear roars? While one of them was inches away from her? Hank was close enough that she felt the heat from his side; she could've reached out and stroked the inky black fur if she weren't tied up. Instead, she tried not to whimper in alarm when Hank blew out angry breaths and bared his teeth.

Sammy bared right back. Sharp white teeth, flared nostrils puffing in and out, and a small pink tongue that was licking its chops…and then hanging out as it panted. Just like a winded dog. In fact, while Cecilia watched in shock, the grizzly collapsed backward onto its haunches and panted. Just sat there breathing hard, and no wonder. It had been roaring and clawing at that basement door for who knows how long.

Outside, the wolves howled again. Closer this time. One sounded like it was freaking next door. The grizzly heard it. Sammy's head snapped up and it pulled its teeth back in a growl. The black bear's ears twitched. The ear nearest Cecilia seemed to twist back toward the front door, but Hank remained steadfast in squaring off with the grizzly. He grunted, low and kind of rolling, deep in his chest. Not a growl, but not really a grunt either. A grumble? Like a cranky grandfather?

Hank lumbered forward. No other way to phrase it on a beast his size. He thudded forward until he was muzzle to muzzle with the grizzly. And when he was near enough to take a big bite of the creature, he extended his long pink tongue and groomed the creature's face.

Lick, lick, and then a nuzzle.

At first the grizzly was having none of it. It growled and turned its face away. Damn, if that didn't look just like a toddler coming out of a tantrum. Cecilia could almost hear the words, *I don't wanna.* But Hank persisted. Nuzzles, licks, even a thick paw stroking against the grizzly's side.

And wow, just watching that had Cecilia softening. It was beautiful, seeing one bear comfort the other. One big, black, and powerful. The other golden brown and frightened. Truthfully, it was the gentlest thing she'd ever seen. And the idea that it was Hank—the huge black man with a scar who had abducted her—made her entire mind twist in confusion. He'd slammed her face into the seat of his car, he'd zip-tied her twice, and he'd even flipped her over his shoulder and dragged her inside here where he'd turned into a beast.

And yet he was also gentle and fatherly as he nuzzled a frightened grizzly. She felt the tenderness as surely as if he were nuzzling her. As if that long pink tongue were stroking up her neck and side. It wasn't sexual, but it was sensuous. In her mind's eye, she felt the heat of his tongue, the wet scrape of it and the reassurance in it as he groomed the grizzly. And she felt the push of his face against her in

a way that begged her to curl her fingers into his ruff and sink deep
into the softness of his fur.

Incredible. And it relaxed her enough that she climbed down
from her awkward place on the bannister. She perched on the edge
of the stair and watched in a surreal kind of envy as the grizzly
continued to settle beneath Hank's ministrations.

And then Hank looked up. The grizzly whined at the loss. So did
Cecilia, though she didn't voice it aloud. Hank lifted his dark face
and turned to Mother. The woman was still on the couch, though
she was sitting there much the way Cecilia was on the stair step. She
had her feet under her and the shotgun in her lap, but at Hank's
look, she set the weapon aside.

"Okay, Sammy. I'm coming over. It's me, Mother. You know who
I am." She took two steps forward. Then suddenly she snapped out
an order. "Say something when I'm speaking to you, child!"

The grizzly's head pulled back and it barked out an "Eep." That's
what the sound was. An eep of startled response, except really deep.
And then it opened its mouth wide. Cecilia heard its breath come
in and out a couple of times, as if it were trying to talk but couldn't
figure out how.

So Hank did a kind of long bark. It wasn't a short burst of
sound like a dog's. More like a rolling symphony of sounds that
were guttural and yet had enough tones in it to make it sound like
conversation. Weird, but amazingly reassuring because it sounded
just like an adult teaching a child how to speak. Especially when he
did it again. Once, twice, and then waited patiently as the grizzly
tried again.

The next sound was almost funny. The grizzly grunted but it came
out very much like a bark. Short, low, and more like a surprised gasp

than anything else. And then the grizzly did it again. And again. Its eyes widened, and it looked straight up at the bear with a kind of look-at-me expression. In response, Hank gave it a long lick with his tongue and a bump with his nuzzle.

Was that the bear's form of a fist bump? Had to be because the grizzly did it right back this time. No longer terrified and suddenly as much like a happy puppy as a three-hundred-pound bear could be.

Until another set of wolf howls cut through the air. Everyone's head snapped up, including hers. She'd begun to relax on the steps, but suddenly she tensed along with everyone else because those howls were really freaking close.

Cecilia didn't know what to do except to look longingly at Hank's clothes. Somewhere buried in his pants was the Swiss army knife that would cut her free. And now that she heard those wolves outside, she sure as hell wasn't running out there. Meanwhile, Mother was stepping forward with her own stern tone.

"All right, Sammy, you've had your fun. Time to turn back now."

Cecilia frowned as she looked at the woman. She'd set aside her shotgun and stood there in front of both bears with her hands on her hips and her legs spread wide. She looked calm but stern, like a mother telling a child it was time to turn off the video games. Her brow was arched, and she looked like she was counting in her head. Definitely a by-the-count-of-three-please look.

Everyone looked at the grizzly. Hank's big bear head, Cecilia from her place on the stairs, and even the grizzly looked down at itself. Time to change back? Like into a human?

Again, Cecilia's mind tried to express that it was impossible, but that was a small, shrinking portion of her mind. The rest was eagerly anticipating the sight. Just where would all that mass go? What about the fur? What would Sammy look like as a human?

And they all waited.

And waited.

Then Mother lost her patience.

"Now!" she snapped. Loud enough that everyone except Hank jumped: Mother from the force of her demand, Cecilia because she was startled, and the grizzly because the child had probably been conditioned to respond to that tone from childhood.

It worked. The huge creature shimmered as she jerked to respond to Mother. There was a golden glow to the transformation, but it was gone in the blink of an eye. The grizzly's golden brown fur seemed to disappear into it and reform into a young black woman. Her pale brown body had a sturdy frame, a sweet face, and neat braids of black hair tucked against her head. And her liquid brown eyes sparkled with triumph as she grinned up at Mother.

"I did it! Mother, I did it!"

"That you did, little girl," Mother said, her tone filled with pride.

Then she looked at the big black bear and threw her arms around him. "Hank, I did it!"

Hank chuffed in a note of clear pride, and his long tongue licked her neck. She was completely naked, but no one seemed to notice. Cecilia only did because her medical mind was cataloging the girl's body and seeing no deformities, no scars, and nothing different from a human girl of approximately sixteen years. If anything, she—

Crash!

The explosion of sound and glass caught Cecilia completely off guard. As did the stinging cuts from the shattered window. She would have screamed. The sound was startling enough. But by the time she drew breath, every part of her had seized up in terror. Because there, leaping into the center of the living room was the largest dog she'd ever seen.

And then she realized the truth.

It wasn't a dog. It was a werewolf, and it had Mother in its jaws.

Chapter 5

Hank heard the werewolf coming a split second before the attack. If he hadn't been so focused on congratulating Sammy for completing her first shift, he might have realized the problem earlier. But the girl had come through the most difficult moment of her young life with flying colors and that deserved a hug. Or a nuzzle, as it were. Which would have been fine if they'd been tucked away in Gladwin and protected by the safety of the largest Michigan pack.

They weren't. They were right in the middle of werewolf territory and these wolves didn't like it when the bears came to play. They'd usually tolerate it because urban living meant close quarters, but this wasn't normal times. The moment the window burst inward, Hank smelled the hybrid stench.

He spun around, his gaze taking in all the details he could in a split second.

A single werewolf had burst in through the large window. Everyone had cringed in the spray of shattered glass. Cecilia was tied to the bannister, dark red lines of blood appearing all over her face and arms. Painful, but not lethal. Sammy was tucked behind him, naked in her human form and completely vulnerable. Fresh from her first shift, she'd be exhausted once the adrenaline wore off. He needed to get some food into her, then she'd probably sleep for days.

Which left the main problem. The werewolf dead center of the living room with his jaws around Mother's shoulder. Worse, the thing was amped up, probably from drinking the tainted water. It certainly reeked of the hybrid stench though it appeared full wolf. Either way, Hank saw no intelligence in the thing's eyes. Just vicious aggression.

Mother was screaming in pain and fury. She was trying to struggle, but he had her held fast. If the thing did what was normal for a wolf, it would clamp down and start to shake its head, trying to snap Mother's neck or at least tear her apart.

Hank leapt before that could happen.

He caught the wolf around the neck, chomping down as hard as he could. He never would have had the chance if the wolf hadn't had Mother in his mouth. Wolves were a damned sight faster than a bear and ten times as flexible. But Hank had size and strength on his side. Which meant when he clamped on a wolf's neck—even an amped-up werewolf—he broke or crushed a lot of vital parts.

Blood burst in his mouth like vile hot copper. He tasted the taint and wanted to throw the thing back out of the window as fast as he could. But he didn't know if Mother was free, so he throttled his natural response. The conflicting urges and the river of blood made him gag, which is a bad thing on a bear. He tossed his head and the wolf landed big and ugly on Mother's favorite couch.

Worse, she went with it. Stumbling sideways as she fell from the dead wolf's mouth.

But this time, Hank didn't allow himself to be distracted. A quick scan of Mother showed she was alive and not spurting blood. That was all that was important right now as he spun to the shattered front window.

The night air was pouring through and Hank smelled what was coming. Damn it. What was already here.

Two hybrids climbed in the window, their eyes yellow with hatred and a stench that made Hank's gagging reflex work overtime. In the background, he heard Sammy scream, "Mother!" as she surged forward. But more gratifying still was Cecilia's bellow.

"Hank! Look out!"

She was warning him of the hybrids. He didn't need her words, but they were satisfying nonetheless. And in a distant portion of his brain, he cataloged the ramifications of her words. She'd called him Hank, so she knew him even in his bear form. She called out a warning, so she'd kept her wits. And best of all, she was afraid for him. That warmed him, but he didn't have time to think of it beyond noting the detail and even that was tucked way in the back of his mind.

The hybrids didn't spare a glance for their fallen wolf. Even if he hadn't seen the madness in their eyes that alone told him they were too far gone to recover. Even the darkest of men noted a fallen comrade and wolves were pack creatures. They could no more ignore a fallen pack mate than they could stop their heart from beating.

So he attacked.

Despite appearances, he hadn't done a lot of fighting as a bear. The military had trained him in human combat and medicine. But that was enough. He took the nearest hybrid first, slamming his massive bulk into it so fast the thing was barely able to snarl through the wolf mouth before it was thrown back out the window. The other hybrid was harder. At least the first had a full wolf face without any humanity in it. The other looked fully human—a man in his thirties—except for the body fur, sharp claws for hands, and curved bearlike ears, plus a hint of a muzzle. Hell, this guy was a bear hybrid, but his hands and mouth were already covered with blood. He'd been feasting on something and it hadn't been kibble.

Worse, he was going for Cecilia, and fuck, he was fast.

Hank saw Cecilia coil tightly, her hands gripping the bannister as her knees tucked into her chest. She was going to kick that thing, but she didn't realize what his claws would do to her legs. Or her face. And Hank was across the room, too far away to save her.

He leapt as fast as he could, but he knew he wasn't going to make it. Fortunately, it was all he needed. The hybrid was distracted by the sudden approach of a big black bear. He twisted his head and extended his claws. But he had already been moving toward Cecilia, which meant he was close enough for her to strike. She kicked him with both feet straight in the face.

Great shot!

The thing's head snapped back, though it would take more than that single blow to keep him away. But now Hank was in position to help. First things first, he swiped at the zip ties that bound her, neatly slicing them in half.

She was free. Hopefully, she'd stay around to help, but at the moment, he wouldn't fault her for hightailing it out of here. Sadly, the precision required to free her had slowed him down. He hadn't wanted to accidentally slit her wrists, so he'd had to concentrate. Which gave the bear hybrid an opening.

He attacked with all the strength in his amped-up claws. Hank felt the bite of those razor-sharp things in his upper arm. The thick bear fur wasn't enough to keep them from digging in and slicing. But it also brought the hybrid in close enough for Hank's mouth.

He swung his head around and bit down on the first thing he caught. His teeth scraped against skull and tore through…he didn't want to know what. Tainted copper blood poured into his mouth again, but he didn't stop. He had to end this because the first hybrid was coming back in the window. As well as another werewolf.

Shit.

The hybrid went limp in his mouth. Dead.

He threw him away, sadly unable to slam him into the oncoming hybrid. The damned thing was too heavy, and he was trying to keep track of all the details. Specifics like where Cecilia was going as she slid behind him. And how badly was Mother hurt? She hadn't moved when normally the woman would be racking her shotgun.

But he didn't have time to look further as he squared off with the wolf hybrid. The other werewolf was heading straight for Mother, but he'd have to go through Sammy first. The girl had just dived across the couch to grab the shotgun. Good for her.

Hank engaged the wolf hybrid. A teeth-and-claw fight, but Hank had the size advantage. In close quarters like this, all Hank had to do was pin the thing against the bannister with his bulk. Not a problem assuming the thing didn't slither away or get lucky and catch a vital organ with its claws.

It didn't, though Hank felt the pinch of a few good hits. And then the thing was flattened against the bannister. Enough for Hank to—

A human arm slid through baring his army knife. Cecilia flicked her wrist across the thing's throat, neatly slicing the carotid. Blood flowed freely, and she hopped back with a squeak. Good lord, the woman could slice open a monster's neck but she squeaked at the blood?

Didn't matter. Hank was both too grateful and too busy to fully appreciate her foibles. He spun around, this time heading for the wolf. What he saw made his blood run cold.

Mother, still down on the floor. Sammy with the shotgun racked and aimed, her skinny body trembling with the effort it took to face down a werewolf crouching two feet away, teeth showing in a growl and eyes narrowed in fury. He was about to leap and who knew if Sammy could get the shot off in time.

Hank roared. It was the only thing he could do to disrupt the coming disaster. He put his full voice into it as he sprang forward. Except his hurt arm wasn't as powerful as it should be, so his push was uneven. And there was a damned coffee table in the way fouling his footing.

The werewolf adjusted, his eyes and his mouth glaring at them both. But he didn't move to attack and for a moment Hank wondered why.

Then he saw.

Three more werewolves came through the window. And a fourth behind that. All creeping in stealthily, one silent paw at a time. Until Cecilia blew out a slow breath and spoke.

"Werewolves in Detroit. We expecting sparkly vampires next?"

He would have snorted if the situation weren't so dangerous. But then something bizarre happened. One of the wolves at the window—the late arrival if he had to guess—snorted as if he were acknowledging the joke. And when he crawled over the windowsill, the others parted to let him pass.

The alpha? An elder? It looked older than the others from the gray on the muzzle, but it was hard to tell, and Hank wasn't familiar enough with the werewolf packs to know one from the other. Whomever it was approached Hank with narrowed eyes. The wolves to either side of Gray Muzzle sneered, curling their lips back to show their teeth. One gave a low growl of warning while the other looked like he wanted to raise a leg and piss on Hank.

Let him try. With one swipe, Hank could disembowel him. Or at a minimum make sure the bastard never had children.

But then Gray Muzzle snapped at the other two, silencing them with a single clamp of its jaws. Okay. Clearly, Gray Muzzle was in charge of the wolves here. So what exactly—

"Yeah, you best shut up," Mother said, her voice weak, but growing stronger as she pushed herself upright. She was bleeding heavily from the shoulder, but her eyes blazed with fury. "Look what you done to my living room. Just look!" She grimaced as she struggled to stand, but apparently got too dizzy. She wobbled on her feet and dropped down onto her couch.

Hank surged forward to help her, but a growl—in unison—from all the wolves stopped his motion. He could do some real damage to those wolves, but it wouldn't be pretty. And if they worked together, they could hamstring him in seconds and then take him out at their leisure. So he waited and prayed that Gray Muzzle was lucid. And restrained.

Meanwhile, Sammy started to help Mother, but the older woman waved everyone back. "You stay right there, girl. Keep a firm grip on that shotgun just like I taught you." Then she turned her dark gaze on the wolves.

"I'm Mother to everyone on this block, and that includes you damned foolish wolves. Just look what you done to my home. Smashed my window. Bled all over my rug. And this here was my favorite couch. How many of you have sat right here and eaten my chocolate chip cookies? Crying about some bully or asking me how to talk to some girl? Huh? How many of you?"

Not a one answered. They were in their wolf form, but at least two of them dipped their heads in shame. And still Mother kept going.

"That's right. I'm Mother, and you destroyed my living room. Now I ask you, what are you going to do about it?"

Silence. Not a single one moved. Then she slapped her hands together in a loud clap.

"I'm talking to you!"

Everyone jolted, but no one wanted to answer. No one, that is, except for Gray Muzzle who walked forward slowly.

Sammy adjusted, moving as if to stand between the wolf and Mother, but Hank puffed out a loud exhalation. The wolves lifted their heads, but the message was for Sammy. She was to stand back and away. She looked at him, met his eyes, and so he shook his head.

With a grimace of distaste, she stepped back and allowed Gray Muzzle to come forward. The wolf walked slowly, respectfully even, until it came face to face with Mother. She stared at it from her seat on her couch. Human eye to wolf eye. Then Mother spoke.

"You got to control your people, Miriam. I told you not to drink the water. I told you—"

Gray Muzzle grumbled, which is when Hank realized that Gray Muzzle was female. And the sounds she was making now were like grumbles of acknowledgment. Like two old women complaining about the stupidity of men over coffee. It wasn't done in words, but damn if Mother didn't understand.

"I know they don't listen, but ain't there someone in your pack got some sense? That you can talk to?"

Gray Muzzle barked softly and then turned her head. It was a mournful look, especially as it was accompanied by a soft whine. Oh hell. The dead werewolf was—had been—a sane wolf. One who might have listened but probably got the news too late. He'd probably drunk way too much of the tainted water before Gray Muzzle got to him.

And now he was dead.

"Ah hell, Miriam. I'm sorry."

And with that, Mother wrapped her good arm around the werewolf and pulled in tight for a hug. Gray Muzzle went willingly and even licked Mother's neck. And when Mother drew back, the wolf nuzzled deeper into the shoulder wound, licking at the blood and tears. Mother hissed, but allowed it. And then she dropped her head on Gray Wolf's haunch.

"You're patrolling, ain't ya? Trying to catch them hybrids?"

A single bark in the affirmative.

"Well go on then. We're good here. Got Hank over there to keep us safe."

Everyone looked at him, and he bared his teeth to show he was ready.

"Sorry about this one," Mother continued. "We'll keep his body safe until you can come back in the morning. But what do you want us to do with the others?"

A low growl. And in case anyone had trouble understanding what that meant, Gray Muzzle went over to the wolf-faced hybrid and lifted her leg. She pissed a long, angry stream on the hybrid before acknowledging Mother with another a nod and leaping out the window. The other three did the same. They first acknowledged Mother with a press of their nose to her hand, gave another lick to the fallen werewolf on the couch, then one by one, they pissed on the dead hybrids. Like they needed the extra stench in here. Mother must have felt the same because as the last one finished, she called loudly to them.

"You'll be cleaning that up in the morning, too!"

The response came first from Gray Muzzle, then the other three. She lifted her head and howled, loud and long, and the others chimed in. It wasn't a frightening sound. More mournful than angry. And it seemed to fill the night with a wild kind of awareness. Mother Nature was in charge tonight. Violent, angry, or even tender. The humans held no sway.

Which was completely thrilling to Hank's bear side. The human mind looked for Cecilia's reaction. Was she terrified? Repulsed?

He found her still gripping the bloody Swiss army knife but watching the werewolves with clear interest, maybe even excitement. And when she noticed he was looking at her, she shrugged.

"How could I have been so blind?"

Because everyone took pains to keep the normals from seeing. But he couldn't say that in his bear form and until they got help, he couldn't risk shifting back to human. He was stronger and a better defender as a bear. So instead of answering, he tried to smile at her.

Bears can smile, though it takes a special person to understand that. It took an ability to see past the baring teeth to the curve at the back of the muzzle. Few people ever got there, which was why bears rarely bothered. But he tried. For her. And she smiled back.

It was a connection, he realized. A moment when bear and woman understood each other, and he exhaled in relief. She wasn't terrified anymore. And she wasn't blind. She was looking at him as if…well, he didn't know how. He just felt it as—

Her head snapped to the side as Sammy cried out, "Mother!"

Hank's gaze shot to the couch, where the woman who had saved them all this night wobbled and collapsed.

Chapter 6

So shifters were real, werewolves were scary, and Hank was both terrifying and kind. None of that really computed in Cecilia's brain, but Mother collapsing? That made total sense.

She crossed quickly to the woman's side, going to press her fingers to Mother's neck except she was still gripping the Swiss army knife and…God. She shuddered as she realized she was covered in blood. And not only that, she'd killed. She hadn't tried to restrain or contain, she hadn't done it as a science experiment. She'd done it because they were being attacked and she knew how to kill the monster attacking them.

And that made her sick to her stomach.

With a gasp, she dropped the knife on the coffee table. Or more like threw it. And then she tried to get control of her shaking hands and the suddenly too rapid beat of her heart.

Sammy, however, had no such problems. She shoved Cecilia back with a glare.

"Who the hell are you?"

Pride came to her rescue. When every other part of her body and mind were scrambling to absorb what had just happened, certain patterns remained solid. Like the one where she defended her credentials to every doubter that she came across. And there had been many.

"I'm a doctor," she snapped. "And I'm trying to help."

Then she forced herself to put action to words as she quickly wiped her bloody hand on the last clean part of her lab coat, then went again for Mother's carotid.

Weak and uneven. Worse, her eyes were panicked, and her breath was gasping, as if she couldn't get enough air.

"Does she have a heart condition?"

"Yeah." Then the girl suddenly brightened. "Yes! Hank gave her pills."

"Get them."

Sammy straightened up, but she needn't have bothered. Hank had already grabbed Mother's big tote bag and was bringing it over. And what a sight that was seeing the bright fabric handles clamped between his bear teeth, a big butterfly tote swinging back and forth. Cecilia grabbed it from him thinking that that was probably the most surreal thing she'd ever seen. And given this night's work, that was saying something.

Meanwhile Sammy started digging in the bag without even pulling it from Cecilia's hand. She yanked out a little plastic baggie of pills with triumph.

"Here!"

Cecilia looked at the bear. Seriously, she looked straight into the bear's eyes and asked the question. "Nitro?"

Hank's head dipped in an obvious nod.

She grabbed a pill and gently opened Mother's mouth to set it underneath her tongue. Then she sat there, holding Mother's wrist as she monitored the woman's pulse. Five seconds. Ten.

Mother's heartbeat stabilized and grew stronger. Her breath evened out, too. And in a moment, her expression eased, and her shoulders drooped.

"I'm getting too old for this wolf shit," she murmured.

"Is there ever an age for wolf shit?" Cecilia asked.

The woman's eyes narrowed then a grin split her face. "Oh hell yes, honey. Those wolves make the best damn lovers you ever seen. Wild and fast. But they do like it doggy style—"

"Mother!" Sammy cried in shock, and Cecilia felt herself chuckle at the hot color in the kid's cheeks.

The woman snorted. "I wasn't born this old." Then she quirked an eye at the girl. "And you're one to talk, parading around naked in front of Hank."

So yes, Sammy had been naked all this time, but everyone had been focused on other things. Certainly Sammy had been until Mother's words. And if she'd been blushing before, now her face burned red hot as she gasped and grabbed the blanket off the couch to wrap it around her thin shoulders. Then with a horrified look at the black bear—who was looking straight out the window as if it hadn't even occurred to him to look anywhere else—she dashed down the stairs.

Mother chuckled, though the sound was weak. "Girl never thinks about clothes. Most shifters don't. It's how I knew she was one of 'em."

"Really? What are the other signs?" Cecilia might've been shaky and splattered with blood, but intellectual curiosity always won out. And suddenly she had a whole new vista of study to explore.

"There's the way they eat. Less cooking, more raw."

"Even before their first shift? That's what this was, right? The first time—"

"Yes. It's a little early for her, but we knew it was coming. Hank could smell it on her."

Cecilia wanted to ask more. Questions piled on top of each other in her brain, but she could see that Mother was exhausted. The woman needed her rest. So she suppressed her need to know in favor of Mother's health, but it was a hard thing to do.

"I want to hear all about it," she said, keeping her tone gentle. "But maybe in the morning. Can I help you to bed?"

Mother gave her a grateful look, but then her gaze skidded around the room at the disaster that surrounded them. "I should—"

"Rest. Hank and I will take care of things tonight. Don't you worry."

Mother's expression was grateful as Cecilia helped her stand.

"And if you give me the name of your cardiologist, I can write up…well not everything." They'd lock her in the loony bin for sure. "But I can tell him about what I saw…" Her voice trailed away. It was in her nature to document everything, especially an older woman's heart episode. But she could see from Mother's face that there were other problems with her suggestion than the fear that she'd mention werewolves in her notes. "You don't have a cardiologist, do you?"

"I got Hank there."

It took Cecilia a moment to remember that Hank had told her at the beginning. "An army medic is a far cry from—"

"He takes good care of me."

Cecilia looked over to where Hank was watching them with a stoic expression. Or simply a bear expression. It was hard to tell.

"No insurance, then?"

Mother shook her head. "The neighborhood takes care of me." And when Cecilia raised her eyebrows at that, Mother shrugged. "The wolves around here ain't that bad. Not generally. It's since this Flu thing that they've gone crazy." She looked sadly at the two hybrid bodies. "Any way to know who they were? Before the Flu got 'em?"

Cecilia swallowed. She hadn't wanted to think about that. She hadn't wanted to look at the bodies and think anything but *monster*. Or *attacker*. That Mother was already aware of the person beneath the fur showed she had a bigger heart than Cecilia. The things—the sick people—had broken through her window and attacked them. Hank was even now standing guard as a bear to make sure no one came at them again. And yet here was Mother thinking of the souls beneath the monster masks.

"I don't know," Cecilia answered honestly. "I'll do what I can before the coroner gets here, but the bodies decompose incredibly fast." That's something they'd learned after the first wave of the Detroit Flu. And they were now on their third.

"Find them. Everybody has someone who cares. A mother should know when her child is gone." There was a wealth of sadness in her tone and Cecilia wondered whom the woman had lost, but she didn't press. Mother needed all her strength to climb the stairs and collapse into bed. She didn't even undress and when Cecilia went to help her, she waved her away.

"Go on and help Sammy. Hank said new shifters are starving at first, before they sleep for a couple days."

Good to know. "I'll bring you some broth to drink. You need to keep your strength up, too."

Mother patted her hand, the gesture maternal and vague. The woman's eyes were already closing. "Go on now."

Cecilia did, listening carefully as Mother's breath deepened into a steady rhythm. She resolved to do some quick research on how to care for cardiac patients, but in the meantime, she had a new shifter to feed and after that, a whole new species to investigate. And though she wanted to make sure the living were taken care of, the bulk of her mind was caught up in the desire to examine the dead.

She'd found her clue and boy was it a doozy. There were so many avenues of research to follow, and all of them so exciting she couldn't decide where to start.

She made it downstairs and headed straight into the kitchen. Hank remained at the front window, his big bear body on alert as he sniffed the night air. He looked over his shoulder at her, and she smiled.

"Mother is resting. I'll check on her soon. She said that Sammy would be starving so…"

Hank left the window to follow her into the kitchen. She smiled as he came close, wondering if this was what it would be like to have a large dog as a pet. One that followed you wherever you went, who listened and never talked back. Who stretched up onto his back legs to paw at a cabinet.

Well, probably not that last one. Damn, he had to be seven feet tall like this. Where did he find the mass? As a man, he'd been over six feet, but somehow during the shift, he'd gained height and at least a hundred pounds. She was still watching him, thinking about the difference between man and beast when he managed to get the cabinet open. But he didn't have the dexterity to pull down a box of protein bars without risking the entire cabinet.

"I'll get it," she said as she stepped forward. He backed up, tottered a moment on his back paws, and then gracefully collapsed down. He didn't touch her, though she felt his heat as he went down. And damn, she'd never been this close to a bear before.

All that inky black fur was beautiful. And the brown muzzle seemed cute and fuzzy. No trace of a scar on the bear, she realized. And were his eyes larger? Yes, they had to be. She wanted to take measurements of both man and bear, but she got lost in the liquid depths of his gaze. He'd dropped to all fours and now they were staring at each other, nearly eye to eye.

She reached out without thought, but then held herself back. "Is it all right?" she asked. "Can I touch you?"

He dipped his head in a nod. She smiled then did what she'd wanted to do from the very first moment he'd changed in front of her. She started at his muzzle, the short brown hair feeling more bristly than she expected. He turned his face into her palm, and she grinned at the feel of his wet nose. His tongue licked her palm, soft and as sensuous as she imagined. It was sweet, the way he curled around her small finger. A single quick lick, almost as if he couldn't help himself, and then he ducked his head.

Her other hand joined the first, and she stroked back along his muzzle, scratching the soft brown fur. He rumbled in appreciation, stretching closer to her until her fingers dug into what would be the ruff on a large dog. Apparently bears liked to be scratched there, too, and she sank her fingers into soft black fur.

No wonder Sammy had thrown her arms around Hank. As a bear, he was just the right size and feel to bury her entire face in his neck while her hands stretched around his back. She flashed for a moment on her favorite childhood books, The Chronicles of Narnia. Back then, she'd wanted nothing more than to hug the big lion Aslan. Now she knew that lions had nothing on bears. Hank was nuzzling softness, hot licks, and exactly the size to make her feel small and safe beside him. Like a child with a big, wonderful pet. Or maybe a woman looking straight at a feat of magic so incredible that it had silenced her scientific mind all together.

Well, at least for a few moments as she held on to him, her face in his neck, her body absorbing his heat and his strength. That lasted for as much as twelve seconds before the questions overran her pleasure.

She drew back long enough to look into his eyes. "You know I'm going to pepper you with questions soon. Am I right that you can turn back to human whenever you want?"

A slow dip of his head.

"I'll take that as a yes. But you're not doing it, right? Because you fight better in this form? And you want to protect us from whatever could come through the busted window."

He nodded again, and if the curve to his mouth was any indication, he was smiling at her. Like a teacher when the slow kid in class finally gets it.

"Okay," she said. "First things first. I'm taking protein bars to Sammy and then some hot soup to Mother." She arched a brow. "Then it's your turn while I look at the bodies. You're going to answer questions while I work."

He'd pulled back as she spoke, giving her room to get to the cabinet, but her last statements had him blowing out a breath. She had no idea what it meant. Could be a *yes*, could be a *no way*. Didn't matter. Everybody in her life learned that once she got going on a research direction, she was impossible to stop. He might as well get used to the idea that she was going to pester him all night.

So she grabbed the box of protein bars and a soda from the refrigerator and headed downstairs. It was a small finished basement complete with TV, couch, and two sets of bunk beds against the back wall. Looked like Sammy wasn't the only one who slept over, but she was clearly the one who'd been here the longest. Girls' clothes littered the floor. A few pictures of her with her friends were tucked into the mirror. And the girl herself was curled up on the nearest bunk, fast asleep.

Cecilia didn't know if it was more important for the girl to eat or sleep. Probably eat. Shifting had to take a ton of energy, so she nudged Sammy awake. "Eat something before you completely crash," she said.

Sammy blinked then nodded. "Starving," she mumbled as she grabbed the soda. She started drinking it while Cecilia ripped open two bars. "How's Mother?"

"Same as you. Needs food and sleep."

"Mmph," the girl answered as she took a big bite of the first protein bar.

Cecilia smiled. "I've got questions, if you don't mind answering them."

Sammy didn't respond as she finished off the bar and started on the second.

"Have you always known you're a shifter?"

The girl shook her head. "Hank told me. I didn't believe him."

Join the club. "How old were you?"

The girl chugged her soda, then set it down empty on the floor. "Later," she said as she curled onto her side.

"But—"

"Leave the box."

"Um…okay. Maybe we can talk in the morning. I'd really like to know how it feels to shift."

Sammy didn't answer, and in a moment, her breath had deepened into sleep. Okay, so no more answers there. It was time to heat up some broth and get some pictures of the bodies before they decayed.

Her steps were light as she climbed the stairs. She made quick work of opening a can of soup. She doubted Mother would be awake to eat it, but she wanted it ready. She grabbed herself a protein bar as she cooked and even offered one to Hank. He nodded, and she had a great deal of fun peeling the wrapper off before tossing it to him. She wanted to know if he would try to catch it with his paws like a man or just open wide.

He opened wide, consuming the whole thing in one bite. And then she finally, wonderfully, got to do what she'd been aching to do for what seems like ages: she got to inspect the werewolf.

Chapter 7

I'm going out to your car."

Hank's ears twitched. He was back in the kitchen trying to peer through the back windows. Bears didn't have great eyesight, so it hadn't helped much. Typically, his nose more than made up for the lack, but all he could smell right now was Campbell's chicken soup and Cecilia. She was a wacky combination of Mother's lemon dish soap and persimmon. He'd had that spicy sweet fruit during his time in the military and he'd never forgotten it. And now that taste was inexorably mixed with her.

He shouldn't have licked her, but she'd been stroking his face, curling her fingers into his fur, and looking at him like he was a Disney miracle and a Christmas gift all wrapped together. So he'd done what bears do. They taste, they mark, and they remember.

"I need my phone, and I think it's in there. I've got your gun and your keys."

Hank padded quietly back into the living room. She was at the front door holding his gun like it was toxic waste, but obviously determined to head out into the dark of a dangerous city gone crazy. Not a good idea.

He moved to her side before she could open the front door. She could have just climbed out the big front window, but she was classier than that.

"You don't have to go with me—"

He snorted. She wasn't stepping one foot outside without him. The wolves were out tonight in force, and no telling who was crazy and who wasn't. But first things first.

He knocked the gun out of her hand. Terrible things happened when untrained people handled a weapon. And she was clearly untrained.

"Hey!" she cried as the gun went skittering across the room. "You could have shot something."

The safety had been on, so he'd taken the risk. And when she went to pick up the gun, he slid in front of her.

"Fine," she finally said. "No gun. I don't like the thing anyway. It was used to abduct me."

He arched a brow at her. He wasn't sure if a bear could do that. They didn't have eyebrows, but she understood the expression.

"Don't look at me that way. It's a fact. And maybe I don't exactly see how you could have done it differently, but that doesn't change the truth. You abducted me with that gun, and now it's sitting in a pool of blood, so I suppose that's just as well."

He jerked his gaze sideways and sure enough, he'd be cleaning that weapon as soon as he was human.

She chuckled at him. He was sure of it. And then she went to open the front door, but he stopped her with a quick bite. He grabbed hold of her once white lab coat and tugged on it. Sure it sported stains of a variety of colors, not to mention a whole lot of blood from the hybrid she'd killed. But that didn't change the fact that it was white enough to draw attention outside and so she needed to get it off.

She looked at him as he clamped down on her coat and promptly misinterpreted what he meant.

"I'm going out there. I need my phone."

He gave her coat another tug.

"I'm not going to call the police or anything, and I'm not running. Everything I want to examine is right here."

Her gesture suggested the two hybrids and the dead werewolf, but her gaze included him. Was she planning on inspecting him? Probably. He'd seen the gleam of scientific excitement in her eye. Did she want to turn him into her personal lab rat? Or lab bear? That wasn't going to happen and yet, part of him was interested in exactly that scenario. If she were the one doing the inspecting. He wouldn't let her bring out the knives or anything, but he sure would love to see exactly how she would explore every inch of him.

And that right there told him that he'd been awake far too long. His libido was running away with his brain. No rest meant no control of his body or his mind. He'd learned from his brother's death that shifters needed control above everything else. And if he hadn't known it then, the lesson had been repeated with every drunk patient he'd seen during his stint as a medic. A lack of discipline created problems. And lack of discipline in a shifter killed.

But he had no choice at the moment. He had to hold it together until morning. Werewolves settled down during daylight. He didn't know why, but Mother had said it often and she knew wolves better than anyone.

Which meant that Cecilia was not going to go outside in an outfit guaranteed to attract attention. With the moon tonight, she'd light up like she was center stage at the opera. So he tugged again on her lab coat, tossing his head to give her the idea.

"What are—Ow!"

He eased up immediately; he didn't want to hurt her. Then he huffed. The woman was a doctor. Why couldn't she understand the basics of nighttime survival? He let go of her coat and then burrowed beneath it. The thing had two big buttons which he couldn't manage in his bear form. Hopefully this gave her the idea of what he wanted.

"Hank!"

She scrambled backward, but ran into the wall. He was nuzzling hard, pressing his nose into her soft belly. The idea had been to jerk his head back and rip the buttons off. But once his head was there against her body and he was surrounded by that heady persimmon scent, all sorts of weird things began to happen.

First of all, he forgot what he was doing. There were too many delicious sensations going on. It wasn't just her scent and the way her hands were gripping his fur. It was the rapid beat of her heart and the giggle she made as he wriggled against her. It was such a childish sound. Like a kid with puppies, and he felt lighter just hearing it.

Then he started burrowing deeper in. Not just her soft belly, but he wanted to feel her breasts against his cheeks. He wanted to lick the underside of those sweet mounds and taste her essence. He had a large tongue and there were so many tastes that she would give him from all over her body.

"Hold on! You're going to pop the buttons!"

She unbuttoned the lab coat, relieving the pressure against the back of his nose. Good because that gave him the ability to draw higher on her body, rubbing his cheek against her clothing and licking the underside of her jaw.

"God, you're just like a dog. Do you want me to scratch behind your ears?"

He should be insulted by that. He *was* insulted, except the feel of her fingers digging into his fur was heaven itself. He couldn't remember any human ever touching him in bear form. Not like this. Not curling underneath his ears to tug upward. Not pressing her face against his as she rubbed her forehead against his fur. Not laughing as she hugged him to her while he licked along her jawline and up to her ear.

"I've never had a dog," she said as she moved to scratch deeper on his neck. "But I imagine this is much better, right? You're much better."

Much.

And what the hell was he doing? He was letting her pet him and play with his ears. She was tugging on them, teasing the shape of them. Did she know how sensitive his ears were? And that what she did was sending bolts of pleasure throughout his body? It was one of the playful rituals of bears before they mated. And he was getting hard. Good God, he'd never had an erection as a bear before.

He licked her again, this time on her face. She squirmed away, laughing as she went. His face dropped lower as he tried to get a handle on his body and mind, but he was still leaning against her, his nose and his ears pressed against her hip and belly.

He inhaled deeply, his nose twitching and his body warming with her scent.

She was in heat, he realized. Ripe and ready for mating. He rumbled deep in his throat, a purr of happiness. He'd never made a sound like that before and part of him was startled. The shrinking human part of his mind. What was he doing?

He took a step backward as he tried to regroup. And in that moment, her head jerked sideways in reaction to a sound. An annoying human sound.

"Hank, your phone is ringing."

He heard, and he didn't want to. He inhaled and was pleased with her scent all over his nose and muzzle. But there was another scent as well. Something sour and—

Hybrid.

He straightened and bristled. He would defend her and the others. The young and the old. The scent wasn't strong. The hybrid wasn't close yet, but it was definitely in Hank's territory.

"Hello?"

It took him a moment to realize what had happened. While his senses were focused outside on catching the hybrid's location according to the wind, she had answered his phone and was now talking to whoever had called.

"Um, no. This is Dr. Lu. He's…um…indisposed right now." Silence. "Yes, I'm a believer. Can't wait to get my hands on the data you…" Another moment. "No, I can't access my phone right now. It's outside where the werewolves are and Hank won't let me go get it."

Hank took another deep breath, his mind clearing as his nostrils sorted through the Detroit smells. What the hell had he been doing? He was protecting Mother and Sammy, for God's sake. There were hybrids out there who could attack at any moment. And he'd been...what? Nuzzling Cecilia?

The enormity of his loss of control was staggering. Anything could have attacked while she was scratching his ears. Anything. And he would have been ass to the room completely exposed. The mental breakdown shook him to his core. Never before had Hank lost himself so completely in the bear. Not even when he'd been a randy teen.

He had to return to human. Forget the fact that he was a stronger fighter as a bear. He wasn't fighting anything while he lost to the animal. It might not even want to hang around but choose to wander off to the River Rouge. That was dangerous for the women he protected and suicidal for him.

So he changed. He made the mental shift to human, the conscious reshaping of his body to the image he saw in his mind's eye, but the bear didn't want to leave. The instincts were running hot, and it didn't care what the man wanted.

Meanwhile, she was talking, her voice calm and professional. Probably giving the sit rep to Simon. That's the only person who would call now. But instead of the thought pushing him back into human form so he could make the report, his bear was sniffing the air inside, drawing Cecilia's scent deep into his lungs.

He stilled, his mind at war. Her scent was intoxicating, but it was also tainted with another smell. No, not her. Outside.

The hybrid. It was closer now. He needed to find it and scare it away. If he couldn't reform himself into a human just then, he'd damn well make himself useful and go frighten off the danger.

He leapt through the window. It wasn't a hard jump, but he heard Cecilia gasp in surprise.

"He just…he jumped out the window." Her voice dropped a note. "That's a pretty impressive leap for something his size."

Good. She was impressed with his prowess. She would be even more impressed when he chased the monster away.

Chapter 8

Cecilia stared at the window, straining for a sight of Hank's furry body. He'd just leapt out the window, and she was still holding the phone and waiting to see if he would come right back. Meanwhile, her mind struggled to hold on to anything in the bursting whirlwind of data that came in too fast for her to process. This whole night had been like ripping aside a curtain to reveal a whole new level of reality. It was shocking and wonderful. It was also completely upsetting that she hadn't even known she was missing it.

That's what she was trying to deal with right then, but it was too much, and she'd gone too long without sleep. She couldn't hold on to facts or details like she should. And as much as she wanted to dig into the corpses around her, she kept staring out the window waiting for Hank.

Why had he left and what had he been doing nuzzling her like that?

She didn't want to think about it, but she couldn't stop herself. He'd been playful and fun, but her body had responded in ways it shouldn't. Her nipples had tightened, her belly had gone hot and soft, and that was nothing compared to the wetness that had drenched her panties.

What was wrong with her? She was hot and bothered because a bear had nuzzled her. A bear. A big, freaking bear. And when he wasn't a bear, he was a big guy with a scar and a taciturn nature who reminded her of her harsh, demanding father. Yuck.

There. That ought to completely kill her libido. Except it didn't.

"Hello? Are you still there?"

Cecilia jolted, remembering that she was on Hank's phone talking to his…well, she wasn't exactly sure who this guy Simon was except that he spoke with clipped authority and acted like Hank should be reporting to him. Kind of like a CO except that, as far as she knew, Hank was out of the military. Either way, he demanded a response from her, so she cleared her throat.

"Um, yeah. Sorry. I was waiting to see if Hank would come back."

"If he left, he had a good reason."

"Uh ye—"

"I've got your GPS coordinates from the phone, but there isn't anyone nearby. Are you in danger?"

Simon's questions helped focus her thoughts. "Not right now. Mother and Sammy are resting. Mother because of her heart, Sammy because that's apparently normal after a first shift."

"Sammy popped?"

She frowned. "I have no idea how to answer that."

"She turned into a bear and then reverted to human." It wasn't a question, but she answered as if it were.

"Yes and yes. Golden brown grizzly of approximately two hundred pounds and six foot nose to tail."

Silence for a moment, and then… "Any other details?"

"Plenty, but I don't know what you consider relevant."

"Good answer. I'd like a full report by Monday. You can email it to me. But for now, tell me how she seems as a human."

"Young African American woman of approximately sixteen years. She's healthy and…feisty." That wasn't a medical term, but it applied. "Once the adrenaline wore off, she fell right asleep. I managed to get her to eat a couple Powerbars, but that was it."

"Good choice. That'll keep her until she wakes. And Mother?"

"Heart condition probably deteriorating with age. She needs advanced medical care, but is fine for now." Then a pause. "Will you be able to help her? She doesn't have insurance."

Silence again as she heard tapping in the background. "She's a werewolf asset. Hank wouldn't even be there without Sammy in the picture."

Somehow she doubted that. There was too much affection between him and Mother. Initially she'd thought Mother was his biological parent, but a closer inspection of the two showed too many differences. It didn't preclude him from being her adopted child though. She really needed to get more details on his history. From a purely scientific perspective, of course.

Meanwhile, Simon was speaking to someone in the background. He'd covered his phone, so the words were muffled, but then he returned a moment later. "I don't have anyone free to help you. We're running food to those who need it and tying down those who are hallucinating. It's our duty to help the people inside our territory."

Pack logic from a bear. Not a surprise as humans could be extraordinarily territorial, but it wasn't generally an ursine trait. Apparently, it was for ursine shifters.

"Understood." She nearly added a "sir" but showing deference wasn't in her nature. That she almost snapped out a salute was a measure of this man's dominance.

"Alyssa and I will come as soon as we're free. Expect us before morning."

She frowned. "I don't understand."

"Hank is one of my people, too. If he needs help, I'll be there. Keep his phone handy. If the situation becomes dire, speed dial number two. Add your thumbprint to his phone so you can use it. His passcode is 'm-y-p-h-o-n.'"

Seriously? His passcode was "my phone" shortened to six numbers? Practical, she supposed.

"Anything else to report?" he asked.

Something along the lines of *I'm not your employee,* sprang to mind. But she didn't say it. She didn't dare at the moment. With Hank gone, she might need Simon's help. So she suppressed her rebellious side and reacted rationally.

"Nothing."

"Excellent. And let me remind you that our information is secret, Dr. Lu. There are real consequences if more people know about us."

"So why bring me in?"

"The situation is dire. This Detroit Flu—"

"No, I get that," she interrupted. "Why me?"

"Ask Hank. I told him to speak to Dr. Hayes. Simon out."

Well, wasn't he a barrel of laughs. This is why she never went into the military. Whenever anyone gave her an order, her first instinct was to give him the finger. Which in a good Chinese girl wasn't normal. In any event, she followed his instructions and added her thumb imprint to Hank's phone. And after checking on both Mother and Sammy, she was able to get down to business with the bodies.

Pictures first of all three—taken with Hank's phone—and then she started taking detailed measurements of the werewolf given that his people were likely to take the body away for burial soon. She couldn't stop herself from looking for Hank every few minutes. She was listening intently to the night sounds but except for the occasional long distance howl, all she heard were normal urban noises. Cars, a couple helicopters, an angry cat. Unless that was a cat-shifter? Did those exist, too?

She really needed to focus. She could already see evidence of decay in the hybrids. Interesting that the werewolf just looked like a normal wolf going through normal animal decomposition. At least as far as she could tell without the benefit of a microscope or even a magnifying glass.

She needed to stop with the werewolf and focus on the far more relevant hybrids. So she straightened and started her regular I-need-to-wake-up back stretches. She froze midtwist with her arms lifted over her head.

There was Hank standing framed by the empty windowpane. He was naked, his cut body lit like he was a Greek God. Or Shakespeare's Othello. Or maybe just Hank looking fierce and terrifyingly wonderful.

"Hank," she breathed, her gaze drinking him in greedily. The harsh angles of his scarred square jaw, the raised line of his collarbone, the taut pectoral muscles, and the bulging biceps. Her gaze took in the narrowing of his hips and the sweet line of dark hair that angled down to his erection. Corded thighs, strong feet, and clenched hands imprinted themselves on her mind.

Wait. What?

Erection. Big, thick, and arrowed straight at her. She saw the wet drop of pre-ejaculate and the way it seemed to pulse as he breathed. She heard that, too. The steady bellows of his lungs. And lord, she heard her own heartbeat rapid and aroused. Her breath was short and quick, her nipples tight, and her body lifted as she stretched out her spine.

She unhooked her hands where she clutched them together over her head. And as her arms came down, she felt her breasts sway as if she wanted him to see her condition: interested and too tired to fight him off. Except, of course, she wouldn't be fighting him.

Wait! Of course, she would! She wasn't an animal who mated with the first hot guy who showed up naked and erect. She was a thinking, rational, scientist. And she couldn't possibly be wet and needy from the sight of him standing there, his gaze zeroed onto her nipples before dropping slowly—sensuously—to look at her hips and thighs.

She swallowed, her mind screaming to act rationally. This was not normal. Do something science-y. Grab a clipboard, take a measurement, damn it, say something! Begin with the basics.

"Are you…okay?" Her voice was breathy, and she cleared her throat midsentence trying to get her mind back online.

He nodded, a quick slash of his chin.

God, how could he be so beautiful just standing there? And how could the musky scent of him have her thinking of ways that he could impale her.

"Um, is this normal?" she breathed.

He tilted his head in an obvious question.

She gestured weakly toward his penis. "Your arousal." She swallowed. "I'm…"

His nostrils flared and his hands twitched by his side.

"Is this pheromones or something? Are shifters deeply...um... erotic somehow?"

He shook his head.

"So, um, you want me." God, how embarrassing to say these things aloud, and yet she couldn't stop herself. She had to know if this was just biochemistry. And if it was, why weren't women leaping onto shifters in every corner of the city? Because, she was not a libidinous woman. She wasn't! But right now she wanted nothing more than to have him press her up against a wall, lift her leg, and thrust right inside. "And, um, I think you can tell my reaction. You can smell it, right?"

He nodded again. Another quick dip of his chin.

"But you don't know me. I don't know you. You just abducted me a few hours ago. Why are we like this?"

This time he didn't answer at all. Not by a twitch of his eyebrow or a jerk of his hips. Which left her with nothing but a pulse between her thighs that shocked her.

"I've never felt lust like this before." She swallowed. "It has to be biochemical."

His eyes narrowed as he thought. He was clearly processing her words, sorting through the facts. She recognized the expression from her own mirror whenever she was faced with a difficult puzzle. And then he suddenly moved.

She tensed, wanting him to come to her. Wanting from the core of her womb for him to do what she was picturing. Up against the wall, clothing ripped from her body, his hands on her breasts as she raised a knee to skate it over his hips. And then the penetration, deep and thick. God, she wanted it. She wanted him.

But he didn't come to her. He passed within touching distance, but he didn't touch her. He crossed to his clothes and pulled on his jeans. Commando. She wondered if shifters disliked clothes like tighty-whities. Maybe they were just another layer to get in the way when changing into an animal. And seriously, who wanted to look at a big scary black bear wearing tighty-whities?

Her mind disintegrated into silly images. It was the only thing she could do to deal with the cutting, horrible knowledge that he wasn't going to touch her. She wouldn't be able to kiss him or feel him between her legs. And honestly, she didn't want him to, right? Right?

But she did. And she hated herself for the irrationality of her own desperate hunger.

So, she turned away. She had bodies to examine, right? Things to figure out. A whole world of science to explore and a dangerous flu to end.

And then suddenly she felt him. His heat along her backside. His breath right beside her neck. Her hair prickled to attention, and her skin tingled from his nearness. She didn't know if she was imagining this, but damn it, it felt so real. She didn't want to turn and find out it was all in her head.

Then he spoke, his words soft and so gentle, it brought tears to her eyes.

"You're exhausted. When was the last time you ate?"

Why did she want to cry? What was happening to her that she was this emotional because he was indeed standing right behind her. Because he was gentle as he asked her a caring question? Because he'd noticed she was drooping with fatigue.

Get a grip!

But she couldn't. Her mind and her emotions were shattered

beyond retrieving. And suddenly, it was too much. She gasped, humiliated because she was crying. Crying! Why? Because he hadn't kissed her? She didn't even know him!

"You've been hit with a lot today. You discovered shifters, and that's never easy. And then the attacks. It's almost four in the morning, and I'll wager you haven't slept much since coming to Detroit."

She hadn't.

"Let me take you to bed."

Her body tightened at his words. Her breath caught on a sob and she wanted to beat herself for it. Sobbing? WTF? Because she knew he hadn't meant the words the way he said them? Because he meant taking her to bed to sleep. Could she be more humiliated? She'd told him she wanted him. And all he'd done was not touch her and be kind.

Kind!

When she wanted him to rip of her clothes off, to force her to submit to him, to penetrate her like they were both animals in the jungle. Raw, passionate, unfettered by rationality.

She pressed a fist to her mouth as the desire pumped through her veins, roared through her head, and squeezed her insides like a vise. It wasn't pleasant, but it wasn't exactly unpleasant either. It was raw and intense. The kind of passion that ripped her mind away until she felt like an exposed nerve.

"Cecilia?" His voice was thick with worry, then suddenly with the sharp bite of fear. "Dr. Lu!"

She didn't know what was happening. The world was moving in a way it wasn't supposed to. Then he touched her. She wanted to cry out, *Not like that!* He was supporting her. Her knees had gone out, and he was picking her up like he would a child when she wanted something entirely different.

She wanted passion to match her lust.

He gave her gentleness as he lifted her into his arms.

She smelled his masculine scent. She felt the strength in his arms as he threw her slightly up in the air so he could readjust his grip. She felt the hard ripple of his abdomen as he braced her against him. And she felt the power in his legs as he turned and began walking up the stairs.

No strain that she could tell. Simply a tight grip as he held her against his chest.

He was as strong as a bear, she realized. And whereas the thought was meant to make her smile, instead it made her whimper.

Mate with me.

She didn't want to think those words. It wasn't real. It was biochemistry gone amok. And yet they were there, a silent desperate plea.

And he was ignoring her as he gently set her down in a bedroom one door down from Mother. There were two twin beds here, and he set her on the nearest one. The sheets were scratchy, thin, and smelled of fresh dryer sheets.

"I'll bring you some soup."

"I can get it," she said. God, she didn't want him waiting on her.

"I'll get it," he said, and she heard the ring of command in his voice.

He wasn't going to bed her, but he was going to take care of her. Did that make the situation better or worse?

"I am not this weak."

"This isn't weak. This is post-adrenaline drop."

Maybe. Probably not, but it was a good enough excuse to allow her to save face. Then his expression shifted as if he were remembering something, and he patted his back pocket before pulling out a crumpled protein bar.

"It's crushed but still good. Start with this."

She reached for it, but he was already opening the packaging. Then he deftly broke a piece off and pressed it to her lips.

He was feeding her?

She opened her mouth to say that wasn't necessary, but he slipped the food inside before she could get the words out. And then she didn't speak because the chocolate and peanut butter paste tasted really good. As in really, really good.

He pressed another morsel to her lips the moment she swallowed the first. And again and again until it was gone.

"Thank you," she said. She really had needed to eat.

"Any medications, conditions, or allergies that I need to know about?"

She snorted. "I'm allergic to cats."

"Mother doesn't have one anymore. The wolves kept trying to eat it."

Her snort turned into a choke. She was lying on her back looking right up into his face. The hard, jagged scar on his jaw was right there and she stroked it with her fingers. She felt his body go rigid with shock, but he didn't move away. His nostrils flared, and his pupils dilated, but he didn't draw away.

"Why doesn't this disappear when you shift back to human? Sammy's skin looked pristine."

It seemed like his entire body was held rigid with control, but when he spoke, his words were calm. Excruciatingly even.

"I got the scar when I was ten. Long before my first shift. It became part of my identity, and so it remains, always part of me."

"How did you get it?"

"I saved my brother's life."

"Then it's a badge of honor."

He quirked an eyebrow. "That's what I told him. He said I'd gotten it when I tripped on my Legos."

She rolled her eyes. "Brothers are assholes."

"He was half right. I was able to save him because I tripped on my Legos. I was sprawled on the ground when he fell on top of me from the roof. We rolled together on impact. I'm not even sure it was a Lego that split open my jaw, but something did."

"Why was he falling from the roof?"

Hank's eyes grew soft. "It was his first shift. Sometimes they're violent things and that's where he was when it happened." He snorted. "He liked to go to calm down."

She smiled because he was smiling. Because he'd just shared a memory of his brother at an important moment in both their lives. And because that made her feel like he wasn't a stranger to her anymore. Not an abductor, not a black bear, but a man with a brother and a heroic scar.

Her fingers trailed across his scar, then up to his lips. They were full and very mobile. She'd been watching them as he spoke. And now she watched them open slightly as she trailed her finger across the lush softness there. Probably the only soft part of his entire body.

"I know so little about you," she murmured, and yet she felt so close to him. "I have brothers," she abruptly volunteered. "One in chemistry, one in biochemistry." She shrugged. "Whole family of science nerds; my dad's a biology professor. Except for my mother who cooked, cleaned, and meddled." She grinned. "It's the Chinese mother way."

He took hold of her hand, enveloping it completely in his as he spoke. "I'm the youngest. Older sister and a brother who's gone now."

She jolted. "Gone?"

He nodded. "Died as a teenager." His eyes were impossibly dark. "He went looking for trouble and found it. It's the grizzly in us, pushes us to be reckless."

She frowned. "But you're so controlled." Even in the middle of the fights, his every action had a purpose, his every motion seemed thought out.

"I had to learn that. My brother's death destroyed my parents, and I wasn't going to do that to them by being stupid. The military helped, as did the training to become a medic."

She shook her head. "I know people in the military. This quietness didn't come from them. It's all you." She wasn't sure if she'd used the right word. Hank was "quiet" in the way of a still, deep pool of water. She felt like she could spend her lifetime exploring his depths and not come to the center of him. So instead, she rested beside him. She drank in his spirit and let herself relax in his peace.

"I had to hit rock bottom," he said, his voice rough. "To that place where I either chose control or self-destruction."

A chill swept through her body. "Suicide?"

His lips curled into a wry smile. "Nothing so dramatic. A lot of booze and bar fights."

"And now?"

He shrugged and his eyes seemed to take on an intensity that belied the warm chocolate brown. It was as though he spoke from the very center of him. "Now I'm looking for my next place in life. I'm done with the military and not sure I'll take to the new alpha. I've got friends and responsibilities, but is that enough to build a full life?"

She understood the question. In her quieter moments between crises, she'd been asking herself the same thing. "I've got my job, medical mysteries to solve and all that. But living out of a suitcase gets old." As did staring death in the face over and over with no one to talk to about it.

Except now she knew Hank, and she knew he would listen if she wanted to share. It was that stillness inside him. It invited her to whisper all her secrets.

"You were never in any danger from me," he said, his voice gruff. "You know that, right? I was never going to hurt you. I protect people."

She got that now. She'd seen it in the way he cared for Sammy and Mother. And she'd seen it when he'd leapt across the room to stand between her and the crazy hybrid. He'd saved her life tonight, at the risk of his own. Hard not to melt when a guy did that.

"I know it's just biology," she said as she stroked a languid caress along his jaw. "Pheromones or something. I know that, but I want it anyway."

He didn't answer. She didn't know if he even breathed.

She trailed her fingers up his cheek and into the short nubs of his hair. His body was rigid. Was he fighting himself? She'd given up fighting sometime in the last few moments. So she stretched herself up to him. Or maybe she pulled him down to her. Either way, their bodies came close. Almost touching.

He held himself back by a scant quarter inch. She felt the heat of his breath on her lips. She saw the torment in his eyes.

"Biochemistry," she whispered.

"No," he said, and she didn't know if he was denying the source of these feelings or just her.

"I love biochemistry," she said. Then she surged upward until their mouths slammed together. It was fast and hard, too abrupt and nothing at all like she wanted because he kept his mouth closed.

His lips were sealed against hers, but she moved across them anyway. She stroked her tongue along the seam. She tugged with her arms and angled her head. Anything to get him to respond.

Nothing.

Nothing at all.

Until he completely changed.

Chapter 9

Hank teetered on cracking ice. The balance point was an ever-shifting kaleidoscope of possibilities. He was a man in his body, but at this moment his mind was more bear than human. The urge to care for Cecilia had come from both sides of himself, so that choice had been easy. He'd carried her upstairs, fed her with his own hand, and now came the inevitable result.

A kiss.

She pressed her lips to his and he gripped the edges of his sanity like a man trying to hold Jell-O together. Thoughts melted away. Morals, decisions, the things a man chooses to think and do—all lost their form beneath the press of her lips.

He tried to hold himself back. She didn't understand what he was. What the animal would do to her wasn't human. It was simple, raw, and would go on for hours. Her wishes wouldn't be considered except in that they got her to spread her legs. And then he would plant himself inside her and stay until he was done.

The only thing stopped him was a disappearing Jell-O mold of human beliefs. And she wiped them away with every stroke of her tongue against the seam of his lips.

His body locked tight, every muscle, every bone frozen. He couldn't draw back, and he would not soften forward. So he trembled on the last pinpoint of balance of neither bear nor man but a denial of both.

But she would not be denied. She teased across his lips with a wet heat that melted the balance point.

His lungs were shut down, but he had to inhale. His body demanded breath and with it came the scent of her arousal. Spiced persimmon. An exotic enough scent that his mind grew distracted by it. He followed it in his head, savoring the wildness of it. Where did it come from? Where would it take him? He didn't even realize it had pulled him off his balance until he was lost in pursuit of her scent.

He didn't find it in her mouth, though he plundered inside it. His tongue touched every part of her there. Teeth, tongue, roof of her mouth. He tasted heat mixed with chocolate and peanut butter and knew that the persimmon was not there.

He pressed her back onto the bed, setting his nose to her cheek and then into her hair. Most of his senses weren't as precise in human form. Though his vision improved, his sense of smell and taste were dulled, so he had to take his time as he followed her scent. He had to taste her cheek and ear; he had to press his nose to the curve of her neck. And he had to breathe there while he learned the details of her scent in minute detail.

And what he learned was that she tasted sweet, but the spice scent that drew him so firmly was not along her neck even though he used his teeth to scrape across her jaw just to be sure.

So he went lower.

Her clothing blocked his path. White cotton with scents that did not appeal to him. His hands knew how to unbutton the garment, and so he did. But the action required his human mind to be stronger and as it surged forward, it began to ask questions.

What was he doing?

Why was he doing it?

And most dangerous of all, are we in control? The answer was a clear no and the human mind pushed into more awareness.

But Cecilia hadn't been idle. As his hands had manipulated a plastic button through its hole, she had helped him, shrugging out of the white lab coat.

Suddenly, his vision was assaulted by the bright primary colors of her top. The pattern was random, the colors extreme, and the human struggled to understand it, but the bear gloried in the brilliance of it. It always liked females it could see easily.

The human was distracted, so the bear surged forward. He chased her scent, and that required the blinding colors removed as well. But this the bear managed easily, slipping his hands under her shirt as she lifted it off for him.

Now he could taste her skin. The heat of her body mixed with the sound of her breath. Sweet tight pants as her scent thickened in the air. He drew his tongue over her collarbone and down. Purple lace interfered with his progress, but she shrugged the bra away.

He found her breasts. His actions here were no different than anywhere else. He inhaled her scent, he stroked with the broad flat part of his tongue, and then he scraped his teeth across her flesh to deepen the taste. When it was not the source of her spiced persimmon scent, he moved on. When he nipped at her nipples, her breath changed, and her hands gripped his shoulders, but they were not what he pursued, so he continued on.

"Hank. Hank, take off your clothes."

She was speaking to him, and some part of him processed her words. He knew that she was willing, and that was enough for him to keep foraging around her body for her purest scent. So he tasted the flesh along her belly. The scent was clearer here, and he moved more quickly. The swipe of his tongue covered more of her skin, and he nipped with his teeth more aggressively. Not deeper, just over wider stretches of her body.

She jolted when he did that. Then there was a long shiver, but she did not draw away. He murmured against the top of her pants. A purr that came from his gut. He bared his teeth, ready to bite through the fabric, but he didn't need to. She pushed them down before touching his shoulders, his head, his face. She was trying to adjust him. Perhaps get him to lift his head, but he would not be stopped. Not by something so gentle as a tug.

Then he found the source of her spice, the taste of her persimmon. On the fur between her legs, on the sweet, flushed center of her.

He licked it as he consumed every drop. If she said something to him, he didn't hear it. If she wanted something from him, he didn't notice. He wanted her spice and her willingness. She gave him both. With every lick, her body stretched open. With every taste, her sweetness flowed stronger.

He felt her orgasm while he was delving between her legs. The undulating movement, the tightening of her thighs, everything that told him she was ready for him came while he burrowed into her sweetness.

And while she cried in delight, a part of him opened up. A connection of sorts. A slender thread that bound him to her and he was so delighted he redoubled his efforts while she gasped and cried in her completion.

Until she tugged at him. Until her body fought so wildly, even he could not contain her.

So he drew back to look at her. Her body was flushed, breasts peaked, and eyes dazed. But most important was that her thighs were spread. She was still flushed with spice and open to him.

He stood up because he needed to shuck his clothing before he mounted her. His hands went to his pants, but his fingers were clumsy. And with the surge of the human in his mind, words spilled from his lips.

"Stop me, Cecilia."

"It's okay," she said, her words breathless. "I liked it."

She didn't understand the bear. Worse, she didn't understand that taking a woman without care was wrong. The human needed balance in all things, most especially with a woman. To simply take according to his desire was wrong. To act without thought was the height of imbalance.

"Stop me," he rasped again.

"Hank, what's wrong?"

He was out of control and that always led to disaster. She pushed up on her elbows to look at him. He needed to draw back. He needed to find that lost center of Zen awareness, but the bear scented her spice and tried to pull his attention back to it.

Something was important about it. Something that the bear wanted him to know so he would comply. So he would release control back to the animal.

He inhaled deeply. He tasted the persimmon on his lips. And the bear pushed him to know the truth.

It had to act now. It had to penetrate her now, because of her scent. Because of her taste, the bear knew it had to be now.

She was fertile.

"A baby," he said. Then he repeated it more strongly. "A baby."

"What?"

"Stop me," he said again. "Or have my baby." He inhaled again and nearly lost himself to the magic of her scent. "A shifter baby. Now."

His pants hit the floor. His organ thrust forward, thick and proud. He paused a moment to let her admire it. Their child would have his strength. Their offspring would survive. She must see that.

"Put on a condom, Hank."

His gaze caught hers and in that moment, he felt his humanity slam forward. The biology burned strong, but her eyes caught his soul. She kept him from toppling into raw need without thought or restraint.

"Hank?"

I choose balance. I choose sanity.

A mantra, repeated over thousands of hours. He latched onto it like the lifeline it was.

"Magic is a force," he said. "Stronger in some than others." It was the first thing his teacher had told him so long ago. And the words came hand in hand with the mantra.

She frowned, and her head tilted slightly in confusion. He couldn't blame her. The last thing either of them wanted right now was for him to lecture her on shifter life. But it was the only way to hold onto his rational mind. That, plus the steady connection of her gaze.

I choose balance. I choose sanity.

"I gave myself over to it," he rasped. "Earlier. To fight the hybrid outside."

Her eyes widened, and her gaze hopped to the window, but he couldn't lose her eyes. So he reached out, his hand jerking too hard, too fast. He stopped a split second before he touched her, and she looked back to him. And that settled him enough to speak rationally.

"You're safe," he said. "But I…" He swallowed. "I want you."

Her expression softened. "I want you, too."

His abdomen rippled at her words, but he held himself rigidly back. She had to understand.

"And babies?" he rasped. "The magic wants babies."

She bit her lip. "Yes, I want children, but not right now. That's why you need a condom."

His bear snarled at the word, and he heard her gasp in surprise. She also straightened, pulling herself into a sitting position while he fought himself. The drive to have her seared him, pushing every cell forward to her. But he kept himself back.

I choose balance. I choose sanity. He voiced it inside his head. He repeated it beneath his breath.

"Hank?"

"I choose balance. I choose sanity."

She nodded, and she gently grabbed his hand, tucking it tightly between hers. "What can I do to help?"

"Get dressed," he rasped. "But hold my gaze."

She complied, though it was awkward. She held their eyes locked together as she pulled on leggings, which hid her fertile scent. The tunic came second, bra ignored. He saw in his peripheral vision that her hands shook, but her gaze remained steady on his.

"I choose balance. I choose sanity."

Then a third voice cut through the air. It was hard and cold. The voice of his alpha, and both bear and man listened. The bear because it had to, the man because it chose to.

"Step into the hallway, Dr. Lu. I will handle Hank."

Like hell. No man came between him and the female, even his alpha. He bared his teeth and forced out words. "She stays."

"Hank!" the alpha snapped, and Hank could hear dominance in every word. "Get control!"

"She. Stays."

Cecilia froze, her hands raised in surrender. "I'm not going anywhere, Hank. I'm right here."

The alpha shot her an irritated look. "You don't know what's going on here."

She snorted. "The hell I don't. He spent the night protecting us. God knows when the last time he slept was. And then he scented…then he." She swallowed. "He wants—"

"To mate, Dr. Lu. He wants you."

She dropped her hands on her hips. "Well, duh. And you getting between me and him is just going to rile him up."

"He's dangerous."

The female bared her teeth at the man. "He's in control. Aren't you, Hank? Remember? Balance. Sanity."

He dipped his chin. He was in balance. He was in control.

"How about you put on your pants?" she suggested.

Hank growled low and deep, but the human mind returned to the frozen balance point of control. And with it came the bear, however reluctantly. They had trained too many times in this for it to refuse.

I choose balance. I choose sanity.

He looked down, consciously seeing the clothing and imagining what he had to do. His body obeyed because he required it to. And when it was done, he looked at the female.

"I am balance," he said to her.

"Yes, balance."

"I am sanity."

"That's good, Hank."

"And I am bound to you."

"Um…what?"

Chapter 10

Too fast, too complicated, and she was too tired to make sense of things. After the best orgasm of her life—and God, if nothing else, Hank sure as hell knew how to give oral—suddenly she was dripping with fatigue and trying to understand words that used to make sense.

"What do you mean 'bound'?" she asked.

The newcomer—she guessed this was Simon—snorted in disgust. "We all think we're bound when we're exhausted, and a pretty woman lets us lick her."

Okay, she wasn't too tired to understand that, and heat bloomed over her entire body. But before she could react further, Hank growled. Yes, an honest-to-goodness growl. Simon drew up short, his expression tightening into fury.

"Don't embarrass her," Hank snapped.

"Don't challenge me. You won't like the—"

A woman's voice cut through the growing tension. "Oh my

God, can we go through one night without a testosterone-fest?" A handsome black woman stepped into the room. Her face was beautiful, but what Cecilia noticed most was that she exuded strength. Not just her muscles but the steel that lay underneath the teasing words. "Here," she said to Simon as she handed him her tablet. "This okay?"

Simon had no choice but to grab the equipment or let it fall to the ground. Then he was glaring at the screen while the woman turned to Cecilia and held out her hand in greeting.

"Hi, I'm Alyssa. That's Simon, chief chest-beater. You're Dr. Lu, right?"

"Um, call me Cecilia."

"Good choice. We're likely to get pretty friendly over the next few days as you get up to speed." Her gaze roved over the entire room. There was no change of expression, just a full awareness of the situation. Hank, Cecilia, and the thoroughly mussed bed.

"Um…" Cecilia began, though she had no idea what she was going to say.

"You've had a pretty eventful night. You understand about shifters now, right?"

"That they exist? Yes. Understand them—"

Alyssa chuckled. "Don't worry about that. Nobody does."

Meanwhile, Simon tapped the tablet before handing it back to Alyssa. "That's fine. And you could have sent that yourself."

"I know," Alyssa said with a grin. "But sometimes you need to take a moment to clear your mind of all the…" She waved her hand vaguely around. "Scents in the air."

Which is when Cecilia figured out that the smell of sex was probably perfuming the entire bedroom. She hadn't thought her face could heat any more, but she was learning all sorts of new things tonight.

"So here's the report," Alyssa continued. "Sammy's asleep, appears to be fine. Same with Mother. Wolves haven't responded to email yet, and Hank has been going full tilt for at least forty-two hours. Cecilia here has been kidnapped, dragged into the shifter world, and attacked. I'll bet she had a bit of a meltdown and now..." She made a vague circle with her finger at the room. "Everybody needs sleep."

Hank straightened. "I will not leave her alone."

Simon grunted. "He thinks he's—"

"Bound to her. Yes, I heard." Alyssa looked at Cecilia. "It's a thing some shifters do with their mates."

"Mates?" Cecilia squeaked, panic making her voice high and tight. "As in sex mate or...um..."

"Forever, uber-married mates," Alyssa said, her gaze hopping to Simon with the kind of warmth that only appeared on the silver screen. And more surprising, the buzz-cut leader softened in response. Their fingers entwined though neither even appeared to notice.

Meanwhile, Cecilia snuck a glance at Hank. Could he really feel that way about her? She doubted it. He looked...fierce, defensive, and more than a little intimidating.

"Look," Cecilia said, thinking about the science. It's what she always did when she felt uncomfortable. "There's a lot for me to study right now before the bodies decompose."

"You need to rest," Hank said, his voice firm.

Yes, she did, but she also needed to get away from all these people with their emotions and things that she didn't understand. "So yes, I had a little meltdown—"

Hank released a low rumble. It was like a warning sound and she had the strongest urge to stroke his arm to soothe him. She didn't. She just looked at him and felt at a complete loss. What was she supposed to do now? Damn, she hated feeling unsettled like this.

Meanwhile, Alyssa focused back on her. "I would have had a massive meltdown if I were you." Then she flashed Cecilia a conspiratorial smile. "I was you, only in reverse. I shot him, then kidnapped him."

"What is it with all the kidnapping?" Cecilia abruptly blurted out. "I mean, you could have just sat me down in a conference room or something."

"No, we couldn't." That came from both men in almost identical rhythms.

"Great," Alyssa snorted. "Shifter stereo." Then she turned back to Cecilia. "You're dead on your feet. Do you think you can sleep? The adrenaline is about to drain right out of you, if it hasn't already."

It was going fast and at Alyssa's words, Cecilia felt her body begin to ache with weariness. Like the words had made her aware of something that had been there for a while now.

"Um…"

"Right." Alyssa's hand shot out on one side, Hank's on the other. They both guided her to sit on the bed. "There's two beds here. Okay if he sleeps on the other?" She shot Hank a dark look. "You can sleep, right? And not crawl all over her."

Hank straightened up as if insulted. "I can rest but—"

Simon interrupted with clipped tones. "Then it's an order. Sleep." That was for Hank. Then he turned to her. "Dr. Lu, we're expecting a lot from you as soon as possible. So get your rack time now."

She wanted to argue, but Alyssa was right. The adrenaline was fading fast and now she was crashing. She didn't even have the energy for the shakes. And though her mind was hopping like a rabbit on caffeine, there was no cohesion to her thoughts. Which meant there was no way she could work.

"Cecilia," Alyssa repeated. "Do you have a problem with Hank sleeping in the second bed?"

"I'll feel safer with him here," she said. Then a split second later, she wondered how that could be. She'd only just met Hank. They barely knew each other, and yet the feeling of safety persisted while she sank into the mattress.

"Then it's settled," Alyssa said. "You two sleep. Simon and I will cover things here. Any science-y stuff you want us to handle while you rest?"

Cecilia's head hit the pillow. The world was starting to spin, and she needed to be lying down while that happened. But even so, she managed to answer the question. "Record the decomposition. I've got baseline pictures on Hank's phone. But a comparison—"

"Got it." The woman snapped off the light and Cecilia heard footsteps traveling away.

"—is important to establish where the breakdowns occur and why. I have an idea…" Her words faltered. She had an idea, but it skittered away from her. She needed to study the cellular structure at the seams. That would provide the biggest clues. There were areas on the hybrids where human clearly changed to animal. The cells at the seam could help her understand the transition process.

Her thoughts continued to spin. She let them drift because she had no strength to control them. Meanwhile, she heard Hank move. She waited to hear the creak of the mattress of the bed next to hers, but she didn't. Instead, there were muted thumps and sounds on the wrong side. The side next to the door.

She cracked her eyes open. "What—?"

"I'm going to sleep between you and the door," Hank said. "You'll be safer that way."

She lifted her head and stared down at the pillow he'd tossed near the open bedroom door. "Don't you trust Simon?"

"He's my alpha and he's sworn himself to protect his people."

She frowned as he stretched out beside her. "So why are you on the floor?"

"Because even powerful alphas can be overpowered." Then he reached up a hand to connect with hers. She was still deciding if she wanted to make such a friendly gesture with him when her fingers entwined with his. Apparently her body wanted to hold on to Hank.

Huh.

She was still wondering how she felt about that when sleep claimed her.

* * *

"Cecilia. Cecilia, wake up."

Cecilia did not want to wake up. The thick fog was comforting, the steadiness of a low rumbling breath nearby marked time in a really soothing way. Though now that she thought about it, she couldn't hear it right now. Still, she remembered it and settled back into its gentle rhythm.

"The wolves are coming."

Her eyes shot open as her legs shoved out from under the blanket. She used their weight to pull her body upright, but she was unsteady and dizzy. Thankfully, large hands caught her. She leaned into their strength and eventually found her balance. And then she blinked as she tried to focus on the sight in front of her.

Male chest. Dark skin. Sculpted pectorals that bunched as they steadied her. Dark nipples. Tight chest hair.

Pretty, pretty, pretty. Male perfection right there to greet her bleary eyes.

She smiled and reached out to touch all that perfection. She felt his heat before her fingers connected. She knew the skin would be satiny smooth and was pleasantly surprised when she felt the muscles twitch beneath her caress. Strength pulsing right beneath her fingertips.

And then her mind woke up enough to collect her scattered attention. Pretty, pretty got pushed aside in favor of something else.

"Werewolves?"

"Yes. I knew you'd want to see them."

Damn straight she would. She just had to wake up.

Hank's hands released her. She mourned the loss of his heat, but she could sit up on her own now. He pressed something to her lips. She smelled chocolate and peanut butter, and quickly opened her mouth.

She closed her eyes a moment, savoring the taste and the knowledge that pretty soon she'd have some blood sugar. She ate another three bites, thinking she ought to be ashamed for letting someone feed her, but at the moment, she needed to get her brain online. God, if only she could have…

"Drink this. Careful it's hot."

Green tea. Yes. Just what she needed.

She managed to wrap her hands around the mug. It wasn't her favorite tea, but if brewed right, it had enough caffeine to wake up a two-by-four. And it was her mother's favorite drink so that brought her comfort. Both aspects were very welcome right then, as was the man who was awkwardly shuffling his feet in front of her.

She quirked a brow at him in question.

"I know it's stereotypical," he said. "Mother likes it, so we brewed a pot. But if you prefer coffee—"

"What's stereotypical? That Chinese people like tea?"

He nodded.

"Most Chinese people do like tea."

"And you?"

She smiled as she inhaled the fragrance. This was quality tea brewed hot, and the caffeine was starting to wake her up. "I like caffeine and chocolate. Hot drinks are a great way to get both."

His eyes took on a mischievous look and she lifted her head to see it more clearly. He had something up his sleeve—metaphorically speaking—and she wanted to know what it was.

"Don't tease me, Hank. Not about my sacred foods."

He reached into his pocket and drew something out. He had angled his body to hide what he was doing, and she was nearly distracted by the cut outline of his oblique muscles. Nearly. Because a moment later he showed her God's gift to exhausted women: an expensive chocolate bar with espresso bean chips.

"Oh my God!" she gasped and nearly spilled her tea while trying to grab the bar. He held the chocolate out of reach, but that didn't stop her from following it with her eyes.

"I stole it from Sammy's stash."

"She'll kill you."

"She won't wake for another day. I'll replace it before then."

"You better. I'd hurt you if stole mine."

He grinned as he squatted down in front of her. "What will you do if I give this to you?"

"Not kill you for teasing me with it."

He grinned as he ripped open the foil packaging. He broke off a piece and held it out.

"Are you expecting me to beg for it?" She would. Despite the Powerbar and the tea, she was still hungry and feeling off her game. Sugar, espresso, and chocolate would give her a needed short-term boost.

"Just a kiss."

Her gaze shot to his, startled enough to search his eyes for extra meaning. His tone had been teasing, even flirty, but in his eyes was a seriousness that belied everything else. That one look brought everything from last night rushing back. Not just the hot times in this very bed, but also the way he'd apologized to her at the hospital before slamming her into the car upholstery and zip-tying her hands and feet. She remembered him as a black bear teaching Sammy how to speak like the best big brother ever, but also the way he ripped apart the hybrid in front of her. All of it came rushing back with a force that had her reeling.

His hand shot out to cup her elbow and she closed her eyes.

"Too soon?" he asked.

"Yeah."

"Sorry."

"Give me the chocolate and you're forgiven."

He pressed the morsel against her lips, but she pulled back without eating. It was too intimate to eat from his fingertips, so she used her free hand to take it from him.

"I, um…I can do it. Thanks."

She watched his expression tighten, but he didn't fight her. He released the chocolate morsel into her hand and then a second later gave her the full bar. She could see that he didn't like it. In fact, she suspected he was hurt by the barrier—however tiny—that she put up between them. It was like he expected their one explosive night together to have cemented an entire relationship, but she barely knew him. Plus, she was a neophyte in this world of shifters. She had to get her bearings before she started eating out of a man's hands. Or, um, did it anymore.

She swallowed expensive chocolate and espresso beans, breakfast of champions. Then she broke of another bit and offered it to him. She thought he'd take it from her hand, but before she could change her mind, he leaned down and wrapped his tongue around it and her fingers.

Wet. Hot. Sensuous. She felt his tongue caress her knuckle and the skin before her nail. Then his lips pressed down as his tongue slipped between her thumb and forefinger, and he sucked the chocolate free.

Her breath caught, and memories flooded her mental landscape. Suddenly she wasn't sitting here mostly dressed with a gorgeous guy and chocolate. She was naked and writhing as his tongue swirled everywhere between her thighs. She felt it delve inside her before sweeping up and around her clit. She felt the suction on her fingers the same way she'd felt it last night.

Too much. Too intense. She was not a physical woman. Or at least not until last night. And certainly not first thing in the morning. She wasn't used to this wet, clutching in her womb or the throbbing in her clit. Not when she was trying to wake up and werewolves were on the way. Werewolves! And damn her nether parts were doing nether things that they weren't supposed to. Not first thing in the morning.

"Cecilia?"

She'd pulled her hand back, and now her head was tilted away with her eyes shut. She was trying to get a hold of herself, and he was too present in her mind. In her mind, her body and in everything.

"Dr. Lu?"

She swallowed. She heard the withdrawal in his tone and knew for sure that she'd hurt him. But damn it, she couldn't worry about his feelings right then. She had to get her own equilibrium back. Which meant she had to focus on the important stuff. Facts. Situation. Science, if possible.

"Tell me about the werewolves," she said.

She waited without looking at him. And when the silence got too strained, she pulled the mug of tea up to drink more. Then their eyes met over the rim of her cup. She couldn't help it. He drew her gaze no matter what her brain told her to do. And once she'd met them, she couldn't look away.

Just like last night. He had brown eyes, slightly narrowed to give them a nearly almond shape. They sat above strong cheekbones in a broad face. Last night they'd seemed to swirl with emotions she barely understood. This morning, she was the one swirling and he looked at her quietly. How could eyes be gentle? How could they hold her safe with steady compassion?

She wanted to look away. She'd always found her balance on her own, usually in a science textbook or a computer screen. But she didn't. She held his gaze and in the quiet, she felt a kinship build between them. Like a tiny note ringing softly but with increasing power. Too quiet to hear, but yet strong enough to feel. It connected them both and she was as terrified of it as she was comforted by its strength.

She wasn't alone anymore, she thought. Not when he was a tangible presence in her…what? Mind? No. She didn't need to think of him to feel him. Spirit maybe, and now she had to believe in that along with shifters and magic.

That terrified her most of all because her entire life was built on science. She worshipped the tangible, not the invisible. And yet here he was, a part of her though he didn't speak, they didn't touch, and she was about to walk away from him.

"It's okay, Hank. I'll just go downstairs and find out." She pushed to her feet and he backed up to give her room. She spotted her bra on the floor and grabbed it. There was a bathroom close by. She wanted to use that and a hairbrush if she could find it. And—

"We'll talk later," he said.

She paused, but didn't turn around. "That's not a euphemism, is it." Not a question. "You really do mean we're going to have a…" What? "A relationship conversation."

"Yes."

Oh hell.

"Werewolves, first. Okay?"

"Okay."

She nodded and fled. And when had werewolves become less scary than Hank?

Chapter 11

Hank watched her rush to the bathroom. His gaze held on the way her bottom twitched as she moved. He inhaled her scent and listened to the sounds of water as she washed. And he had to fight his bear to remain still in the bedroom, simply absorbing Dr. Cecilia Lu through all his senses without actively stalking her.

He waited an extra long time. He held himself still and breathed, hoping the desperate need to be with her would fade. It didn't. And that was how he knew he was well and truly fucked.

His bear had bound itself to her.

Why her, when she was a scientist, the one person guaranteed to fight everything he was? Not just his bear, but the fact that he was a poor man with little education. She was a good girl with a PhD and a string of specialties behind her name. Words he hadn't even known before he'd looked her up on the Internet. What exactly did an epidemiologist do? He hadn't a clue. Virology, he guessed, was about viruses. But then he'd linked over to one of her papers.

He hadn't been able to understand the title, much less the contents of the paper.

And he was a big black army medic turned muscle for a Detroit grizzly clan.

He blew out a breath and closed his eyes. He needed to find his balance point. Some way to settle into a Zen calm that would allow him to sort through his feelings dispassionately. Instead, he thought of her white lab coat that hid a wild tunic of blinding colors underneath. He thought of the way she'd fought him in his truck, screaming and kicking when most others would have given up. And then the way she'd lit up with excitement at the idea of examining the hybrid bodies. She was smart, fought like a demon though she had no training, and rolled with the punches like a regular street kid.

He liked her. If they had met in the normal course of life, he would have enjoyed her company while they shared a burger or went to a movie. He would probably have asked her out for a date and allowed things to progress in the normal way.

But he wasn't normal in any sense of the word. "Muscle for the Griz" wasn't exactly something to put on a tax return. And he sure as hell couldn't tell that to a woman with multiple PhDs. The two of them didn't fit and they weren't going to have a future after the crisis was over.

So why in the hell was his bear determined to have her? Her and no other? Because no matter what Simon had said, Hank had bonded to Cecilia. He would pursue her, watch her, dream about her, and most likely stalk her for the rest of his life. It wasn't something he could control, and it wasn't something she could stop.

She was about to come out of the bathroom, so he straightened and went into the hallway. He ordered himself to leave. She was coming downstairs to see the werewolves. He could wait for her there.

He didn't. He leaned against the wall until she emerged. Her face was pink and wet from a fresh scrubbing. Her hair was pulled back in a ruthless ponytail, and her colorful tunic over black leggings was smooth as if she'd just gotten it from a laundromat. Her lab coat was back in the bedroom, and he wondered if she wanted it. It would please his bear to give it to her, though he preferred this brighter, less professional attire.

She pulled up short as she saw him waiting for her. He guessed she would nod at him and rush past. It's what most women did in his presence. Instead, she gestured to him.

"Are you going to put on a shirt?"

He shook his head. He didn't bother explaining that it was downstairs, and she was upstairs. He hadn't been able to force himself to grab it despite the fact that he'd walked right past it to get her tea.

She folded her arms and mimicked his pose as she leaned against the frame of the bathroom door. "You just like standing there looking all big, bad, and hot?"

Yes. If she thought he looked hot.

Then she frowned. "Wait. The werewolves are coming. You don't want another piece of clothing interfering if you have to go grizzly. Right?"

He shook his head. "I went bear last night. Won't be able to shift again until tomorrow." And that was assuming he got some more rest.

"Really?" Her eyes brightened, and she straightened up. "Is that normal? How often can others shift? Are bears different? What about the wolves? And the hybrids?"

His lips twitched. She was like a kid in a video game store with her questions. Which character can do what and how often?

"Faster than normal, some as little as once a year. Wolves can go more often, though that might be hype. Cats won't tell anyone shit, though we think they're similar to wolves. As for the hybrids?" He shrugged. "Looks like they can do it whenever they want. One of their advantages." He quirked a brow. "The smell being a distinct disadvantage. At least from Vic's perspective."

She took a step forward. He loved that. All he had to do was answer some questions, and she went from running away to eagerly standing beside him. "Who's Vic?"

"Simon's beta. He's a hybrid. One of the few who stayed sane. Alan's another. He's with the Gladwins."

"That's because the change seems to destroy the frontal cortex. But not for this Vic? Or Alan? Can I meet them?"

"Yes—" he began, but then he cut off his words, holding up his hand to quiet her as he sniffed the air. "They're coming," he said in a low voice.

Her eyes widened, and she started to head downstairs. He stopped her by pressing his hand into her belly in a quick block. It wasn't meant to be anything more than a gesture to stop her, but the moment his hand connected, his mind was flooded by sensations. The softness he felt there, the joy of being able to freely caress a place so vulnerable, the sweetness of her gasp, and the visceral memories of what they'd done the night before. It all surged through him, hard and fast. His nostrils flared and his dick throbbed.

But that's all that he did. And when she turned to quirk an eyebrow at him, he shook his head. "Stay behind me."

She nodded slowly. "Werewolves not so tame?"

"No shifter is tame. Don't ever forget that."

He watched the information sink in. He saw her swallow as she squared her shoulders. And then suddenly, her brows narrowed. "Neither is the Hong Kong B virus, but I handled that just fine, thank you very much." Her expression shifted into a grin. "Surprised you, didn't I?"

Yes.

"You thought you could spout some B movie lines and I'd be all aflutter."

"Most people would be on the floor drooling after what you saw last night."

Her face paled and he regretted reminding her of the uglier parts of last night.

"Well, I'm not most people," she said.

No kidding.

"And besides, this is an answer to my prayer, so I can hardly look a gift horse in the mouth, can I?"

He frowned. "I have no idea what that means."

She blew out a breath. "For the last three days I've been praying—actually praying—for a clue. Some way to get a handle on the Detroit Flu. And then, bam, you kidnap me and suddenly I've got more clues than I can follow. So, I've set this down to divine intervention. You want me to handle werewolves with care? You got it. You want to be my big scary bodyguard? Whatever floats your boat. But if you keep me from following any one of my divinely given clues, then I will find a way to...to pinch you in a way that hurts. A lot."

A laugh burst out of him. A single, wild bark of sound that he hadn't made in years. Not since being forced into the Griz and becoming the muscle for Nanook, the asshole that Simon defeated a very short two days ago. And now suddenly, this little spitfire threatens to pinch him, and he was choking back humor.

Balance.

Well, hell. There it was. That balance point of calm that he'd lost last night. He felt as if all the world had settled, which allowed him to smile at her and nod.

"If you stay behind me while the wolves are here, then you can pursue any clue you want."

She snorted. "The wolves are the clue, but for the moment I'll bow to your greater wisdom. I'll just think of you like protective gloves or a fume hood."

Not images he liked, but he'd take it. Especially as he heard the wolves enter with heavy tread and that very particular dog scent. Pissed-off canine. Gah.

"Just remember, they're touchy, aggressive, and don't like insults to their manhood. Treat them like unstable TNT. With fangs."

He saw her eyes widen at that. Secure that she had gotten his message, he started down the stairs. The scene spread out before him as quickly as the smell. Five werewolves in their human form had come in the front door. Three others stood as wolves outside the broken window looking in. Simon stood next to Mother, facing them. It was her house, so he allowed her to stand beside him, but Hank could see that the alpha was in position to protect her if needed. And way back behind all three dead bodies—one werewolf, two hybrids—stood Alyssa with tablet in one hand, gun in another. Sammy was probably still sound asleep downstairs.

Hank should be beside his alpha, acting as protection and support. Simon hadn't called for it, but it was Hank's place and he itched to go there. But his job was to protect Cecilia. No one had said that, but his bear was adamant on this point. It was what happened with bonded males, and so he accepted it with a grim sense of fate.

At least he could get to a compromise location. He gestured Cecilia to stand with Alyssa as he moved to a halfway point in the room. And he waited while everyone pretended to like each other. The wolf alpha started. He looked to be a man in his fifties with pale silver eyes, distinguished in his expensive suit.

"Mother, we've come for our dead."

"Where's Miriam? She okay?"

"She's resting. It's been a long night of corralling hallucinating normals. Antwone was our only casualty."

"And them." She gestured to the hybrids. "Do you know who they were?"

The man barely gave them a glance. "They're gone now." His eyes narrowed on Simon. "But you have a hybrid beta. How did you manage to control him?"

"Vic controls himself," Simon responded. "How many hybrids in your territory? Have you told everyone not to drink the water?"

"We have control, but you are well out of your territory."

It was like watching two men play completely different video games while in the same room. It looked like they were talking to each other, but neither seemed to be interested in the same thing. And even Mother's interest was somewhere else. For her, each of the three dead shifters used to be a person. Someone's child, someone's friend. She wanted to know if the families had been notified, if those who grieved had been comforted. It was why she was able to stay so neutral while sitting on the bad side of the wolf lands.

Sadly, everyone ignored her.

"I'm here for Sammy," Simon said. "She matured last night."

"Then why are you—"

"And I stayed to protect Mother from attack. Isn't she favored by your pack?"

The alpha—named Emory Wolf—didn't like being interrupted, but he didn't quarrel. Instead, his gaze landed on Cecilia. Hank tried not to react. He really did. But the moment the guy's eyes lingered too damn long on her bright, beautiful form, Hank felt his hackles rise and his hands shift into claws.

Wolf noticed. The bastard saw everything and he chose to poke at Hank by moving the conversation to Cecilia.

"I don't remember this woman in my territory."

Cecilia opened her mouth to speak, but Hank shot her a warning look. He hadn't needed to. Simon spoke, his tone level and with the exact same amount of steel underneath as he always used.

"Dr. Cecilia Lu is from the CDC. We've brought her into the clan so she can help."

Wolf's brows rose. "Help what? There is a poison in the water. You said as much. The weak ones die, the strong ones evolve. She cannot help that."

Cecilia snorted. "Pull that attitude out of the dark ages handbook?"

Well, it had been too much to hope that she could keep silent when someone—even as cold and powerful a man as the werewolf alpha—challenged the benefit of science. And just as Hank feared, the man bared his teeth at her, showing his elongated canines.

Instead of being frightened, the insane woman took an eager step forward. "Is that normal for you? I mean in your human form? Those canines are at least forty percent longer than typical for a human male. Are you able to partially change into a wolf? If so, then perhaps the hybrids are more wolf than—"

"I am a full shifter!" the man snapped. "And the hybrids are nothing but rabid dogs."

The venom in his words was clear and Hank wouldn't have been surprised if he whipped out his dick and urinated on the bodies as proof of his contempt. Meanwhile, Cecilia would not shut up.

"I get that. It's their frontal cortex. Deteriorates for some reason. But if you can partially change, then that's important. That's… oh my."

"Oh my" was right. The alpha's eyes had gone yellow-green and fur popped out along his arms. His jaws elongated, and his teeth looked sharp and white as he growled at her. But he didn't strip out of his clothes and he certainly didn't shift the whole way. It made him look like the big bad wolf of Disney cartoons. A beast in human form. Except his hands stayed human, though they extended slightly as if he wanted to change but was holding himself back.

It was enough to silence Cecilia, and it was a damned impressive show of control. No other shifter that he knew of could consciously halt the change midway. For everyone else, it was all or nothing, and Hank couldn't suppress a grudging respect.

Cecilia, on the other hand, was walking closer as she studied the alpha. And she was patting the pockets of her tunic as if looking for her phone, which was mercifully still in his car. Fortunately, she'd gotten close enough that he could grab her arm and hold her back.

"What are you doing?" he growled at her.

"You want me up to speed. This is how I get up to speed."

He grimaced and turned to the alpha. "She is trying to help.

Is there a wolf who could answer her questions? Someone young, perhaps, and not busy right now."

There was a long pause as the wolf alpha stared at her, and Cecilia continued to inspect the man, clearly not nearly as intimidated as she should be. Everyone else remained poised, waiting for a response with seeming calm. Did no one else see the implied threat in the man's furred face or long white teeth?

In the end, Wolf straightened, his expression turning cagey as he shifted back into human. Cecilia gasped audibly, her eyes practically dancing with interest. Everyone else pretended they'd seen that a thousand times before. Then the alpha spoke with sudden decisiveness, as if he were the one giving commands here.

"She will come with me. I will answer her questions."

Hank's bear reacted violently to that. It surged in his mind, roaring in a way that had his entire body prickling with fur. Or it would have if Hank hadn't shifted last night. He wasn't strong enough to change right now, and that was probably a good thing because it gave him a moment to control his reaction, though his words came out fast enough.

"She stays with me."

The wolf grinned, his completely human teeth flashing. "Then come with us."

Simon spoke, his voice so calm, it could have been a recording. "He stays with me."

Mother snorted. "And you all can sit at my table and talk all you want. So long as someone is fixing my window and making sure those bodies are handled respectfully." Her gaze narrowed. "Or maybe I'll just find me a nice home in bear country and find other children to help."

It was an empty threat. Mother had lived in this house for thirty years, and she had much more fondness for the dogs than the bears, probably because her husband had been a wolf. Plus the dogs popped out children like rabbits. Always a new puppy to care for, though they were completely human until adolescence. And though she'd cared for a variety of different breeds—Sammy being the most recent bear—she wasn't going to up and move to Griz territory.

Meanwhile Wolf gestured with a single flick of a finger. Like the smallest tick of a tail, it was a signal to gather Antwone. "We will take our own." His gaze landed on the more wolflike hybrid. "And that one." His gaze slid to Simon. "Care for your own."

"And my window?" Mother pressed.

He arched a brow at Simon. "Shared costs? They would not have come if the bears hadn't been here." He sneered as he said the word "bears," as though he was referring to rats.

"Are you saying you can't control your own? Because mine did nothing wrong."

Wolf's expression turned condescending. "You are a new alpha just arrived in Detroit. In this city, we share the burden."

Simon didn't say a thing. He simply turned to Alyssa who had been tapping on her tablet. "Not according to Nanook's records. He's detailed every dime he thinks is owed—"

"Nanook is dead," Wolf snapped, his eyes flashing yellow as he referred to the old Griz alpha. The one Simon had killed two days ago. "There are no debts."

"Agreed," Simon said, his voice again excruciatingly calm. "New slate. No debt. But if I fix Mother's window, her block and the ones north of her become mine."

Every single wolf reacted to that. The ones who were wolves

growled. One even howled. The humans bared their teeth and made sounds that had Hank's skin crawling. But not a one moved forward, though Hank was braced for it. And Simon—coldhearted machine that he was—didn't even blink. He kept his body relaxed and his attention square on Wolf.

And then one of Wolf's men stepped forward. He was an older man with thick muscles and the slightest bit of gray around his temples. He didn't speak, though. Simply waited for Wolf to acknowledge him, which took another excruciatingly long minute.

Eventually Wolf nodded. Then the man spoke.

"I will fix the window, Mother. In thanks."

Hank had no idea what she'd done for the man, but it was enough to break the impasse. Especially when Mother smiled and added her two cents. "Your boys turned out to be fine men. I'd be grateful for the help."

So it was done. The wolves picked up the dead Antwone with reverence. The wolflike hybrid, not so much. They had body bags with them, and whereas the wolf was settled with care, the hybrid was all but thrown inside. And given the smell, Hank really couldn't blame them.

Cecilia opened her mouth to say something. Probably to ask to autopsy the bodies, but Hank squeezed her arm to silence her. She subsided with a mulish pout, and for that show of intelligence, he was profoundly grateful.

It took a surprisingly short amount of time. The werewolves were quick and efficient, as if they were used to picking up bodies and whisking them away. Meanwhile, Wolf turned his attention to Cecilia in a way that made Hank bristle from his bear's protective instincts.

"What have you learned about the Detroit Flu?"

Cecilia shook her head. "Inconclusive so far, but I'm excited to take another look at our data. Now that I know more."

"And who will you report your findings to?"

She opened her mouth to answer, but then abruptly frowned, her expression uncertain. She looked to Hank, but he couldn't tell her what to say here. She was in on the shifter secret, but that only meant she was in the same vise of uncertainty that they all lived in. How to keep their existence a secret in a modern city?

"Who would listen?" she finally asked.

"You will send them to me," Wolf said.

Simon interrupted. "Actually, she'll send them to me, and I'll pass them on to all the alphas. As part of my clan, she is my responsibility."

Meanwhile, Cecilia had run out of patience. "Look, as fun as it is to visit feudal society, I'm here for the science. We all need a cure for the Detroit Flu, and I'll happily email my results to anyone who will listen."

Hank sighed. "No, Cecilia—"

"Agreed," Wolf cut in. Then he pulled a crisp business card out of his pocket. "Here is my card." He held it out to her but only by a few inches. It would require her to cross several feet to take it from him. She went without hesitation while Hank fought every instinct within him to let her go even that distance. He didn't release her arm, though. And he was prepared to yank her backward if Wolf did anything suspicious.

He didn't. But that didn't mean Hank wasn't ready to tear out his throat just for getting near Cecilia.

And then the bastard had the gall to smile at Hank. A slow,

knowing smile that taunted while Hank fought his inner bear. Bears didn't give way to wolves. Ever. But if a pack coordinated their attack, then an outnumbered bear would lose every time. And innocents could die in the process.

He wasn't willing to risk Cecilia that way, so he kept a fierce hold on his instincts. And the moment she had Wolf's card in hand, he jerked her back behind him. Meanwhile, the wolf alpha looked to her.

"I'll have three wolves visit you tomorrow night, Dr. Lu, at your hotel. To answer your questions."

"One," Hank corrected.

Which is when Cecilia snorted, clearly impatient with the territorial posturing. "Two? Okay? Send two."

To which Simon answered: "Agreed." And since Simon was the bear alpha, Hank had no place to argue. But he could assert some protections.

"And I'll be there," he said. Cecilia opened her mouth to argue, but he cut it off with a hard squeeze on her arm. "To help. With the science."

Wolf exhaled loudly, the sound derisive, but he didn't bother to argue. And a moment later, he turned on his heel and left like a damned military dictator. His men separated enough for him to leave first, then they filed out with paradelike precision. Men on four sides, wolves extending in a perimeter beyond.

Pompous ass.

Still, Hank watched closely to make sure every single one left. And while he was peering out the window, all his senses on alert, Cecilia rounded on him with a huff.

"And now can I use your phone? I need to record my impressions of that testosterone-fest. Was that just human male? Or are all you shifters prone to that kind of display?"

Hank didn't bother responding. Turns out, he didn't need to because both Mother and Alyssa answered together.

"Both."

Chapter 12

I need to get back to the hospital."

Cecilia had finished recording her impressions of the meeting on her phone, which Hank had handed over as soon as the wolves had left. Now she really needed to get to the lab for serious work. She was itching to look at the CDC's existing data with her new understanding. Not to mention studying the data that Simon had emailed her. But she couldn't start doing that until she had a computer larger than her hand.

"I can call an Uber—" she began, but Hank cut her off.

"I'll take you. I just want to make sure everything here is settled first." His gaze went to Mother where she was sitting and sipping tea. The man was obviously super protective of her and Sammy, and Cecilia couldn't damn him for it. In fact, it only made him more attractive to her.

"Kennedy reports five more cases of the Flu, all fatalities." That statement came from Simon, his tone so bland he didn't even look up from the tablet he and Alyssa were using. And wasn't that nauseatingly cute? Two people cuddled up together on Mother's couch as they discussed personnel, whom they were protecting, and where.

Actually, that was cute. And reassuring. It felt good to know that Simon, in addition to the exhausted police, was looking out for Detroit's residents. Meanwhile, Cecilia looked at Hank who was busy making omelets for everyone. And lord, they smelled heavenly. She was about to ask who was Kennedy when he answered as if he'd read her mind.

"Detective Ryan Kennedy. He's one of us."

"Grizzly?"

Hank nodded as he brought her a Denver omelet that had her stomach rumbling with hunger. One bite later, she nearly forgot everything else. "Oh my God," she gasped. "This is good!" It's hard to screw up an omelet, though she'd managed it a few times. But overall, that also meant it was hard to make an amazing one. Hank had done something to simple ham and eggs that made her taste buds weep. "Are all shifters great cooks?"

"Just my Hank," Mother answered with a grin as she accepted her own plate.

The man in question grinned back as he ducked his head, obviously pleased and a little embarrassed by the praise. "Alyssa, you're next."

"Thanks a million, Hank."

Cecilia watched the exchange, noting that he had served her first, Mother second, Alyssa third. The women first, starting with her. In most pack hierarchies, the alpha male would come first, but Simon hadn't been fed yet. And she had no idea what it meant that Hank had given her food before any of the other women.

Clearly standard pack structure didn't apply here, but in other
things—like that bear versus wolf clash earlier—pack structure had
been well in evidence.

She just wished she knew what it all meant. Hopefully her
notes would make sense later. That's what she did when she got
too exhausted to make conclusions. She focused on details, wrote
them all down, and tried to sort them out later. She sighed as
she tucked into her omelet. Maybe they were right. Maybe she
needed to eat first and mentally regroup before trying to sort
through data she couldn't fully process yet. She was still eating
when someone drove up in a large truck, followed quickly by a
police cruiser. Apparently, it was what everyone had been waiting
for because Alyssa hopped off the couch, Hank left kitchen
duty, and Mother said, "About damn time," into her tea. Simon
didn't appear to react at all as he continued to study something
on the tablet.

Two men climbed out of the truck's cab, one so old as to be
considered elderly, the other barely out of adolescence. But both
had barrel chests and thick arms as they pulled a body bag out of
the back. Behind them came a uniformed police officer who looked
more like a California surfer dude than a cop, especially with his
too bright smile.

Cecilia recognized that smile. It was the one she wore when she
was so exhausted she could barely see, but still had to appear fresh in
front of patients. She guessed this cop was on his very last legs.

Meanwhile, the three knocked politely on the door, though they
could see straight in through the busted window. Hank opened the
door and two headed straight for the hybrid's body while the cop
crossed to Simon's side.

"Report," Simon said, his voice almost casual as he looked up at the men.

The cop answered, his tone frequently betraying his exhaustion for all that he kept his words light. "Looting is contained but that's because more people are home puking. We got reports of monsters everywhere, most hallucinations. A few not. And regular shifters—the ones who ought to be helping—are just mean."

Simon nodded as if it were exactly what he expected, then he gestured at the cop's uniform. "Since when do gang cops dress up?"

The man snorted. "Since we're supposed to show that the police are everywhere." He rolled his eyes. "Which we aren't. We're down to less than half now." Then he turned and abruptly extended a hand to her. "Detective Ryan Kennedy, here to serve and protect," he said. "And you are…"

Cecilia smiled. It was hard not to respond to his easy charm. "Dr. Cecilia Lu. CDC." That was all she got out before Hank released a low grumble from her opposite side. Detective Kennedy quickly lifted his hands in a backing-off gesture.

Meanwhile, Simon started talking to the other two. "How are you two? And your families?"

The younger man flashed a quick smile. "We're all bottled water, nothing else."

"And beer," the older one said with a grin. "You said we can drink the beer."

"Anything that was made outside of Detroit."

There was more byplay. Simon had gotten all the information he wanted. It was Alyssa who asked for more details about grandchildren and jobs. And then the younger one looked sadly at the hybrid before nodding at Detective Kennedy.

Ryan explained the exchange a moment later by holding up his phone to show to Simon. "We think we know who this is. Pretty sure this is the same kid."

Cecilia stretched to look. She wanted to see what the person had looked like beforehand. And she was greeted with a smiling picture of a high school boy in his football uniform celebrating a win. The face itself hadn't changed that much. Just added fur and those rounded ears. If you shrank the muzzle down, then it was the same boy. Especially since the tattered shirt he wore was the same as in the photo.

"He changed during practice."

"You know the family?" Simon asked.

"Not well," said the detective. "But enough to tell them—"

"You'll come with me then." Simon straightened and got off the couch.

"Where are you taking the body?" Cecilia asked

"Wherever the family wants," Simon answered. "You got enough from him?"

The CDC needed data, always. But weighing that against the shifter secret and the family's grief was hard. "We'd like the study the body if we can. In a lab. With—"

"They won't let you," Detective Kennedy said. He looked at Simon, but his words were for her. "They know about us. The boy's mother has the gene, though she never changed. She knows to keep it quiet. Just bury the dead and grieve in peace."

Simon didn't answer. He just looked at her, his expression flat. It was like he was trying to tell her something, but she had no idea what. So she looked to Hank who was equally silent, but his eyes were filled with sorrow. Yet another dead child. Was this the one she'd killed? She wasn't even sure because parts of last night were a blur. Plus, she'd been specifically blocking that information from gaining prominence in her brain. She'd studied the body as she would have any tissue. Disease first. Method of death, irrelevant if it didn't pertain to the disease.

He'd been a violent monster ready to kill. She'd protected herself and others. And frankly, it wasn't the first time she'd had to put a sick animal down. Her PhD research had been on monkeys and she'd inured herself to killing them years ago. It was simply part of the job.

But now she saw that the hybrid monster was a boy who had played football and had a family who would grieve. Sure, she'd known in her clinical brain that his higher cortex was all but gone. Even if there had been a cure, he would never regain human function. Closest analogy was that he was a rabid animal and had had to be stopped.

But she hadn't thought about the family. Or that he'd been playing football just a day or so ago.

"Dr. Lu?" Simon pressed. "How important is it for you to study this body?" A simple question asked without emotion.

"Not." She swallowed. It was a lie. They always needed more data, but she couldn't be the one to dissect the body. Not now that she'd seen that picture. And she couldn't trust anyone else to see what she would see now that she wasn't blind to shifters. "Let them bury him however they want."

Simon nodded then gestured to the men to gather the body. They worked as efficiently as the wolves while everyone watched.

Everyone, that is, except her. She had to look away. So she turned aside and her gaze collided with Hank's. He crossed to her then.

He didn't speak, but he put his arm on her and she let him fold her into his comfort.

"You understand now, don't you?" he said, his voice low. "That these are people—our people—who are being changed in horrible ways."

She swallowed. "I always understood that."

"But you didn't feel it. It was always a disease to you."

She nodded. "If I think of the people—of the families—it tears me apart."

He nodded, his expression grave. Then he curled her into his arms and pressed her head to his shoulder. He was still shirtless and she was well aware of the heat of his skin, the scent of his body, and the steady, solid beat of his heart. Any other time, she probably would have gotten aroused, but not this time. She clung to him as she allowed the picture of the boy to sink through her consciousness. It slipped inside until it settled right next to Brittany's Facebook video, which was filed along with all the faces and memories of other people and families she'd treated. Victims with one huge difference.

Most of them hadn't died in vain. She'd used their information to fight their disease. And she'd already won. She hadn't saved the victims, but she'd solved the mystery of the virology. Even when they couldn't stop the thing, she'd helped put in place systems to prevent it from ever happening again.

Except for the Detroit Flu. This monster was still in full form and at the moment it was winning.

"You'll figure it out now that you know the truth," Hank said, and his faith warmed her.

Simon spoke, drawing all their attention. "Miguel just texted he's on his way to cover Sammy and Mother. That means Hank can take you to the hospital now." He took a breath and his gaze settled heavily on Cecilia. "I'm sorry I ordered Hank to kidnap you. I wanted to show you shifters at our home base where we could control the situation. I thought it was the safest way."

She nodded. And though Simon was the one who spoke, it was Hank who made the apology real. She felt him squeeze her arm. She heard his exhale. And she knew, in her heart, that he felt miserable for what he'd put her through. At another time, she'd examine how she knew that. She certainly couldn't deduce that from his heat or his breath. But she knew, deep in her heart, that he felt real pain for her and was desperately sorry.

"I can see that it was necessary," she said. It was the truth. Hank could not have gone furry in the hospital, and she wasn't going to believe any of it without seeing.

"Hank will take you wherever you want," Simon said. "He can answer any questions you have, then—"

"I'm not leaving her," Hank interrupted. "The wolves are coming tomorrow night."

Simon was silent for a moment, his gaze hard on Hank. And here again was another undercurrent she wasn't sure she understood. Though she guessed the man was not used to being interrupted.

Simon narrowed his eyes. "Perhaps it would be better if Vic spoke to her. Until you get some real rest, you can't shift."

She felt Hank stiffen by her side, then he spoke through clenched teeth. "I would appreciate Vic's backup."

"But you're not leaving her." A statement, not a question.

"No."

Simon shook his head. "You haven't bonded, Hank. Not yet at least."

Hank didn't answer. He simply stood there with his arm wrapped around her and his entire body bristling with defiance. And in the silence, Cecilia managed to insert her question.

"Someone is going to explain this bonding thing, right?"

Hank nodded. "That will be my job. Soon."

She sighed. She feared she wasn't going to like that conversation at all. "Can I get a shower first? And maybe another omelet?"

To which Mother burst out with a cackling laugh. "I like a practical girl." Then she waved at Simon and the others. "Go on. Let him get this girl a shower and let me get some rest. I'll let you know when Sammy wakes."

Simon frowned. "Miguel isn't here yet and the wolves—"

"Are going to fix my window. That's them pulling up now. And they'll help me clean, too. I practically raised those boys when their mother ran off. I'm going to be just fine."

Cecilia hadn't even realized that another two trucks had pulled up. Construction trucks and four men were already piling out. That was enough for Simon who nodded at his men. They started carrying out the body while Alyssa shut down her tablet and began gathering her things. Everyone was moving except Detective Kennedy who seemed to shift awkwardly from one foot to another, his gaze on Hank.

It wasn't long before Hank noticed. The man probably saw everything, but he didn't ask. He just waited until the cop finally spoke.

"So you mentioned a mantra or something. That helped you sleep."

Two statements, but good God, did they expose a significant problem. No one looked as exhausted as this guy did and then asked about sleep aids. Not unless he was haunted by something big. And now that the detective stood closer, Cecilia could see the red in his eyes and the way his expression kept sagging before he propped it up again with an extra-brilliant smile.

"It's not a magic spell," Hank said gently. "It's just a way to focus the mind—"

"To quiet it for sleep, right?"

Hank shrugged. "Eventually. Yes."

"I'll take it."

Cecilia turned to look at Hank. What exactly was this magic mantra for people too haunted by something to sleep? But instead of answering, Hank turned and rummaged around in a messenger bag. A moment later, he pulled out a plain tan notebook, the kind used by artists to sketch in. He held it out to the detective who took it with a frown.

"What am I—"

"The greatest meditation is a mind that lets go."

It was actually comical seeing the cop's expression. He just held the notebook and stared at Hank like the man had spoken Greek.

"Say it after me," Hank pressed. "The greatest meditation is a mind that lets go."

The man echoed the words, though his expression had already shifted to tolerance. As if he had realized that Hank had no magic words. Meanwhile, Hank was nodding.

"Great. Now write that down. Once for every page in that notebook."

"Write—"

"But each page has to look different. Do it in calligraphy or in paintbrush."

"I don't do calligraphy."

Hank snorted. "You do now. Every page, a different style, a different way. Pen, crayon, whatever. Take your time with each page. Make it look like art."

The detective slowly brought the notebook to his side. "And this will help me sleep?"

Hank shrugged. "Eventually. At least it did for me."

"How soon?"

Hank grinned. "About three notebooks worth." The guy's eyes widened in horror, but Hank didn't let him interrupt. "Unless you want Dr. Lu here to prescribe—"

"No pills. Not with the city like this." His tone was firm, his expression as closed down as any Cecilia had seen.

"Then start writing," Hank said. And then his words softened. "Ryan, there really is no easy way."

The detective answered with a grim shrug. "I don't care about easy. I just want it to work."

Hank nodded. "The greatest meditation—"

"Is a mind that lets go. Got it." And it looked like he did or that he would at least try it. Then he abruptly pulled on a carefree grin. "Okay, bossman," he said to Simon. "Let's go…" His words slowed, and his shoulders drooped before his jaw immediately clamped shut.

Right. They were going to notify the kid's family. Not an easy task and certainly not one for a man already haunted by something. Simon obviously understood because he shook his head.

"I got this. You go—"

The detective held up his hand. "You're new, so I'm going to explain something. I know the family. I know the Griz. It's disrespectful to them for you to do this without me." Cecilia heard the weight of his words hit the room. They were going to notify a family of a loss. Simon was the leader of the Griz, but it was Detective Kennedy who carried the full weight of the clan. At least in this. And her heart went out to him.

What other burdens was he carrying? And which ones kept him awake at night?

She wanted to ask, but knew that now wasn't the time. Especially as Alyssa touched her arm then passed her a handwritten note with a phone number and email address on it. "I know things are happening fast, and you're going to need to catch up."

Understatement of the century.

"Ask me any questions you have. If I don't know the answer, I'll connect you with someone who does."

"Thank you," Cecilia said, her gaze shifting away from Detective Kennedy. She didn't have the brain space to sort through the mystery of a haunted cop. She had to focus on the medical problems. At least that was her plan until Alyssa waggled her eyebrows at her. "And don't worry about this bonding thing. It's not all gloom and doom, like they think." She shot Simon a significant look. "At least it's worked out pretty well for me."

No way to answer that, not when every cell of her body flushed with heat as she abruptly became hyperaware of Hank's presence at her side. While she suffered a hot flash of embarrassment, Alyssa was all business as she grabbed Hank's arm.

"Don't forget to check in. We need you slept and recovered ASAP."

He gave her a clipped nod.

Then she flicked his bare chest with her finger. "And get a shirt on. You look like a cover model prancing around like that."

"My shirt is covered in blood," he growled. "I don't have—"

Alyssa spoke up, her voice pitched to the room. "Anybody got a spare shirt?"

Every single one of the shifters—wolves included—raised their hand.

"Someone loan one to Fabio here, will you?" Then she gave them a jaunty wave before following Simon and Detective Kennedy out the door.

Chapter 13

Once Cecilia had gotten the okay to leave, there was no way Hank could hold her back. She barely gave him enough time to get a shirt on before she was at the door impatiently tapping her foot. She did manage to hug Mother good-bye and promised to return soon with some tea that she thought the woman would like. But beyond that, she was all too happy to leave.

He couldn't really blame her. Even he felt overloaded by the events of the past twelve hours, and he hadn't just discovered shifters.

Still, he was cautious as he escorted her to his car. He opened the front door for her and she eagerly hopped inside. He climbed into the driver's seat quickly, his borrowed shirt pulling too tightly against his neck.

"Okay if we swing by my place first so I can get a change of clothes?"

She glanced at him, her expression wistful. "Personally, I enjoyed the Fabio look, but yeah. It's fine."

She already had her nose back in her phone. Every free moment

she had was spent scribbling notes on the nearest pad of paper or
staring at a screen of numbers. When she gasped, he immediately
tensed, scanning the environment for threats. Nothing appeared,
but they were still in wolf territory. The looting wouldn't be a
problem. It was over a mile away. Unless things had changed, which
they were prone to do.

"What is it?"

She looked up from her phone, her expression tight. "It's nothing really."

He turned to look at her. She was lying and frankly, she wasn't
even trying to hide it.

"Is it work? Are they worried about your abduction?" He forced
himself to say that last word because it was exactly what he'd done.
No sense in trying to run from it.

"What?" She frowned at him like she'd forgotten, but then she
shook her head. "Actually, it's rather depressing that no one noticed
I was gone. Not a one."

Ouch. "That's not a problem with shifters. We're pretty protective of our own. We like knowing where everyone is and that
they're safe."

"I bet your teenagers love that."

"Um, yeah," he agreed catching her sarcastic tone. "That's number
two on the teenager hate list."

She turned to him. "Number two? What's number one?"

"Body hair. Especially with the girls. That's a biggie."

She snorted. "I'll bet."

He stayed quiet while he backed out of Mother's driveway and
headed toward the freeway. The road was eerily thin of traffic.
Though some of the city tried to keep on with life as normal, most

of it was either hunkered down and sick or outside and creating havoc. None of that required the freeway.

Meanwhile, she didn't go back to her phone, so he knew there was something really bothering her.

"If it isn't work—"

"It's nothing. I forgot a phone call, is all."

"You were being abducted, attacked, and learning things."

She sighed. "Yeah, but I forgot long before you came into the picture." Her head dropped back against the seat. "I often forget. I get deep into a problem and just lose track of time."

"Sounds normal."

"Yeah. He knows it, too. He forgets me all the time so we're even on that score."

His ears pricked up at the pronoun. Just what kind of "he" was he? It didn't sound like a boss or father, and she wasn't wearing a wedding ring. But that didn't mean she wasn't dating someone or even married. And boy was he screwed if she was married.

He didn't comment. Didn't know how to ask his questions and his bear was much too ready to tear apart any rival. Best if he didn't press the point right now. Besides, she'd start talking again eventually or go back to her phone.

Rather than have her mentally disappear on him, he reached out and touched her arm. He meant to comfort her with a touch. Instead, he was comforting himself, feeling the heat of her skin, the vibrancy of her body, and the thrum of their connection even if it was only in his head.

"Tell me about him," he said.

She looked at him, obviously startled. He was, too. He was normally the one who just sat in silence and waited. Got most of his information that way. And yet in this, he was pushing for more connection, probably much faster than she could handle.

And then she started talking.

"He's a chemist. Our labs were on the same floor in school, but it was our mothers who set us up."

Definitely a romantic relationship. "How long ago was that?"

She shrugged. "Three years? Four?" She looked down at her hands, twisting her fingers together as if missing a key piece of jewelry. "Our mothers keep hoping for an announcement."

He swallowed, using the motion to shove down a howl from his bear. Meanwhile she glanced at him as if he needed an explanation.

"A wedding announcement, you know. A proposal."

"Yeah," he said, his throat painfully tight. "I got it."

"I didn't. He didn't ask. Probably because he wasn't sure I would say yes." She chuckled. "Yu likes knowing the answers to questions before he asks them. Out loud at least. Scientifically he's all about tearing apart the biological mystery."

"You?"

"Y-U. Actually, it's Jian Yu, which means 'building the universe.' But Yu likes being the universe, so he shortened it. He also likes the joke. You—as in someone else—seeming like the universe but it's actually him because it's Yu." She waved her hand. "Don't worry if you don't get it. His brain can be pretty convoluted at times."

"Sounds like a dick." The words came out with a growl, and Hank gripped the steering wheel tighter. He was out of control here. That was not something he would ever say normally. People's choices in partners were their own, and everyone was a dick in some ways. And yeah, she was smart enough to call him on it.

"He's just smarter than most people and so has found ways to entertain himself in his own mind."

Hank turned to her. "And do you come into that picture anywhere? Or is it all about him?" Which was a fat load of crap considering how Hank had made love to her last night. It hadn't been about her at all, and he was ashamed to remember how selfish he'd been in the way he'd touched her. Ate her. And fuck, now he was hard just thinking about it.

Fortunately, she didn't seem to be able to read his thoughts. Her gaze had shifted back down to her phone. "I love talking science with him. His mind…" She shook her head. "He's brilliant."

"And so are you, so you understand each other." Marriages had been built on less substantial things.

"Yes, we do. Which is why when we miss scheduled phone calls, neither one of us takes it personally."

Except she obviously did. Something about it bothered her. He took a stab at the reason. "How long since you had something together that wasn't about science?"

She snorted. "Well, I thought he was a good kisser." Her gaze shot to his. "Until you kissed me. Hell, I didn't even know it was possible to be that good at it."

Hank didn't know how to respond. He hated the idea that she'd been kissing this jerk, but then she'd turned the compliment to him and he flushed with pride even as he tried to figure out her meaning. Yeah, okay, so he'd been good at it last night. That was all about patience and attention to detail. And actually wanting to lick every part of her just for the sake of tasting her. But his driving force had been getting between her thighs. About locking in the bond so that babies could be created. It hadn't been about her as a person. They barely knew each other, though damn it, it felt like they'd been fated since the beginning of time.

Fucking bonding magic. It screwed up the progression of a normal relationship. Made it impossible for him to take his time with her and learn the things he wanted to about her. To see if they fit for real instead of just biologically.

Then she spoke, clearly smart enough to follow his thoughts even though he hadn't said a word out loud.

"You said you were bound to me. What exactly does that mean?"

"It's about the magic," he began. But then she rolled her eyes as she looked away and he had to grip her arm tighter to get her to listen. "I know you think it's stupid. I know you don't believe, but you didn't believe in shifters yesterday either. What don't you believe in today that you will tomorrow?"

She wrinkled her nose at him. It was pretty adorable, but her words were serious enough when she spoke. "Fair point, but you're fighting an entire lifetime of conditioning here. Science is real. Magic is superstition."

"Yeah, I know. You don't have to call it magic. Hell, it could be a really amped-up biological imperative to make special babies. We don't know why, but it's real."

"The bonding."

"It's not uncommon for a shifter to lock on a person. Like really lock on. Base-of-the spine, gut-instinct, completely-without-rational-thought lock on."

"How long does it last?"

Hank squirmed with that. He didn't want to answer, so he took the distraction of his exit to maneuver the car down to his neighborhood. Everything looked quiet from where they were cruising through, but there was evidence of problems. A few broken windows, police tape, and at least a half dozen people peering nervously out windows.

"Hank? How long does it last?"

"It's lifelong."

"A permanent mating. Like with apes and wolves."

He nodded. "Also swans, eagles, and beavers."

"And others," she said, her voice softening. "Lots of other species…" She looked at him, her eyes wide and a little frightened. "So that's why we…that was last night…why I…"

"It's one sided, Cecilia. Just on the shifter side." He looked her straight in the eye. "On my side. But it was powerful and that's how I knew if we did it, you'd get pregnant. Magic does shit like that. Condom breaks, birth control fails. Hell, if it's really strong, you get twins or triplets."

She shuddered at the thought and it was like she'd put a knife in his gut. The idea of having his children was physically repulsive to her and that cut. It cut deep.

"But it was strong for me, too."

"As far as we can tell, it's always on the shifter side." He tried to smile, but he doubted he did a good job of it. "We're the magical creatures. Normals are…well, normal."

"But I wanted to with you. I mean I really wanted—"

"That's sometimes happens in really stressful situations. Soldiers will react that way and—"

She held up her hand, and he cut off his words with a click of his jaws. He stayed silent while she stared out at his neighborhood. He'd barely gone a block before she started again.

"So I chose last night, but you…you were forced?"

"No! I wanted—"

"You said magic forced you. Magic wants the babies and all."

He grimaced. "Um, yeah."

"So how do you know that what you felt last night was real? I mean, it could be biology, right? Magical biology, but still biology. No choice at all."

He was silent as he pulled into his spot under an aging carport. And while he put his car into park, he thought about last night. Had he chosen her with his mind? Had he wanted her because he liked her? Or because her scent, her taste, her body made him lust like never before?

And in the silence, he felt her touch his arm. It was a light caress, but his entire forearm reacted to it. His muscles twitched, his skin heated, and his nostrils flared as he inhaled her scent. He wasn't reacting to her personality. This was biology, just as she said.

"Hank, I'm so sorry."

That was not what he wanted to hear from her. Not an apology. Not an admission that he'd locked on to her purely out of animal need. He was a thinking man who had learned the value of control. He did not want to believe he had no choice in a mate. He liked her as a person. She was smart and she wore blindingly bright clothes. And she hadn't cowered in the fight. Wasn't that enough to say that he'd chosen her?

No.

This was magic, pure and simple. And it was because she and he would make strong magical babies. That was always the result of a true bonding.

He turned to look at her. "You still have free will, Cecilia. You don't have to choose me."

She arched a brow. "I think I did last night."

"But that was stress and yeah, maybe there was biological imperative involved. But it's not a life sentence for you."

"But it is for you?"

He shrugged. "Simon says not."

"But you say yes."

He didn't know how to answer that. In the end, he took the coward's way out. "I say that I need to change my clothes and get some things from my apartment. I need you to come with me. I can't leave you out here."

She looked around the parking lot. It all seemed safe and quiet. But he knew that bad things could strike anytime, even in broad daylight.

"Please don't fight me on this. I really need to keep you nearby."

"This the magic thing again?"

He shrugged. "It's my job to keep you safe. You're the only shifter-aware doctor in Detroit right now. We need you."

She frowned. "That can't be true."

"It's not," he admitted. "But the others are pediatricians, a dentist, and a podiatrist. Not much help."

"You'd be surprised." Then before he could say more, she held up her hand. "I'll go up with you, Hank, if you promise to get me their names and numbers."

He frowned at her. "You know you could get those from us just by asking, right?"

She sighed. "I was teasing you. Trying to lighten the mood. Don't shifters make jokes?"

"Of course, we make jokes. We're just like everybody else. Except for—"

"Going furry. And magical bonding. And gang territories in Detroit."

"Humans have that last one. And some normals are pretty hairy, too."

"Fair point. So is there a reason we're still sitting in your car debating this? Why aren't we already up in your apartment?"

He sighed. God, she was smart, but she needed to know it all. "Because the minute I get you up there, in my place…my den, so to speak, I'm going to be on you like white on rice."

She blinked. "What?"

"If this is all magic or biology, then I won't be able to stop myself. I'm going to want to make babies with you like it's my primary reason for living. Which it will be. To propagate the species and all."

Her eyes widened. "Um, so why am I going up there?"

He shrugged. "We have to know, don't we?" Then he amended his statement. "I'd really like to know if I'm bonded that deeply to you already."

"We just met twelve hours ago."

He didn't answer. Just held her gaze until she sighed.

"So, tell me what you want me to do."

"Ever shot a Taser before?"

Chapter 14

Hank lived on the third floor of a very modest apartment complex. Given his size and health, they could have been on the upper floor in a matter of minutes, but he went to the basement first to check on the washing machines and furnace, then door by door to make sure everyone was okay.

It didn't take a few minutes. It took an hour, which actually was okay by Cecilia. It allowed her to watch him interact with the tenants. He was unfailingly kind, accepted grouchy comments and complaints with aplomb, and even hugged a few babies while he was at it. Every few doors, he'd ask Cecilia if she minded if he took another few minutes for him to check on Mrs. So-and-So or Mr. This-and-That. He'd tell her something quick about each one, introduce her, then get pulled into a discussion about whatever was going on in their lives. He always reminded them not to drink the water as he added their to-do tasks to his phone, and then on to the next door.

More than one female tenant gave her a thumbs-up behind Hank's back and whispered, "He's a good 'un."

Yeah, she was beginning to see that.

By the time she made it up to his apartment, she'd forgotten she had a Taser in her lab coat pocket. And wasn't it weird that not a single person commented on the blood splatter?

"So, you're popular," she drawled as he finally opened his door. It wasn't even locked, and that startled her even more.

"I'm the building superintendent. A good one is always popular."

She cried bullshit on that. He cared about the people in the building and made sure they were okay. That wasn't just being good at his job, that was being a good person. She might have made a comment, but she was too busy being stunned by his apartment.

First and foremost, there was a mile-high stack of water bottle cases by the door. He grimaced as he looked at it then sighed.

"I told them to just come up to my apartment to get these. I left the door unlocked for them. But some of them can't climb or carry so well and others…" He shook his head. "Well, they're just lazy."

"Because they know you'll cart it down for them?"

He shrugged as he hefted three cases. "I'll just be—"

"A minute. Yeah, I know."

"Sorry. I didn't mean to lie. I meant to come right up here, but then I thought I better check on—"

She waved him into silence. "Take your time. I'll just work on my phone." And she would have. Except, of course, looking around his apartment was much more interesting.

She didn't know what she expected. Something like her own messy two-bedroom apartment back in Atlanta. Dishes in the sink, half-dead plant, papers and books everywhere, not to mention an embarrassing laundry pile. Even her hotel room looked like that, minus the plant. She had not expected to step into a Japanese Zen garden.

The furniture—what there was of it—was minimal. A bed, a small table with four chairs, and large cushions for people to sit on while drinking tea. There were books in a low bookcase, a high-end tablet, and plants. Lots of little plants in tiny planters next to a zillion rock gardens with tiny Zen rakes for the sand. And, by the way, all of the sand had pristine patterns around the rocks and miniature toys. She saw army soldiers near a Hello Kitty who drank tea with a troll.

She tried to picture it. Big man with a scar using his huge hands to pull a tiny rake through the sand around a Hello Kitty doll. It didn't fit. Well, it didn't fit until she added one of the kids from downstairs. Little Kaylee who had pigtails and a dress with juice stains on it. Put her next to Hank and Cecilia could absolutely see it. And she would bet her next paycheck that the toy soldier came from one the little boys she'd met on the second floor. The elderly woman on the first floor had asked about the air plant she'd given Hank for Christmas, and he had responded that it held a place of honor. She looked around. Ah, right over there at the window. It had to be one of a dozen tillandsias basking in the sunlight in a coiled wire hanger.

Wow. Talk about not judging a book by its cover. Hank defied any stereotype she could imagine. Which didn't surprise her at all. Nothing he'd done in the last twelve hours was even remotely predictable, though he'd always been quiet and steady, even in the most heated times. Kind of like he had the peace of a Zen master or what she imagined a Zen master would be. She'd never met one. But given the number of books about Buddhism and meditation on his shelf, she'd bet he had. They filled the bookshelf along with medical textbooks.

And way back in the corner, half covered by a well-tended fern, were two pictures. One of him in his unit. He was grinning and mock choking the guy next to him. And another of what had to be his family. Mom, dad, the older brother he'd mentioned, and an older sister with pigtails of her own and a very serious expression.

"That's was taken a year before my brother died." His voice was quiet, but she didn't even jump. He filled her thoughts so much, of course he would be standing behind her when the questions started piling up. And he would start with the biggest one in her mind. She'd wondered when the photo had been taken and where his family was now.

"Your brother seems so happy here." She turned to look in his eyes. He stood so close, crowding her against the bookcase, but not in a scary way. His eyes were serious, his expression sad, but she didn't feel any tension off him. Just answers. And a need to touch her as he stroked her arm.

"He was always moody. Happy-go-lucky one moment, then steeped in dark thoughts the next. It got worse when adolescence hit. Plus, shifters get antsy. There's a kids' camp in Gladwin for just this kind of thing. It's run by the grizzlies, but all shifters are welcome."

"He didn't go?"

"He did. But then a few months later, he went to hang out with the Griz. Got into a pissing match with the leader at the time. A big asshole named Nanook."

Her brows arched. "Like Nanook of the North? From that old documentary?"

He shrugged. "Guess so. The bastard was powerful and touchy as hell. Roy never came home."

"I'm sorry." She touched his chest and his muscles rippled beneath her fingertips. "Were you close?"

"We were brothers."

Not an answer. She and one of her brothers never spoke because he was an ass. But the answer was in the way his gaze lingered on the photo and the quiet yearning that echoed in the air between them. Was she imagining it? Or did she really feel that?

"What about the rest of your family?"

"Mom and Dad split up after Roy died. Dad was never comfortable with shifter stuff, and this was the last straw. He passed from a heart attack a couple years ago. Mom's the shifter. She moved to Traverse City soon afterwards."

"More wild places to roam?"

His lips curled into a soft smile. "Better skiing. She's started freeheeling it since she got tired of snowboarding."

Of course, she did. "And your sister?"

"In Alaska right now studying wolves. It's the family shame. You'd think she'd be interested in bears, but no. It's all about the dogs for her."

"Is she a shifter, too?"

He nodded. "But not a strong one. She had her first change at nineteen and then never since."

He took the picture from her hand and gently set it back in its place. She was about to ask about his unit and the guy he was fake choking, but he didn't give her the chance. He stroked her cheek and his eyes turned dark and hungry. She thought for a moment of the Taser in her pocket, but she didn't grab it. She didn't feel any threat from him. Just the same hungry intensity that simmered inside her.

"I like you here among my things," he said. "I like you looking at my family and not shying away when I touch you."

She didn't know how to answer that. Especially since her mouth was dry and her heart was hammering in her throat. And yet, deep inside, she was calm. Quiet. As if this was exactly how it was supposed to be.

"Is this the magic?" she whispered.

He shrugged. "I don't know. Does it matter?"

It should. It absolutely should. She wanted to believe that her emotions were her own. Her desire, her interest, even the throbbing in her womb. She wanted those to come from inside, not some mystical force.

"Hank—"

"Do you have the Taser?"

"You know I do." He'd given it to her and made her put on her lab coat to hide it in her pocket.

"Good. Grab it and be ready."

She pulled back so she could look at him more squarely. "You want me to Tase you?"

"I want you to hold it." He took a deep breath, and damn it, it was hard not to notice how his chest expanded and his shoulders stretched wide. "I'm going to kiss you, Cecilia. I'm going to kiss you once, and then I'm going to go take a cold shower." He paused. "Is that okay?"

"Um, I think the cold shower is going to suck."

His expression lightened and his lips curved up. "Yeah it will. But if I can leave you alone, then I'm in control. I can walk away from you because that will be my choice."

She nodded, understanding where he was going. But what if she didn't want him to walk away. "What if I...what if I can't control myself? What if the magic is too strong for me?"

Then his lips did widen into a smile. "Then I'll tie you up and go take my cold shower." He arched a brow. "Unless you want the shower?"

She shook her head. "I'll take the kiss and no more." At least that was her plan. And she knew it would be just as much of a test for her as it was for him. They had to know that they controlled themselves. That they were the ones who...

Her mind was still talking, but her body was completely ignoring her. She'd already put her hands on his shoulders and was drawing him in close. Her lips met his eagerly, moving in a wholly instinctive way. She touched their mouths together, feeling his breath, the texture of his lips, and the way he smiled just as they met. She wanted to push forward hard, but he kept himself back, and he held her in place with his hands on her hips.

Hot hands like brands on her hips. Hot lips moving across hers, teasing with his tongue and teeth as he nipped at her lips but didn't push inside.

Damn it, it was frustrating! She wanted a kiss, not a tease, but he would not be hurried. And when she was just about to say something, he spoke in that low growly tone that she felt at the base of her spine.

"I only get one," he said. "I want to make it good."

"I'm an all or nothing kind of girl," she answered. She'd always been that way. Completely into her current project or unconscious. Completely in a book, oblivious to all, or eating something while surfing the Internet. This slow windup was driving her crazy, but she had to respect a man who took his time. Mostly because she hadn't known they existed.

And since he wasn't going for the gusto, she might as well. So she stuck out her tongue, coiling it underneath his top lip, pressing it against his teeth, doing whatever she could to speed up this process. Because suddenly, her breasts were heavy and aching, her womb was pulsing like the prelude to a great orgasm, and…wow, even her toes had curled tight in her shoes.

He let her tease him. His tongue barely touched hers, his mouth cracked just a fraction, but it was a ruse. She knew that because his hands were gripping her hips with a kneading motion in his fingertips. A slow roll of pressure, from front to back, and a steady pull closer. His mouth might not be opening to her, but his lower body certainly knew what it was doing. She felt the heat of his groin against hers and the hot brand of his erection as surely as she felt her heart thrumming in her clit. He hadn't touched it, but by God, her entire body was doing the work for him.

She let it. She let herself go flush against him, thighs bumping, groins pulsing against each other, and her breasts pressed into his chest. She didn't thrust against him. She wanted to, but she held back. She needed to know—just like he did—that she had some control over this situation.

So she pressed herself against him but no more. And her tongue still fluttered against his teeth, darting in and out and only occasionally catching the very tip of his tongue.

Then she started to smile because this was fun, this holding back. Especially since waiting built the desperate hunger in her body. When would he break? When would she? Could he feel her like she felt him? Did he know that her nipples felt rock hard against his chest? Did he realize that her groin felt so liquid it would accept his penetration without a whisper of complaint? Would he—

He broke.

Suddenly, he slanted his mouth over hers and pushed inside. Where before she'd been stretching up to him, now he towered over her and pressed down. Her back arched, but he held her hard against him. And then he began to thrust.

Above and below, in equal measure.

OMG, it was hot.

His tongue mastered her in seconds. It took control of her mouth, dueled with her tongue, and managed to touch every part of her. Her mind was still yammering away. Something about the differences in their physical dimensions, but that it wasn't an insurmountable problem.

Meanwhile, with every thrust of his tongue, his groin pushed against her. Every time he coiled in her mouth, his hips ground a hard circle into her pelvis. The timing was impressive. What it did to her body made every part of her heat to near orgasmic explosion. And what it did to her brain was shut it the fuck up.

Perfection. And Cecilia was ready to strip naked and let him plunder her however he wanted.

Then he stopped.

The movement was abrupt as he ripped his mouth away. He held her hips back from him, even though she shoved forward as hard as she could. And while she panted and the blood roared through her ears, he spoke in a low groan.

"We. Stop."

No, no, no, no, no! Her mind was wailing at that. Her body, too. But she nodded because that's what he wanted: proof that they could stop.

"Cold. Shower," he gasped.

Was that a statement of intent? They hadn't separated an inch. In fact, the only reason their mouths weren't fused together was because their foreheads were pressed hard against one another while they both fought with the emotions rioting inside.

"Can I watch?"

His hands spasmed on her and she gloried in the hard grip on her hips. God, what she wouldn't give to have him pounding inside her while he held her like that.

"We're in control. Not the magic. You and me."

She nodded. Her breath had slowed, but her heart was still thundering. And her clit pulsed with every rapid beat. "Okay if I finish myself off? While you're freezing in the shower?"

His laugh came out grudgingly, like gravel rolling onto the ground. "Okay if I do, too?"

She snorted. "Now I really want to watch."

He grinned. "Me, too."

Then he straightened up. He pulled his head back, his shoulders next, and then he stepped away. The last part of him to leave her was his hands. They lingered on her hips, lightening in pressure slowly until just his fingertips brushed her thighs. Then his arms fell to his sides.

"See?" she said as she made an effort to straighten up. God, her knees were weaker than Jell-O. "We're in control. No sex here. No shoving me against the wall as you thrust inside. No bending me over the table or mounting me in any way. Nope, nothing like that happening here." More's the pity.

His nostrils flared, but she saw humor light in his eyes. "Not helping."

"I'm just thinking if magic makes the sex hot, why not enjoy it?" She let her head drop back and she ended up falling backward until her back connected with the wall. "I didn't think my nipples could get this tight. And I think I need to change my leggings. I'm so freaking wet—"

"Are you trying to get me to attack you?"

She straightened up. "Will you?"

"No! We agreed that we wouldn't do this. We're proving—"

"We're in control. No magic." She stepped away from the wall and threw her arms out wide. "Well guess what? I'm so hot and horny I can't even think straight. So no, we're not in control. I mean yes, you haven't thrown me over your shoulder and taken me back to your cave, but hell yes, I want it. It's taking all my willpower to not strip naked right now."

He growled at her, not in fury, but in raw hunger made audible. Need radiated out of him. "I will not give in to this. Not until you choose it."

She gaped at him. "I'm choosing it, Hank."

He shook his head. "No, you're not. You just said it's the magic."

"You said you were the one with the magical compulsion, not me. I'm completely normal so the magic doesn't work on me. Right?"

His expression tightened, and his hands balled into fists at his side. "I don't know."

She stared at him while her body throbbed. And in the silence, she realized he was all about control. His every action was balanced, his every thought chosen. Which meant this was about him establishing control over his own body. He didn't want to be compelled by some mysterious force. He wanted to choose, and she had to respect that. Even if it meant she was left all revved up with nowhere to go.

"Okay," she finally said. "You need to stop, so we stop."

He nodded. "I'm going for that shower now. Don't leave the room. I'll know. Even in the shower, I'll know, and I'll come get you."

"Are we back to kidnapping again?"

He opened his mouth to argue, but then froze. She watched as realization flowed through his entire body. He curled inward then in defeat. His eyes grew bleak, and his knuckles went white where they gripped the doorknob.

"Yes."

"So the magic will let you take a shower, but it will compel you to follow me if I leave."

It wasn't a question, but he answered it anyway, and his one word came out dark. "Yes."

She stared at him, finally realizing that this was a lot more serious that she'd thought. The ramifications of how they were apparently bound together were horrifying. Was he doomed now to follow wherever she went? To want to bed her no matter what else was going on? At the moment, that sounded A-okay with her, and that was even more disturbing. What if this wasn't magic but a ramped-up biological urge? What if she was doomed to want him forever? She had a job to do, a flu to end, and patients to save. It was her guiding mission. And yet all she wanted right now was to follow him into the bathroom, strip naked, and get it on.

"Okay, this is bad," she murmured.

"Yeah," he answered. "I'm going to shower now. You staying?"

She nodded. "Yeah. Can't have your naked ass chasing me down the street. What would Mrs. Stotts say?"

"She'd probably pull out her cell phone and start taking pictures."

Cecilia smiled, though the expression felt difficult what with the clit throbbing and all. "Go on. Take your shower. I'm going to see if my nipples can cut glass."

It took him a moment to process her words. His gaze dropped to her chest and the obvious bumps even through tunic and coat. As expected, his nostrils flared, and his hands tightened, but he didn't move for her. Instead, he slowly lifted his gaze.

"Let me know the results, will you?"

She gave him a thumbs-up, then watched with an aching pain as he disappeared inside the bathroom and firmly shut the door.

Chapter 15

The cold shower didn't help. Neither did coming out of the shower to see her sitting at his kitchen table with her phone in one hand and furiously scribbling on his grocery list pad with the other. Her brow was furrowed, and she was clearly focused on something scientific he hadn't a prayer of understanding. But the sight of her working at his kitchen table was so powerfully domestic that his belly tightened with need. He wanted to see her there every day and every night. He wanted to feed her when she forgot to eat. And he wanted to pleasure her when she became too stressed to think.

"I can feel you staring. So either bend me over this table or let's get to the hospital. There's someone I want you to meet."

Her words short-circuited his brain and lust leapt to the fore, but he'd promised not to take her...for some reason he couldn't remember. Then she looked up, her gaze confused and her lips incredibly kissable.

"Hank?"

"You don't help my control. You know that right?"

She shrugged. "I know. But it's fun to test your limits."

"And if you cross too far?"

"Screaming Os until I'm hoarse?"

He swallowed. Damn it, he'd put on fresh jeans and they were too damn tight. "Is that what you want?"

She threw up her hands. "Can't I want both? Screaming Os and my job? But since we're being all self-denying in the name of freedom from magic, let's get to the hospital." She grabbed his notepad and headed for the door.

"Don't you want your lab coat? It's got your ID on it."

She blinked and patted her hips as if her ID were somewhere in her leggings or tunic. He took a step forward and grabbed her coat from on top of his large beanbag cushion.

"Oh!" she breathed. "Thanks. There are too many things to remember, and you're taking up half my brain space."

Only half? He might be insulted if he didn't know just how huge her brain was. And wasn't that a surprising turn-on? He'd never gone for dumb girls, but brainiacs were never his type. Until now.

"This way." Opening the door for her nearly undid him. She stood right beside him, her hair up in a messy bun. He smelled the passion on her, perfuming everything she wore. He knew what that tasted like, he knew what it would feel like to run his fingers through the dark silk of her hair. And how he wanted to tame her lips and her mouth.

"Hank," she said, his name cracking as desire and denial fought in her voice. "This is going to be a problem for me."

"Yeah," he agreed. "Me, too."

"How do we stop it? Or at least…" She shrugged. "Quiet it to a dull roar?"

Screaming Os filtered through his thoughts. As well as all sorts of wicked things he could do to her all over his apartment. "Come on," he said. "I'll tell you all the stories I've heard about bondings."

She nodded and took a step into the hallway. "Do they end happily?"

He shook his head. "If they did, they wouldn't be stories. They met, they humped, they lived happily ever after doesn't make for a very good tale."

"So it's more like they met, someone stalked, someone said no—"

"And someone lived miserably ever after."

She sighed, and he couldn't help but agree. Romantic souls liked the idea of being fated to another soul, but he was horrified by it. He'd spent his life learning how to balance his needs and his bear's needs until they lived in harmony. This hunger he had for Cecilia wasn't rational, and it certainly wasn't balanced. He didn't want to lock on to Cecilia unless he chose it and she wanted it. Right now, he couldn't tell if this desire was a choice or a compulsion, and he wasn't going to act on it until he knew the answer.

So rather than focus on that, he kept a wary eye on the environment as they moved to his car. Things seemed to be quieter during the day, but violence could erupt any moment, especially with the city on edge. The poison seemed to ramp up everyone's aggression, not just the shifters, and those that could, hid inside as much as possible. Or stayed perched over a toilet throwing up. In any event, he and Cecilia seemed to be the only idiots who needed to drive all over the damn city.

Meanwhile, she kept talking, showing him that her mind was on the problem even while she scanned the area as much as he did.

"So the magic wants magical babies."

"That's the common interpretation."

"What happens afterwards?"

He frowned. "After what?"

"Humping, pregnancy, bam beautiful baby."

"Rinse and repeat until we're too old or dead."

He saw the news hit her. She paled and her steps hitched.

"Were you hoping to get pregnant and then be rid of me?" The question came out harsher than he intended. The idea that she'd conceive his child and then kick him out of her life was so infuriating that he grew murderous at the mere thought.

Her eyes widened in surprise. "What? No! And for the record, I want children. I'd love a couple kids and a husband who is there for me and them. I just haven't had time to think about it."

Her words warmed him, gave him hope well out of proportion for what she was saying. But he took the joy and held it close. Maybe, if he played his cards right, it would be possible for them.

"For the record," he said slowly, his voice thick with need. "I want kids, too. And I'd be there for them and for my wife."

She nodded, but she didn't quite meet his gaze. "Okay, common interest has been established. But what about the magic? How long before it eases up?"

"Never," he ground out.

"And you're okay with that?"

He opened his mouth to answer. Sure, growing up, he'd always expected he'd have a wife and child someday. Maybe a whole bunch of kids. But not recently. Not since...

He winced. "After my brother died, Mom all but forced me into the military. She said it would instill discipline, burn off the aggression."

"Get you past shifter adolescence?"

He nodded as they made it out to the parking lot. He held her back, his hand on her belly as he sniffed the air. Nothing unusual out here. Just the urban scents of exhaust, waste, and dog poop baking in the sun. And her. Always her, perfuming the air until he wanted to breathe it all in, straight down to his soul.

"This way," he said, guiding her to his car. He hadn't thought he'd needed to, but she'd started heading in the wrong direction.

"Oh. Right," she said, quickly adjusting. "So you went into the military for discipline. Did you get it?"

"Not like she thought." Not like anyone thought. "Two firefights later, I lost my best friend."

Her hand stilled on his car as her gaze shot to his. "The guy you have in a choke hold in the picture."

He nodded. "Charlie was my best friend. And after losing my brother…"

"Double punch. Hank—"

"I went wild. Got drunk every chance I got and into fights. Shifted a few times that should have got me killed or at least exposed, but I got lucky."

"What happened?" she asked the moment he climbed in behind the wheel.

"A shifter I met in a whorehouse taught me Zen Buddhism."

She laughed, the sound bubbling out of her like a temple fountain. "Seriously?"

"Seriously. I honestly don't even know why she was there. She wasn't working, that's for sure. But one night she started saying things to me. Simple things."

"What is the sound of one hand clapping? That kind of thing?"

He smiled in memory. "More like, the greatest goodness is a peaceful mind." He glanced at her. "That one stood out."

She smiled. "I'll bet. You were grieving. It must have felt like your brain was going to explode."

"More like my entire body. Into a bear. Then my friends would probably shoot me in self-defense."

"So you discovered Zen at a whorehouse."

He smiled. "I discovered the woman who taught me Zen there." He shrugged. "She later told me that she was sent in a dream to find me and bring me peace."

"And it became your spiritual focus?"

He nodded. "The greatest worth is self-mastery." He arched a brow. "I spent every moment I could at the temple studying. She had books on the history of shifters, scrolls that outlined the force of magic. They look like physics textbooks, but the words were all about the magic or the force or whatever the hell you want to call it." He turned his attention back to the road. "And she taught me to feel it at a level no one else does."

Cecilia abruptly pushed forward. "You feel magic?"

He nodded, pushing himself to admit what he had told no one else. "Imagine standing in an electrical current all the time. First, you have to be aware of it, then you can sense changes in it. Like when it pushes you to do something."

"You *sense* that?" she stressed.

"Yes."

She leaned back in her seat and looked at him. "You're a pretty fascinating guy."

He didn't think so. He felt like he'd bounced around a lot in his life. He'd gone into the army because his mother has forced him.

He'd picked medicine because he was a terrible shot. And he hadn't truly studied anything until he'd met the woman who'd taught him discipline, silence, and magic.

Meanwhile, Cecilia's expression had turned wistful. "My grandmother tried to get me into Buddhism." She shrugged. "I preferred to worship at the altar of science."

That made sense.

"But now that I know magic is real…" Her voice trailed away, and he shot her a quick glance.

"You're giving up science?"

"Hell no. But I might become an alchemist. That's the word, right? People who put scientific methods to studying magic?"

"I thought it was more about turning copper to gold."

She shrugged. "Well, that could be helpful, too. Do you know how underfunded the CDC is?"

No, he didn't. But he had fun asking her about it and hearing stories about the lengths her coworkers had gone to get toner for their printers or extra lab coats after getting burned or gassed or spilled on.

He was smiling by the time they made it to the hospital. He could have sat and listened to her stories for years, but they were here. And worse, the moment he put the car in park, her expression sobered, and she touched his arm.

"I need you to explain something to me." He didn't respond, but waited patiently for the question. It took her a moment to realize he wasn't going to speak and then she fumbled with her words, unusually embarrassed. "So, um, can you sense…you know by smell or something?"

"Sense what?"

"If someone can…" She waved vaguely at his body. Then she frowned. "If there's magic there? If they can shift?" Her hand gestured included the two of them. "You said you can feel the magic—"

"Just in a general sense, and it's everywhere."

"Right. But not everyone can shift."

She was asking if he could tell if someone had shifter DNA. It was valid question, and frankly, she was adorable in the way she fumbled, worried that she'd embarrass him or something. So even though he was smiling, he answered as honestly as he could.

"I can usually scent it right before someone changes, if I'm standing close enough. And sometimes it's really obvious if someone's a shifter, though that's not a hundred percent. We were pretty sure with Sammy for the past year, but it wasn't certain until yesterday."

"I need to understand the biology of shifters. And I need you to talk to a hybrid girl and her parents."

His entire body tightened with alarm. "No. No talking to parents. No explaining things. Not my job."

She arched her brows. "You explained them to me."

"That *was* my job. Not anyone else."

"Didn't Simon say you'd help me with whatever I need? Isn't he your boss or something?"

Yes. Simon was both his alpha and his boss. The Griz paid him to do a variety of tasks, but initiating someone into the shifter world was delicate, and not something he ever wanted to do again.

He opened his mouth to argue, but she stopped him with a shake of her head. "There's no one else." Then she hopped out of his car and headed for the hospital.

He would have argued further, but they were rapidly surrounded by people. Whereas he had made a point of driving through the quiet parts of town—Alyssa sent regular updates on any violent outbursts in the city—the hospital was one place where people would come. Not just because of the Flu, but because of injuries and all the regular reasons people sought medical attention. So he buttoned his lip as Cecilia seemed to power walk through the huge building.

No one stopped them. She clearly belonged, and he did his best to make it clear he was with her. And while people eyed him warily—they always did given his size, race, and his big damn scar—no one questioned them. Pretty soon they were back on the floor where they'd first met what seemed like years ago but was really just yesterday.

They went first to the same lab she'd been in before. Her coworker was awake today instead of drooling on his shirt. He greeted her without looking up from his microscope.

"Get some sleep?"

"Yeah," she answered. "You?"

"Enough."

"Any news?"

"Couple DOAs came in. More of the same. Am working them up now."

"Brittany?"

He sighed and sat back on his stool, his eyes focusing with surprise on Hank. Neither said a word though and he ended up speaking as if Hank wasn't there.

"Mom just came through the quarantine. She's been in California visiting relatives." His expression looked sad. "They're bringing Brittany to consciousness now. Taking it really slow to see if Mom can help calm her down before she's fully awake."

"Good," Cecilia said as she grabbed a tablet from her workstation and started tapping. "This is Hank. He's going to help."

Her coworker flashed him a grin. "Great. How?"

Cecilia waved at him without even looking up as she headed out the door. Hank followed her, thinking that anything he said was likely to get him into more trouble, not less. So he kept his mouth shut as she took him down the hall to what she'd called "the Weird Ward."

"We talk to Mom and Dad first," she said in a low voice. "To find out if they're part of your club."

"I can't—"

"Give it a shot, Hank. We're all clutching at straws."

Fair enough.

They crossed into Brittany's room. It was a normal hospital room if you counted a dozen or more machines whirring away as normal. A pale blond teenage girl lay unmoving, looking like she belonged on the set of Hollywood's latest teen flick rather than with IVs sticking out of her...black bear arms. A closer look showed him that beneath artfully arranged blond hair, her ears were furry and rounded. Definitely a bear. And now that he looked at the silhouette beneath the sheet, he guessed that her hips and legs had bearlike dimensions. At least some. And then, of course, was the usual hybrid stench. Not strong, but definitely present beneath all the antiseptic smells.

"My money's on Peter, the father," Cecilia murmured as she turned to greet the parents. Mom was holding her daughter's hand and surreptitiously wiping away tears. Dad stood back a step, his expression stoic, but anyone with eyes could see the pain burning underneath.

"You'd be wrong," Hank whispered back. Shifters held pain

differently than full humans. This man was large and broad, built for football, though he was obviously aging. Broad shoulders, straight spine, probably had some military experience in his background. But his gaze remained trained on his child. Shifters—especially those in pain—couldn't resist scanning the environment for threats. Even if their body was tall, they tended to stand in defensible positions in a room. Tucked into a corner or braced near an exit. It was rarely conscious, but a trained observer noticed.

Brittany's father stood with his back to the door and his gaze never wavered. He was completely and wholly there for his wife and child. And when Mom looked up at Cecilia and Hank, he wrapped her in his arm and provided comfort in the way men do: with a touch, but no sound. Shifters were more likely to nuzzle and murmur. A purr or a whisper. Some sort of sound that soothed the animal inside even as it was meant to comfort someone else.

The dad was not a shifter. But the mom, on the other hand, did all those things. She placed her back to the wall, she scanned everyone and everything. And when she cried—tiny little drops leaking steadily out of her eyes—she whimpered slightly and cleared her throat. "Hello, Mrs. Randolph. I'm Dr. Cecilia Lu. I'm so sorry we had to meet under these circumstances."

"Call me Abby—" Her voice cut off as she cleared her throat again. Trying to help, the father grabbed Brittany's untouched pitcher of water and poured her a glass. Hank's nose twitched. It was hard to isolate scents in this place. Between the antiseptic smells, the various scents of terrified people, and of course the hybrid defensive stink, catching the stray waft of tainted water would usually be beyond him. But he was hyperalert in here, his animal side also watching for danger, and that scent was a big one.

"Don't drink that!" he snapped just as the mother pressed the cup to her lips.

She gaped and drew back, her eyes wide as she stared at him.

"Smell it. Can't you smell it?"

She sniffed carefully, her brows drawn together in a frown. The dad did the same, inhaling cautiously over the pitcher.

"I don't smell anything," he said.

Hank crossed over and took the pitcher out of the father's hand. Yup, the taint was there, strong and nauseating. He set it aside with a heavy thump. Meanwhile, the mom was frowning over her glass.

"This is Hank," Cecilia said, her voice soothing in the awkward silence. "He's here to help. He thinks the Detroit Flu is carried in the water."

"Do you smell it?" he pressed the mother.

She set down her glass slowly. "Maybe." She looked at him, and her eyes narrowed. Then her gaze hopped to her daughter, to the clawed hands and the furred arms.

"You know," Hank said quietly. "Or you guess, at least." His gaze moved to the father. "Is he blind?" The term wasn't universal among shifters, but it was common enough in Detroit.

"What?" Mr. Randolph said. "What is he talking about?"

It took two tries for his wife to answer, but she managed it. "Yes. He's...blind."

"And you? Who taught you?"

"My mother. I...um...I never..."

She'd never shifted.

Mr. Randolph stepped forward. "I'm not blind. What—" He stopped when his wife grabbed his hand.

"It's slang, honey," she said, her voice still cracking with strain.

Meanwhile, Hank kept pressing. "What about your siblings? Brother, sister—"

"My brother did it once. We aren't...we don't..." She shook her head. "It's never been a big thing for us."

He looked at Brittany. "It is now."

She swallowed, fear tightening her features as she took a half step backward toward the corner. Her gaze roved the room, and she clutched her free hand to her chest, her fingers curled into claws. Her husband turned to her, and she tucked tighter into his arms as she made tiny, almost inaudible whimpering sounds. Hank sighed. She was definitely half-shifter and her daughter, therefore, had enough DNA to activate, at least partially. Which made her a hybrid, although they already knew that.

But he needed more information if he was going to help. "What clan are you?"

It took Abby a moment to answer. She was busy breathing her husband's scent and squaring her mind for what was ahead, but eventually she straightened and looked back at Hank. "Black bear. From the Grand Rapids area."

One of his own. There were few of them in the Detroit area, and technically she should have reported herself to the local bear clan when she moved here, but she'd never shifted. Most people like her just forgot. It wasn't part of their lives, and they rarely told their spouses.

"Don't drink the water," he said clearly. "We think it activates your DNA."

Which is when the father's eyes lit up. "So you know what this is. You know how to cure it?"

Cecilia hedged. "We have an idea. I thought Hank here could talk to Brittany as she comes out—"

"No," Hank interrupted. "It has to be her mother." Then he looked at the woman. "Do you know how to do this? Did you see with your brother? You keep her eyes closed and get her to remember."

"There were triggers words with Owen. We all practiced them in case…" Her gaze went to Brittany. "But she doesn't know anything about this. I never—" Her voice was rising in hysterics. She wasn't melting down, but she was terrified, and he couldn't blame her. To have thought that this part of your life was done and then have it endanger your child? Even he could see that it cut at her.

"That's okay," he said quickly. Brittany was stirring. Her breath was deepening, and her hand twitched. "Think of a time when she felt powerful, pretty, or smart. Did she win something that made her feel really good about herself?"

"We just went shopping for prom dresses," she said, her voice uncertain.

"No, no," the father interrupted. "She's a mathlete. Remember how happy she was when they'd just won regionals? She's the only girl on the team."

"And the captain asked her out," Mom continued with a nod.

Hank smiled. "Perfect. Take her back to there. Don't let her fully wake. Speak right in her ear."

"And get her to remember being—" Her words cut off.

Being human. That's what she wanted to say, but her husband was standing right next to her getting frustrated the more they excluded him from the conversation. She'd have to tell him the truth soon, but maybe now wasn't the time. Not with Brittany starting to stir for real.

Cecilia noticed, too, and she gestured for Abby to come to the girl's side. Meanwhile, Hank pulled the curtains closed. This was a moment for privacy. And as they watched, both parents gripped their daughter's clawed hands, but Abby was the one who spoke as she stroked her hand over her daughter's eyes. She kept them closed as she murmured into the girl's ear.

"Hey, honey, I'm back. It's Mom."

Brittany took a deep breath and started to move, but Abby kept her from opening her eyes. "Don't wake up, honey. Not just yet. Just listen to my voice, okay?"

She didn't really wait for an answer, but Brittany must have heard because she stayed quiet except for how she tried to snuggle tighter toward her mother.

"I'm just going to talk to you for a bit," Abby said.

Hank whispered. "Climb into the bed with her. She needs to smell you."

Mr. Randolph frowned at that, but didn't argue. He helped his wife climb in and settle beside their child. Pretty soon she had Brittany snuggled against her chest as she stroked across the girl's forehead.

"Do you know what I've been thinking about?" Abby asked. "I've been remembering that day you won the mathlete regionals. Do you remember? The trophy was so heavy you almost dropped it. What was that boy's name who caught it? The captain of the team? The one who asked you out to the movies to celebrate? George? Jeremy? John?"

"Jordan." The name was mumbled but it came out clear enough.

"That's it. My God, you must have gone through half my makeup that night."

"Did not. I have my own." The girl's voice was stronger now, still slurred from the drugs, but definitely conscious.

"And then you came in and got mine. I tried to help you, but you said I had the stroke wrong. Like you're supposed to circle blush on or something."

"Mmm-hmm."

"A circle, honey? Come on. It's blush." She held up her daughter's clawed hand. "Can you show me it again?"

"Mommmm," the girl grumbled. It sounded just like every teenager who wanted an extra hour of sleep.

"Just like you did that day, remember? You'd just won regionals. That was exciting. My God, you're so smart."

Her father spoke up. "We're so proud of you honey." His voice broke on that as he gripped the furred hand.

"We are. And that night you went out to the movie with Jordan, but only after you showed me how to put on blush in a circle." Abby opened her daughter's fingers like you might spread the pads on a pet's paw. "Show me how to put on my blush, Brit. Please?"

The girl huffed back, her eyes still closed. "Can I open my eyes, Mom?"

"Not yet. I've got a surprise for you, and I just need you keep them closed. Come on, honey, how do you—"

"Like this, Mom." Her hand flicked in a very specific motion that Hank didn't even try to understand. But it was a hand. Somewhere between the beginning of the motion and the end, Brittany's hand went from a thick bear claw to a normal girl's hand. It even sported soft pink polish on her nails.

Her father gasped suddenly pulling Britt's other hand to his mouth. "Oh Brit," he murmured. "Oh thank God."

Abby was smiling, too, as she pressed her kisses to her daughter's face, surreptitiously wiping away the tears that fell. "That's great, honey. That's really great. Thank you."

"Can I open my eyes now?"

"Yes, honey. Go ahead."

And here was the really tense time. Because sure, they'd gotten Brittany to revert to full human in the twilight before fully waking up, but that didn't mean she'd keep the form. Not when she remembered where she was and why. From what he'd seen of other hybrids, any kind of fright could bring on the shift. And sometimes all it took was the memory of what they'd been not five minutes before.

Which meant they had to somehow keep Brittany calm while they explained to her exactly what she'd become.

Chapter 16

Score one for the good guys! Cecilia grinned as both parents hugged their normal-looking child. It was a beautiful moment made even more striking because Cecilia couldn't help but imagine holding her own child someday. One who had Hank's quiet strength and Cecilia's smart mouth. The kid didn't even have to be magical. She just wanted the whole idea of it.

Up until now, kids had been a someday kind of thing. Sure she wanted a family that shared makeup tips and teased about mathlete boyfriends but it hadn't been high on her priority list. Not until Hank had started talking about babies. Suddenly she was thinking about children in a very real, very present way. And with a man she hadn't even known yesterday morning. Was it possible? Did she want it?

Yes, absolutely, but maybe just not this exact second.

In her confusion, she turned to Hank. She wanted to see what he thought of the beautiful scene still playing out in front of them. But when she saw his face, she immediately sobered. He was worried.

She saw it in the narrowing of his brows and the tight cast to his shoulders.

"Hank?"

He looked at her, and his gaze immediately cleared. No worry. Just warm brown eyes and a mouth that—

"Why am I in the hospital?" Brittany asked, her words becoming sharper as her body continued to clear out the drugs.

Cecilia's gaze jerked back to the family scene. Oh hell. Brittany had woken up enough to ask questions. And from there, it was a short step to remembering which could lead them right back to panic. Obviously, the parents knew that as well.

"Honey—" her father began, his voice tentative, but his daughter was there before him.

"My arms!" she cried as she lifted them and spread her fingers. "My hands! They were…" She frowned as she moved them every which way. "I thought…"

Her mother started speaking, low and urgent. "Brit, you need to listen to me, okay?"

"Keep her calm," Hank instructed. "Show her what she looks like."

"Everything's fine," her father said clearly.

"I've got a mirror in my purse," Abby said as she rolled out of the bed and started rooting around in a large designer purse. It sat in the corner with her luggage, probably because she'd come right from the airport to here. "Here you go," she said as she pulled out a compact and flicked it open.

Brittany grabbed it, using it in the way of most teenage girls, efficiently moving it around to look at her face, her hair, her entire body with narrow-eyed intensity. "My hair is awful."

"But look at your complexion, Brit. It's all peaches and cream."

Abby's tone was warm, but Cecilia could hear the notes of strain underneath.

Her daughter used the mirror to inspect her face in minute detail. "It is nice," she murmured. "What have they been feeding me in here? Look at that. I don't even need a facial."

Abby chuckled at that, but there was still that nervous tone, and this time, Brittany was awake enough to notice it. She took a deep breath, her gaze still in the mirror, and then she slowly set the compact down. She looked at her parents first, then at Cecilia, and finally at Hank. She took her time at it, and everyone waited until she seemed ready. Then she folded her hands in her lap and looked right at her father.

"Okay, Daddy. What's going on?"

"It's all good news, honey. You've had the Detroit Flu, but look at you now. You're all better." He made a gesture at the monitor. "No fever, great blood pressure, and..." He grinned at her. "Well, I don't know what the other stuff means, but you're fine now. Look, you're great!"

Brittany relaxed at that, but her smile was still careful as she turned to her mother. "So why do you look so scared?"

Abby took a deep breath. "Well Brit, it's because I have to tell you something. Something about Grandma Teak and, um, me. And now, about you."

Brittany's gaze went to Cecilia. "I remember you. Dr. Lu, right?"

"Yes—"

"But what about him?" Her gaze pinned Hank with a steady, no-nonsense glare. "Who are you?"

"Hank's here to help explain things. After your mother does."

Then everyone's gaze went right back to Abby. She was clearly nervous, but in the end, she took a deep breath and spoke. "Well, honey, you know what werewolves are, right?"

Brittany snorted. "Sure."

"What if…well, what if I told you that your grandmother is a shifter, too? But instead of being a werewolf, she changes into a bear?"

Brittany blinked. Once. Twice. Then her mouth split into a wide grin. "You're telling me Grandma's a Care Bear? Like on TV or something? Did she finally get an acting gig?" She glanced over at Cecilia. "She's been doing dinner theater forever. At least since I was twelve."

Meanwhile, Peter shifted uncomfortably. "Abby, why don't we talk about this later? I think you're a little overstressed."

"No, dear," Abby's tone took on an edge. "I'm trying to explain. Werewolves exist, and Grandma's one of them. Except she turns into a bear."

Husband and daughter stared for two full seconds, and then burst into laughter at the same exact moment.

"Good one, Mom."

"What were you doing out in California? Is this a new Internet challenge or something? See if you can get your family to believe in werewolves?"

Cecilia narrowed her eyes, watching denial play out right in front of her. It was the blindness, for lack of a better word. No one would think that Abby was talking about a TV show or some Internet challenge. It just didn't work with the situation. And yet there they were, laughing as if she'd just told a good joke.

Which is when Abby turned to Hank. "They aren't going to believe unless they see."

Hank nodded, obviously already aware, but he held up his hands. "I shifted yesterday. I'm burnt until tomorrow."

Abby looked to Cecelia, but what could she do? "I just found out yesterday."

"Mom—" the girl began, but her mother straightened and took on that Mom tone that every child knew well.

"Listen to me. Both of you. Brittany, your grandmother can change into a bear. And now, apparently, so can you. Sort of. Not completely. It's why you had furry hands, remember?"

Brittany just stared at her. Peter, too. Both of them just froze, as if their minds fuzzed out for a second, maybe more. And then Peter turned to his daughter. "All the kids at school have been asking about you. I've got your phone somewhere." He started patting his pockets. "I'm sure you want to see it."

"Yes!" Brittany cried, reaching over to her father. "Did I miss the history test? I hope so because I haven't studied at all."

He finally found her smart phone and handed it over. Brittany thumbed it on and then promptly buried her face in the screen while Peter looked on with an indulgent smile. He looked so relieved. His daughter was well. They both seemed to have forgotten that Abby was even there.

What now? She supposed they could wait a bit until Brittany was stronger. Abby apparently was thinking the same thing because she sat back on the bed with a defeated huff. But again, Hank understood things better than they did. He spoke in a low tone.

"She has to understand now. Otherwise, something will spook her, she'll shift, and you'll be right back here again, forced sedation and all."

Abby spoke, her voice choked. "But maybe she won't change again. My brother never did."

Hank shook his head. "Hybrids can change at will. No apparent limit as far as we can tell."

So they had to show her and Peter. It was the only way through. "Is there anybody you can call?" Cecilia asked. "Someone who can…" Her voice trailed away at Hank's expression. He didn't even speak, but she knew the answer. The city was insane right now. All the shifters were probably out patrolling, trying to keep the city and the secret safe.

"She has to see it happen," Abby said, her expression taut. "They both do."

Clearly, she was thinking something. Cecilia watched as her jaw tightened, and her eyes narrowed in determination. It was as if she was steeling herself to do something. But what—

Oh hell. It all happened so fast. And once started, it still took Cecilia a moment to process what was going on.

Abby grabbed the pitcher of water—of *tainted* water—and starting guzzling. Hank reacted first, leaping forward with a jerk.

"No!" he cried, but Abby was prepared. She twisted away, draining the pitcher with surprising speed. Peter looked up, startled. Even Brittany set down her phone.

"Mom! Thirsty much?"

Abby set down the empty pitcher and looked at Cecilia. "I'm going to change now, right? That's what you said."

Double hell. "It's what we guess, Abby. We don't know for sure."

Peter shot to his feet. "Did you just infect my wife?" he demanded. "With the Detroit Flu?"

Infect? The woman had just guzzled it of her own choice.

Meanwhile, Hank stepped protectively in front of Cecilia. "Calm down, Mr. Randolph. Your wife is just trying to make you see something."

"Don't tell me what my wife is trying to do! Who are you exactly? Why are you here?" The man's voice was rising in anger, and Cecilia watched with a fascinated kind of horror. The man wasn't acting rationally at all. Was this how the magic worked? First with laughter, as if everything was a joke, then with misplaced anger. Hank hadn't done anything, and yet Peter was suddenly furiously aggressive. And on a man of Peter's size and build, Cecilia ought to be afraid.

Except she wasn't. Hank stood between her and Peter, a large, intimidating presence all his own. But instead of adding to the tension, he remained a quiet mountain of stability simultaneously protecting her and speaking in soothing tones.

"I understand your concern," he began. "But you need to focus on your wife. See her clearly."

Peter frowned, his gaze hopping to Abby and back. Abby who, incidentally, looked absolutely normal as she finished off the glass of water that had been set to the side earlier. So now the woman had a big dose of whatever was tainting the water. Just what did that mean? Was she about to sprout fur, too?

Abby turned to her husband and spoke in a level tone. "There's something I've kept from you, Peter. It's about my family."

"Stop this!" Peter commanded. "We're here for Brittany. I don't want to hear about anything else right now."

Abby took a deep breath as she looked to Cecilia. "How long will it take?"

Like she knew? "We don't even know if that's the real cause."

The woman nodded, her arms wrapped tightly around her belly as she turned to her daughter. "Brittany, honey, I'm not going to let you go through this alone. I've never done this before either. If this is the only way to get you to see, then I'll do it. I don't care if I have to drink an ocean, I'm going to be right beside you the whole way."

A touching statement of strength. Cecilia's heart melted at the words, especially since she understood a little of what kind of danger the woman was in. Abby had a lot more shifter DNA than her daughter. And if Brittany had turned into a hybrid, then what would happen to her? A full shift? A half shift? Most of the hybrids lost cortical control, meaning they got massive brain damage and lost rational thought. The last thing they needed was a crazed hybrid here. Or worse, a crazed bear.

"Let's all just take a breath," Cecilia said in her most official tone. "Peter, Dr. Hank here is a well-respected authority on the Detroit Flu, and I trust him completely. His insights have been invaluable in finding a cure for your daughter."

Hank turned slowly to give her a heavy look and no wonder. She'd just changed his first name to his last and given him a doctorate to boot. Thankfully, people tended to respect people with extra letters after their name, so Peter appeared to settle down, helped no doubt by the fact that absolutely nothing was happening to his wife. She was standing beside her daughter's bed, her entire body tight with worry, but with no physical changes.

Kind of anticlimactic, actually. Cecilia glanced at Hank who shrugged. He had no more idea how long it would take than she did. And in that moment of indecision, Brittany lost interest.

Her head went back into her phone. A minute later, she was chuckling. "Mom, look what Mr. Delgado posted on Instagram."

She turned her phone so her mother could see. "It's supposed to be a math joke, but it's just lame."

Abby turned to look. "Um, okay. Oh, I get it." She chuckled, though it sounded forced. "Funny."

Brittany rolled her eyes. "No, it's not. Regular people won't get it. Smart ones will just think it's dumb."

Abby smiled. "Well, I guess you're one of the smart ones, then."

And just like that, everyone settled. Peter stopped bristling. Brittany kept scrolling through things on her phone and showing them to her mother. Cecilia and Hank just stood there awkwardly.

Cecilia touched Hank's arm. "Should we leave?"

He shook his head. "I can't. If she changes…"

He needed to be here. He was the only one somewhat prepared for what would happen.

"And you need to be ready to sedate Brittany."

Cecilia started. "What? She's fine."

"But she'll get frightened if her mother changes. And then…"

"And then she'll shift, too." The last thing they needed was for Brittany to start screaming again. "But it's also possible that nothing will happen, right?"

Hank didn't answer except to shrug. No surprise there. Cecilia was the one with multiple PhDs, and all she'd done so far was stand behind Hank and watch. Then something even worse happened.

A knock sounded on the door. Everyone turned as Brittany's other doctors came pushing in. They must have heard—or seen on the video feed—that she'd reverted to normal. And anyone who was even tangentially involved in Brittany's case was bustling in to see. They wanted to inspect Brittany's arms and face, take new blood, run new tests, and so on. Cecilia was glad. She wanted all those tests done. She wanted to see how the girl's blood chemistry may or may not have changed. And cell slides would be fascinating. Not to mention a bit of analysis of the few stray hairs that had fallen to the floor when the girl had changed back to full human.

But what about Abby? Just how long did they have until the tiny hospital room was bursting with bears?

Chapter 17

Security! Security to 5L immediately!"

Hank tensed but he didn't move. It was the third security call today, this time to a hybrid four rooms down. Didn't these people have noses? Couldn't they tell the hybrid was about to pop? There was always an extra pulse of stench before the monster went TA—terminally aggressive. That's what Hank called it. That moment when the thinking mind ended and the adrenaline kicked so high that the animal creature inside everyone went wild. At that point, rabid dogs were more sane than the poor people who finally succumbed to the poison.

Hank peered out Brittany's hospital room window to the commotion in the hallway. The curtain was still drawn for privacy. Even though it had been five hours since Abby had drunk the poisoned water—with no obvious effect—they didn't want someone watching if she did pop. But he and Cecilia had stayed in the room because her change was coming. It was just a matter of time and possibly more water.

As he looked out from behind the curtain, he could see two security officers run down the hall, guns out. Then there was a crash inside the hospital room and a man screamed in terror. He knew about the patient in there. A guy in his twenties just starting to make his way as a chef when someone decided to poison Detroit. Hank hadn't seen him, but Cecilia had showed him the chart. The guy had shown up in the ER with a wolf's snout after biting the arm of his sous chef. The cops had managed to restrain him and bring him here in handcuffs. That was two days ago, and the guy's brain scans revealed steady deterioration.

Beside him, Cecilia straightened up from her seat in the corner. When it was clear that Abby wasn't going to shift immediately, Cecilia had brought her work into the hospital room. She'd been nose deep in her tablet, but now headed toward Brittany's door as if she could help the hybrid down the hall.

He grabbed her arm and shook his head. No way could she do anything at this point, and the resignation on her face said she knew it. The bitter condemnation in her exhausted gaze also told him she was furious—not at the bastards who had created the poison—but at herself for not curing the disease.

"Maybe if we tried—" she began, but her voice abruptly cut off when three gunshots rang out in rapid succession.

Gunshots on a hospital ward. The thought made him want to vomit.

Behind him, he heard Brittany "Eep!" in surprise. He turned around, ready to grab her if she went hybrid in her fear. Fortunately, her father was there, gently stroking her face.

"It's nothing honey. Probably something on the TV."

It wasn't, and everybody here knew it. But since there was

nothing she could do, Brittany nodded at her father and picked up her phone with shaking hands. Hank never thought it would be a good thing for a teenager to spend more time buried in her phone, but at the moment, he'd take it. Anything that kept the kid calm.

Meanwhile, Cecilia was as tight as a bowstring, her face and her body aimed toward the hallway.

"I should…" Her voice trailed away, and he arched a brow at her. What could she do now? The young chef was dead. His story was over, and there were a dozen medical personnel handling the aftermath. Cecilia's gaze took on an angry, determined look. "I should solve this fucking problem," she said under her voice. Then she softened as she focused on him. "I can't thank you enough for being here. You're the only one keeping us calm, and you haven't wavered an iota."

He felt his insides still at her words, and his breath caught as the meaning sank in. She saw him. She knew that he was doing everything he could to keep the situation from spiraling out of control. Abby was about to do her first change, and that was never a safe thing. Her daughter was a new hybrid, and her husband didn't know about any of this. He couldn't imagine a more volatile situation. Hell, he'd spent the last five hours prepared to leap into action at the first hint of a problem. Most people didn't notice how alert he was. He was so quiet, sometimes people forgot he was even in the room. But Cecilia saw him. Cecilia knew his strength, and he couldn't be more pleased.

"I'm here," he said, the words pushed through his tight throat. "Whatever you need."

"I know. And I'm grateful," she said as she gave him squeeze. Then she put on her game face and went back to what she did best.

She returned to her tablet and the pages of data there. Her brain was working a million miles a minute to solve this medical disaster, and she was absolutely determined to do it or die trying. In the face of an overwhelming problem, she had found her battleground in science and taken her stand.

He admired the hell out of that. Especially since he'd long ago given up fighting and just accepted the world's ills. Which gave him peace but no satisfaction. While she had no peace and, at the moment, no satisfaction.

But she still took the time to see his value.

And so he fell. He gave up resisting and fell totally and completely in love. It might be the magic, it might just be hormones, but suddenly he didn't care. He loved her for who she was, and inside he felt the bond to her strengthen from "compelling interest" to steel chains of *I will always be hers.*

He tried not to hate that part. This bond didn't say anything about her belonging to him, only that he was locked in to her. That no matter where he was or what he did, all she'd need to do was crook her finger, and he would be there for her. To protect, to love, to do whatever she wanted.

He was forever destined to love her. Zen detachment was gone. If she hurt, he would hurt. If she was frightened, he would destroy what scared her. If she was happy, then he would throw confetti and cheer as if she stood on the gold medal platform at the Olympics.

He was hers. Forever. Whether she wanted him or not.

His knees went weak as he started to see the ramifications of what had just happened. He understood now why there were stories of bonded shifters who went crazy. His body, mind, and soul abruptly depended on her. He could not have peace unless she was at peace.

He would not experience joy unless she was happy. He could not exist except in a space where she too lived and thrived.

His breath shortened as he adjusted to the chains. His mind, however, still reeled. What if she didn't return his affection? What if she saw him as a big, dumb black guy and ditched him tomorrow? What if she was kind now, but then left when the crisis was over? When the Detroit Flu ended and she was sent off to somewhere else to fight a different outbreak? What then?

He didn't have many friends and no family nearby, but he still had a life here. If she left, he would go with her. No question. He'd abandon his home, the people in the building he cared for, and he'd walk away from the Griz—his shifter clan—without even looking back. He had to be near her. He had to be able to give her anything she wanted, whenever she wanted. And he would be grateful for her attention. A slave to her for the rest of his life.

His hands shook, and he had to grip the doorknob for support. He was a man, damn it, not a lapdog. A powerful man with a strong mind who had always forged his own way. He'd gone through his shifter adolescence with a measure of control that his brother hadn't found. He'd gone to war and seen such destruction there, but had found Zen peace in the midst of atrocity. And even back here in Detroit when Nanook had compelled him with a special mind-fuck ability to go on drug runs, he had found his own thin road through. He never killed anyone, only stood there as an apparent threat. And if Simon hadn't defeated Nanook, then Hank would have made his own run at alpha. In truth, he'd been prepared to attack on the very day that Simon showed up.

He was slave to no one!

And yet, he was to her. And that thought brought him to his knees.

"Hank?"

She noticed his change. Even with her nose in her work, she still noticed him. That brought him a little comfort until he realized that she wasn't looking at him. Her eyes were on Abby.

He looked over and immediately went on alert. It was hard to shift away from his own personal crisis, but Cecilia was in danger now, and that snapped him into lightning focus. Abby was about to change. She'd probably heard the gunshots and had her adrenaline spike enough to kick her over.

Her hands were knotted into fists, and her breath came in short pants. Her eyes were narrowing, and her lips were pulled back in a growl. She was about to shift, but was it into a black bear or a hybrid? And would she have any brain left when she was done?

Hank straightened to his full height. Cecilia had set her tablet down and stood as well, but he edged her behind him toward the door. There was precious little room to maneuver in here. He would have to keep Abby contained and calm—and bring her back—all in a space barely large enough for a hamster.

"Mom?"

Brittany was paying attention. Faster than her father who was still too deeply settled in his denial and his own tablet.

Hank spoke quietly to Brittany. He needed her to understand and not freak. "She's showing you that she can change, too. She's shifting into a black bear. Don't be frightened. It's normal."

Abby's eyes started to bulge out and there was panic in her gaze. Shifting could be painful, the first time even more so. It felt like your body was shattering as it went to an energy state, but it was only your thoughts that actually broke. All those notions of who you are and what your body is burst with a very real psychic pain. At least that's how he'd felt. Abby, too, apparently, because her mouth split wide in a scream.

Her husband leapt up. Even he couldn't ignore a woman's bellow.

Cecilia was at the door, abruptly jerking it open to scream out into the hallway. "Everything's fine here! We're just having a discussion. Don't come shooting! Do *not* call security!" Then she slammed the door again and blocked it shut with her body. "Your turn, Hank. I'll hold them off as long as I can."

He wanted to laugh. There was no taking turns like in a game. This was Abby's show. It all depended on how she handled sharing her rational mind with the animal inside. And nobody did that well the first time, but he did try to help.

He held up his hands and spoke clearly. "You're okay, Abby. Just go with the change. This is how it's done."

Fur was sprouting all over her face and body. Black fur infused with a golden glow that would disappear once the change settled. Her nose was elongating as her face became darker, thicker, and distinctly bearlike. She growled at him, the sound low and threatening. And then her chest started expanding, hips, then legs.

Only the first change went this slow. Soon, she'd get the hang of doing this almost instantaneously. But for right now, it was like every part of her popped in individual sequence. And with every change, she released a sound of half anger, half agony. Which is when Hank realized that she'd made a classic new-shifter mistake.

Her clothing was too tight. He'd checked that before. She had on a loose blouse that ripped easily, pants with an elastic waistband that adjusted though it looked pretty silly on a big bear, and cheap sandals that broke the second her feet started expanding. But he forgot about her bra.

Her eyes narrowed, and she looked down at her chest. Her claws started ripping at the heavy elastic, shredding the blouse and drawing blood through her furred chest. She cut it slightly, but then she must have really looked at her hands, now big furred claws. She drew back in shock, her head tossing back as she roared again, but that only banged her against the equipment there.

Meanwhile, her husband bolted upright and started screaming. No big surprise. His wife was now a bear. But that was nothing compared to what Brittany did. She went full hybrid, and the stench nearly brought Hank to his knees. It certainly made her father start choking. She also leapt out of bed, disconnecting all her monitors in the process, which began a series of beeps and bings. And then she saw her own arms. She'd been pointing at her mother, but with furry arms and clawed hands. Which began a whole other series of screams of horror.

Hank tried to divide his attention. He didn't want to take his focus from her mother. Abby was the most dangerous one here at three-hundred-plus pounds of panicked bear, but Brittany was equally lethal with her claws and younger mind. At least Abby's mind understood what was going on.

Thankfully, Cecilia kept her head. "You stay with Abby. I've got the other two."

He wanted to shout her a warning, but he didn't have a chance. Not with Abby spinning around as machines blared at her. She had no special awareness of her body and her bra chose that moment to snap in half, ricocheting painfully into her arm. She threw her arm over her head with a roaring yelp and then banged into another monitor.

Meanwhile, Cecilia faced the other family members and snapped at them in her doctor voice.

"Settle down this instant!"

Would have been better if she hadn't started gagging. God, Brittany sure could turn on the BO. At least the father was out of danger. He'd dropped to his knees as he retched into the biohazard wastebasket.

Abby turned to her husband, but Hank waved his hand to get her attention. Then he let fly with his best boot camp sergeant imitation.

"Freeze, now!"

At least he got it out without coughing, though the stench in this closed room was making his eyes water. Better yet, Abby's gaze locked on his.

"Abby! You understand what happened?"

The bear straightened to her full height, but then couldn't keep her balance. It was hard to manage in a body suddenly so different. She only remained upright for a couple seconds, and then she teetered forward. She was going to fall and he needed to get out of the way fast.

"The bed," he said as he pointed at it. "Fall forward onto the bed."

She did. It was clumsy, but she managed it. And more than that, he now knew that she had kept control of her mind. The bear wasn't in control, her thinking mind was. Excellent. There'd be more adjustment, but for the moment, he could work with that.

Thankfully, Cecilia had gotten Brittany past her initial terror. She was still panting, the whites of her eyes way too present, but she was staring at her mother, not her own body. Way better to focus on how her mother had changed. Cecilia was talking, her voice low but clear now that Abby had stopped roaring and Peter had stopped retching.

"That's your mother, Brittany. She can change into a bear. Just like she told you."

Brittany swung her face to Cecilia, shaking her head in denial.

"Don't give me that crap, young lady," Cecilia snapped. "You see it. You know it. Don't be willfully blind. That's your mother, and she needs you."

Abby didn't need Brittany. In fact, she'd taken this massive risk just to help Brittany. But whatever got through to the girl was fine by him. And apparently saying her mother was in trouble worked because Brittany slowly got it together. Her breath evened out and her arms dropped as she stared at the bear leaning on top of her bed. Which is when the father finally looked up from the waste can enough to process his surroundings.

"My God," he breathed.

"Nope," Cecilia said almost cheerfully. "That's your wife. Don't be an ass and abandon her." Then she turned to Brittany. "She did this for you, remember?" She squeezed Brittany's huge furred arm. "She didn't need to do this. It was really hard and scary for her, right?" Cecilia glanced at Hank.

He nodded. "And painful. First shifts suck."

"But she did it for you both. So you would see that it's not scary. It's a good thing. Pretty cool, actually, right?"

He didn't expect Abby to answer, but she did. The bear opened her mouth and did a kind of soft grunt—very restrained and very anxious—but it got through to Brittany.

"Mommy!" she cried then suddenly she was climbing onto the bed with her mother and throwing her arms around Abby's neck.

Perfect, right? Would be except for the heavy bangs on the room door. "Dr. Lu! Dr. Lu! Open up."

Cecilia turned to bellow out the door. "We're fine! Stay back!"

Hank worried that they wouldn't listen, but a moment later, things quieted down on the other side of the door. Apparently, Cecilia's doctor voice carried true authority. Meanwhile, it was now up to Peter. Would he accept the evidence of his own eyes? Just how much did he love his wife and child? Maybe not enough, given how much he was staring.

It was as if the words were written on the man's face. An endless stream of: *This can't be true, this can't be true.*

Hank wanted to shake him. He wanted to force the man to really accept what he was seeing, but he knew that any distraction would likely make matters worse. The battle was all in Peter's head now and at the moment, it was fifty-fifty which side would win.

Mother and daughter noticed. Brittany still had her bear arms wrapped around her mother's neck. Her lower half had gone bear, too, which was just as well given that she was in her hospital gown. Abby was nuzzling her child, making soothing bear purrs as her tongue licked long swaths across Brittany's forehead revealing the girl's bear ears. But the longer Peter stayed silent, the more the two noticed that he wasn't part of them.

Abby looked at her husband and made a low moan. Brittany opened her eyes and turned to stare at her father.

"Daddy?" Her voice hadn't changed much. A little deeper maybe, but Hank could still hear the little girl in that one word.

Apparently, so could Peter. He blinked his eyes and wiped away his tears. And then he took a deep breath as he squared his shoulders...and dove into the big hug.

All three, hugging it out on the bed. Bear, hybrid, and human. Hank rocked back on his heels and blew out a slow breath in appreciation. Family unity in the scariest of situations. It never failed to steal his breath. Cecilia seemed equally effected as she entwined her fingers in his.

"Sometimes life doesn't suck in the least," she murmured, her eyes sheening with tears.

He smiled. So did Peter who was now rocking backward to stare at the two women in his life. "I never want to hear one word about how I'm going bald," he said. "Not when you two can do this whenever you want. It's just not fair," he said as he ran a hand over his nearly bald pate.

Brittany chuckled as she rocked backward. Abby, too, though the sound was more a rumble as it came through her bear body. Then there was another knock on the door.

"Dr. Lu? Mr. and Mrs. Randolph—"

"We're fine!" Cecilia snapped. "And you're interfering with therapy!" She turned back to the threesome on the bed. "This isn't going to last long. You need to change back." Then she looked at Abby. "And I need to get behind you to turn off those alarms."

The *beep*s and *bing*s were continuing, but she'd have to climb over Abby's back to get to them. Then Hank saw a better way. He scooted around and pulled the plugs. All of them. As many as he could reach.

The silence was heavenly. At least until Cecilia gasped at him in horror. "You just lost all the data!"

He looked at the suddenly dark machines. What could he say? "Oops."

She blew out a breath, but then turned to the family. "Brittany, human now. Abby? Do you know how to do it?"

The bear shook her head and Brittany just stared at her hands and thick arms obviously starting to climb back into hysterics.

"Don't you dare," Cecilia snapped. "Remember how your mom got you out of it before? She got you to remember that day when you won that mathlete thing."

Peter took up the reins. "Remember that day clearly, Brit. You won because you're so smart. And that boy asked you out. What was his name?"

"Jordan," Brittany said as she closed her eyes. "Jordan and I kissed," she murmured as she clearly relived the event. And again, in that soft yellow glow, Brittany returned to human. Right at the exact moment her father drew up short.

"You kissed? What do you mean you kissed?"

Brittany gave her father a very human eye roll. "Dad, I'm sixteen. I've been kissed before."

"You have not! I mean, you have? When?"

Cecilia held up her hand and the two abruptly stopped. "It's Abby's turn." She looked at Hank.

"Same thing Abby," he said. "Remember who you are. Remember that you're Brittany's mother and Peter's wife."

"We're here for you, Mom," Brittany said, her voice strong.

"Yes..." Peter's voice cracked, and he had to clear his throat before he could speak again. "Yes, honey. Remember our...remember..." He softened, right there before their eyes. His shoulders relaxed, and his face took on a nostalgic glow. "I remember the first time I saw you on our wedding day. We should have picked a church with air-conditioning. I was sweating bullets in that tux. And then the doors opened and there you were with your father. I've never seen anyone look so beautiful before. You were so perfect, I couldn't believe how lucky I was. That's what I kept thinking. About how I was so damned lucky to be marrying my best friend."

The bear opened her mouth. At first Hank thought she was panting or trying to speak, hard to tell. But then came the golden glow, the fur dropping into it. Her face pulled in and there she was. A full human leaning against the bed with her eyes on her husband.

"Peter," she whispered.

He didn't answer. He was too busy kissing her.

Hank watched it, his heart squeezing tight. Right here was the best of human kind. The happy result that everyone longed for. Mom, dad, and kid buried in love. He remembered that kind of love from his own family, but it just hadn't seemed to be in the cards for him. Girls shied away from him when they saw his scar, but the real problem started after his parents split up. Everyone thought it was because of his brother's death, but the reason was that his father couldn't handle what he'd learned about his own children—that they changed into animals—so he'd left. Hank had realized then that any woman would not only have to see past his scar but his shifter nature, too. Wasn't going to happen, he'd thought, but now suddenly he had hope. If there was a future for these three, then maybe he and Cecilia could make it work. Maybe Cecilia—

His thoughts froze when he caught Cecilia's expression. She was focused not on the sight in front of her, but on her tablet, which she'd grabbed sometime in the last minute. She wasn't seeing Mom and Dad find themselves despite the massive revelation. And she wasn't seeing teenager Abby groan as she threw a blanket over her mother's bare shoulders. No, her attention was away from the love and deep into the science. He could see the scans she was tapping as she apparently studied the last of the data that had been uploaded from whatever machines he'd unplugged. And she wasn't smiling; she was frowning in annoyance. Because he'd screwed up her data.

Hell. Had he fallen in love with a woman who was all work, all the time? Someone who couldn't stop long enough to live a full life?

"Damn it! Damn, damn, damn it!" she cried.

Everyone turned to look at her as she started stabbing with her finger on the tablet.

Hank shifted, his protective instincts looking for danger even though his mind knew she was angry at something on her computer. "What is it?" he asked, his voice tight.

"The data! It's corrupted."

"I'm sorry—"

"No, you don't understand. Not just that data," she jerked a finger at the machines. "All of it on Brittany." She dropped the computer on the bed while she threw up her hands. "It's like there was a glitch or something in the records. Our one good outcome, gone!"

She threw up her hands in disgust and glared at the ceiling as she obviously tried to get a hold of herself. Hank wanted to reassure her. He wanted to suggest maybe it was on the backup or the server or the cloud, but he knew it wouldn't help.

Thanks to the magic, the data was gone. He knew it as surely as he knew his own name.

"I'm sorry," he said.

She glared at him. "It's the…the magical force thing?"

Hank nodded. It didn't make sense, but this wasn't the first electronic glitch that had helped hide shifters.

"Fucking damn magic!" she spat. "I'm so done with it." Then she grabbed her tablet and jerked open the hospital room door. She was about to stomp out when she noticed the circle of medical personnel and security who stood there. "What?" she gasped, obviously startled.

"Dr. Lu, is everything all right?"

"No!" she snapped, and then she abruptly moderated her tone. "I mean, yes, of course everything's fine. Brittany's cured. She's fine. Let her go home."

A cheer went up from everyone standing there.

"But how?" one of the men asked. Dr. Thorton, according to his ID. "How was she cured?"

Everyone looked at Cecilia, himself included. How to explain Brittany's miraculous recovery?

She grimaced, looking defeated even as she spoke with clear authority. "I don't think she had it in the first place."

"Of course, she did. Look at her files."

"Don't bother," Cecilia said, her voice tight. "It's corrupted. We'll have to try to reconstruct it from memory."

The men looked at Cecilia, then again back at Brittany. "So she never had the Flu to begin with?"

"Well, obviously she had a flu," a nurse said. "Just not the Detroit Flu." The woman smiled at Brittany. "Honey, you are so lucky. You dodged a big bullet here."

Literally given that the two security guards were just now putting their guns away.

"So what do we do now? Just discharge her?" Dr. Thorton asked.

Cecilia blew out a breath. "She's fine. She's healthy." She glanced back at the Brittany and her parents. "Hank will get you all the information you need." She dropped her hands to her side. "I'm going back to the lab."

She walked away, her steps clipped and angry. Behind her, the other doctors were still talking. "So our one good case isn't a case after all? They all die?"

"Looks that way," Dr. Thorton said. "Bloody hell."

Hank watched everyone disperse. He knew from experience it would feel weirdly surreal. People going through motions as if nothing life shattering had happened here. As if they couldn't wait to get rid of the strange people who challenged their grip on reality. And not a one commented that Abby was wearing a blanket around her torso rather than a blouse.

All back to normal. Denial or magic or something else. He didn't know, but he'd seen it before. And now Cecilia saw how the shifter world survived in the shadows.

Clearly, she wanted nothing to do with it.

Chapter 18

Cecilia could barely breathe. She made it to the lab where Dennis was again asleep on the couch. The man could sleep anytime, anywhere, and through anything. But since he often worked through the night, she couldn't complain about his work ethic. Just be jealous of his peace of mind.

How did this happen? How was there magic in the world that nobody saw? And when solid, scientific research could bring it to light, bullshit happened. They shouldn't have lost all the data. Not from simply unplugging the machine. At least they had video. Unless...

She crossed to the monitor at her station and pressed the keys to bring up Brittany's room. Sure enough, there was the whole family packing up, hugging each other, and getting ready to set off on their new shifter-aware adventure.

She hit another key for the playback. She wanted to go back an hour and see everything in minute detail. Every...

She wasn't even surprised when the recording showed snow. Lots and lots of white noise static with no image.

She dropped down onto her stool in defeat and started to rationally, logically consider the possibilities. Shifters existed. She was biologically and romantically drawn to one of them. The Detroit Flu was a shifter poison that activated magical DNA, if you had it. Most of them went crazy except for the lucky few like Brittany who joined the magical ranks. And, by the way, evidence of this truth was zapped somehow. Pfft. Gone.

She took a deep breath and spoke aloud to her monitor. There really was only one logical answer. "I need a CT scan. I've got a brain tumor."

Dennis shifted on the couch. He answered without even opening his eyes. "You're not crazy. You're just brain fried."

She frowned at her coworker. "No really. Dennis, I'm seeing people change into animals. I'm watching data disappear in front of my eyes. And I'm hot for a guy I'd never go for normally. It's a tumor. It has to be."

He opened his eyes and blinked them wearily at her. "I'm too tired for games."

"I'm not playing."

He sighed and shut his eyes. "You don't have to create a brain tumor to be taken off this case. Just invent an emergency at home. Or call in your vacation days. You can be out of here in a few hours."

"The city's quarantined."

"Fine. There are really important samples that need to be analyzed in Atlanta. Highly contagious. Must be hand delivered."

She glared at him. "Are you trying to get me fired?"

"Yes. Then I can have your job and with all your special perks."

She had no special perks and wasn't even paid as well as he was, and they both knew it. "Dennis, I want to have this man's babies.

Like I want to ride him for the next hundred years in between raising his children."

He shifted on the couch, stretching his legs into a more comfortable position. "So you're horny. Who isn't?"

"Me. Ever. Not when there're lives to save. A flu to end."

He snorted as he folded his arms across his chest. "Welcome to puberty. I knew you'd get here eventually."

She threw up her arms. "I've been through puberty, thank you very much. And have no need to revisit—"

He shifted and glared at her, his expression annoyed but not unkind. "You're fried, Dr. Lu. As in sizzled in a pan and done. So go. Get your freak on. Ride this guy until you both pass out from exhaustion because you're not doing us any good here."

She stared at him. "He can turn into a bear, Dennis. A big black bear."

He snorted. "Never would have guessed you'd be into costume kink, but whatever. Yabba dabba do!"

She rolled her eyes. "That's *The Flintstones*."

He lifted his head a moment as he obviously sorted through his childhood memories. "Oh right. Play ball!"

"That's Yogi Berra."

"Fine," he huffed. "Only you can prevent forest fires." Then he rolled onto his side on the couch, firmly putting his back to her. "Kill the lights when you leave, will you?"

"You have a hotel room, you know."

"Yeah, but it's right next to yours and I don't want to hear you being smarter than the average bear."

She stared at Dennis. Damn it, she was actually in crisis here. Logically it made way more sense that she had a brain tumor than that shifters existed and magic corrupted data files. But she knew what she'd seen. She knew Abby had changed into a bear. Hank, too. And then there were the werewolves and Sammy and…

She dropped her head in her hands. "I need a CT scan."

Dennis didn't answer, but Hank did. She hadn't heard him come in, but the big man was incredibly quiet. Even his voice was soft, soothing her ragged nerves.

"Let me take you out to dinner."

His hand was warm on her shoulder, big and comforting. She felt it like a drop of oil on a turbulent sea. It expanded across her churning thoughts, quieting them though she didn't know how. Normally when she was upset, she hated it when people touched her. But not Hank. She wanted to crawl up inside him and stay there forever. Instead, she thought about dinner.

"Is there anything still open?"

"I can cook."

Of course, he could. He was the most perfect man ever.

"I don't even know if you're real," she said. "Maybe I'm hallucinating you."

Dennis groaned from the coach. "He's real. Go away. Get your freak on."

She dropped her head against Hank's large, comforting chest. "What do you think?" she asked.

"About what?"

She tilted her head up. She saw his broad shoulders and large, dark face. Never in a million years would she have predicted being attracted to a man like him. He wasn't an academic. He was a man of few words, and God knew everyone in her circle talked until forced to shut up. He was a building superintendent in a not-so-spectacular area of Detroit. An army medic and, she now guessed, a Zen master. None of that added up to anything she'd ever imagined in a man. And yet, looking at him now, she wanted to kiss him with everything in her. Worse, she wanted to go to bed by his side and wake up with him in the morning. She wanted to hear about his days and could think of no one better beside her when she wrestled with her own demons. She wanted him forever and always.

What was that if not a brain tumor? And yet, part of her didn't care.

"So do you want to…um…get our freak on?" she asked.

His eyes blazed hot and his nostrils flared, but there was no other indication that he'd even heard her. She wasn't sure he breathed.

"Hank?"

"Yes."

She frowned at him. Was that a *Yes, I want to get our freak on?* Or a *Yes, what are you asking me?* She opened her mouth to ask him to clarify because honestly—brain tumor here—she needed things very clear. But her words were stopped when his hand touched her face. He was a large man and his hand was no different but she hadn't realized just how gently he could touch her.

His fingertips barely skimmed her skin and left a tingling wake as he skated along her jaw. Then his thumb stroked across her cheeks to her mouth. She didn't even think he touched her lips, but they plumped and tingled just from the thought. And from the dark intensity in his eyes as he watched her.

Her fears shorted out. Brain tumor? Psychotic break? Magic was real? All those confusing thoughts kept screaming, but she couldn't hear them when he looked at her like that. When he leaned down as she stretched up to him.

Their breath mingled, but again, he didn't touch her. He just breathed her in as she ached for him.

"Please," she whispered.

He closed the distance between them, but he didn't press deep. Lip to lip now, he brushed back and forth as her breath caught and her head dropped back. His other hand caught her, supporting her head as he pressed deeper, harder against her mouth. In that moment, she opened all of herself to him. Her heart, her head, and her body, and he thrust inside with a hunger that matched her own.

He plundered her mouth and she dueled with him without restraint. Animal hunger. Desperate passion. She had no words for this, no other experience that matched the need that pounded through her blood. Her arms wrapped around his shoulders, drawing him closer as she stretched higher.

His tongue became wilder then. The thrust and parry seemed harder now, more powerful as he owned her mouth, but she didn't give way. As he started to take from her, her passion roared through and suddenly she was dueling with him as if her life depended on it. Her life felt poised in the balance as she thrust and took from his tongue, his mouth, his hunger.

She clutched his shoulders harder. She used him to pull herself up along his torso. She even curled a leg around his as she tried to climb up for a better angle. His right hand left her face, dropping down to her thigh as she wrapped herself around him.

Need clawed at her, irrational and overpowering. She dove into it, throwing away her rationality as if it meant nothing. All she needed was him. Right now. Right here.

She would have done it, too. She would have ripped off her clothes right here while Dennis pretended to sleep six feet away. She would have, but Hank kept control. Where before he was holding her against him, pressing the bulge of his hot penis against her groin, now he gripped her hard and pushed her back.

She didn't want to go. She fought him, straining to keep them connected, but he was stronger and relentless. He held her back while she whimpered in distress.

"Not here," he said.

"On-call room?" she asked.

"No." He swallowed and took an unsteady step backward. Again, she tried to keep him close, but he refused though his gaze seemed to burn. "I'll drive. Your hotel?"

She nodded and headed for the door on shaky legs. He remembered her tote bag, which held purse and tablet. And while Dennis muttered an amused, "Yabba dabba do!" she flipped the lights off.

"Still *The Flintstones*," she returned as she shut the door. Then linking her fingers with Hank, they headed to his car.

Neither spoke much on the drive, though he attempted conversation twice. The first time, he said, "Do you want to talk about this?"

"No."

Then five minutes later, he tried again. "We don't have to—"

"Yes, we do. It's the magic, right?" Or the brain tumor.

He looked at her, his gaze serious. "On my side, yes. You're still free. You can still say no."

Could she? She didn't think so. Not with this need clawing inside her. Her face must have said as much because he shook his head.

"You aren't magical," he said firmly. "You don't have to feel this way."

"But I do feel like this."

His expression tightened. For a moment she thought she saw joy, fierce and powerful. But a second later it was locked down and hidden away. A statue of Buddha had more expression than he did. And then he asked one last question.

"What if…" He halted as he turned a corner. "What about the baby?"

Not *a* baby. He'd said *the* baby as if a child was a foregone conclusion if they did this.

She closed her eyes and dropped her head back against the seat. The idea of carrying his child thrilled her. And that confused her. In her mind's eye, she was looking at a serious little boy or a giggling little girl. One would play with a chemistry set, another would tear after a soccer ball. And she had no idea which child would do what. She thought of holidays and birthday parties. Of baby snuggles and that moment when Hank brought home a puppy. All those scenes flashed through her head and she wanted it. Oh God, how she wanted it.

But she couldn't say that aloud. She was a career girl. She's spent most of her life in study just so she could have this job with the CDC ferreting out the secrets of stubborn viruses and deadly fungi. Bacteria were almost boring because she understood them so well, but there were always more mysteries to solve, more contagions to conquer. She loved her job with an all-consuming passion.

Except for right now when the passion was completely focused on him.

"You sure I'm not magical?" she said. It certainly felt like she'd been taken over by something.

He shrugged. "Not in the way I am." Then he repeated his words loudly. Firmly. "You are *not* bound by this."

Yeah, she was. She already felt the link between them. Solid chains that heated her blood and made her womb ache to be filled.

"I want this," she said firmly. Not just the sex, but the whole thing. Husband, kids, white picket fence—whole shebang. She just hadn't expected it to happen this fast and with a man she'd only met yesterday. Brain tumor or magic didn't matter. She wanted him, so she pointed to the extended stay hotel parking lot. "Turn here. My room's in the back." She had a kitchen, a desk/sitting area, and a very large bed.

He didn't say anything more as he parked. She hopped out immediately, her keycard in hand. She was inside in a moment, already stripping out of her clothes. He followed a step behind, quietly shutting the door as he watched her toss aside tunic, bra, leggings, and panties. She was naked beside her bed within seconds, and it felt so good.

Then she turned to wait for him.

He stood there at the door. He hadn't moved and yet she thought she could hear his heart racing and his breath short and quick. She could see the bulge in his jeans and knew how very large and hot his penis was. There were things she wanted to do to him, but it all culminated with him inside her. With the pounding release and the grasping pull of her womb as she took his seed inside.

"We do this," he finally said, "we do it my way."

"Any way. I don't care."

"I do. You do whatever I say or I leave right now."

She tilted her head. "Could you? Leave, I mean."

He didn't answer for a long moment, and then he shrugged. "I could try."

He could, and she would let him. But they both knew where

they would end up. Right back here on her bed or on the floor or wherever they landed with him inside her.

And then, to her absolute joy, he stripped off his tee.

Dark glorious muscles revealed to her hungry gaze. Broad shoulders, perfect flesh. Except for the scar on his face, there were no flaws. Not even a mole. Probably a benefit of being a shifter, she realized. Then he toed off his shoes and pushed down his jeans.

His penis sprang free, large and proud, and though she'd seen it before, she again marveled at his size. He was a big man everywhere, and her body was only average. But even as she had the thought, she knew they would fit. At this moment, she believed even her bones would adjust to accommodate him.

"Lie back," he commanded.

She did. It took her a moment to scurry backward on the bed, but pretty soon she lay dead center, her hands spread at her sides, and her legs softening open though her knees still touched. He prowled closer to the bed. No other word for it, especially since she'd only flipped on the far light. That put him in silhouette as his dark form slipped through the shadows toward her and the bed.

Her heartbeat sped up and her mouth went dry. Wild thoughts ran through her head of what he could do to her. God, she'd only known the man for a day and here she was willing to let him do…what? Whips? Chains? Would she even say no?

And then she stopped thinking as he made it to the edge of the bed. She opened her mouth to speak. His name. A question. Hell, she didn't know what. But the tension in her body was growing unbearable. She wasn't used to being on display like this, and though his gaze was more than complimentary, it still made her feel self-conscious.

But when she opened her mouth, he made a swift sound of denial. Half bark, half growl—it silenced her before she'd even found her voice.

"I'm going to go slow, Cecilia. Very slow. The only word you can say is, 'no.' Do you understand? It's the only thing that will get through."

She nodded, too mesmerized by his intensity to risk anything else. He was still prowling, his motions steady as he seemed to stalk her. First one side of the bed, then sliding around the base to crawl up by her feet.

She heard him inhale, long and deep. Then he released a kind of purr from the back of his throat. Appreciation, and she flushed at the sound.

He moved up the bed on all fours, his powerful arms outlined by the light. He set his mouth to just above her left ankle, skating his teeth across her skin enough to make her shiver. Her legs loosened then, slipping even farther apart.

He scooped an arm under her left knee, drawing it up as he kissed up the side of her leg. Lips, tongue, teeth. He moved up her leg, thrusting his tongue in the crook made by the bend of her knee, and then drawing her leg wide as he kissed the inside of her thigh.

She tried to draw him higher on her body. She crooked her foot behind his back and pulled, but he went at his own pace. Slow, steady, and inevitable. She was dripping by the time he made it to her groin.

This close, she could see the tension in his body. There was sweat on his forehead and a trembling restraint in his movements. And yet, he still worked her body as if he were helping with a leisurely bath. A squeeze on her thigh, followed by a lick and a kiss. Every inch of her leg was held or caressed. And when he had adjusted her left leg to where he wanted it, he moved back down to her right knee.

At least he didn't start back at her ankle. Was it possible to orgasm just from a tiny bite on her kneecap?

He pressed his nose to her inner right thigh while his hand stroked up to the crease between leg and groin. He kneaded her there, dipped his fingers into her moisture, and thrust two fingers inside.

She arched up with a cry. Finally, penetration. Not the kind she wanted, but her body didn't care. She gripped his fingers and squeezed her legs around him until she grew weak with the effort. It didn't move him an inch, though he did continue to scrape teeth and tongue along her inner thigh.

He kept pumping into her. Two fingers. Three. He did it casually, as if he barely noticed the rhythm he set inside her while his mouth tasted her thigh.

His mouth was so close that he had to adjust his position. Her legs were fully spread, blocked open by his broad shoulders. His fingers were large and callused as they thrust inside one last time before pulling out to play in her curls.

She should have felt embarrassed. Hell, she did feel embarrassed by her own lack of shame. But the need was too strong and she was without words to cry out, so she did everything she could to encourage him silently with her body.

He found her clit. His thumb rolled over it while she bucked beneath him.

Orgasm hit like a freight train, speeding through her mind and body as it obliterated everything. But when it eased, she realized he hadn't moved. He was poised above her, apparently ready for when the first rush passed.

She lifted her head an inch to see him better. It was all the strength she had. She met his gaze and saw a dark triumph there. Joy at her orgasm. Pride that he had given it to her. Then he ducked his head and put his tongue to her clit.

Another contraction hit, fast and hard. Her belly pulled with the force of it, and she cried out in shock. He eased off her for a second, maybe two, then he returned. His tongue was thick and sweet where she was most sensitive.

She nearly said it then. "No" was on the tip of her tongue. It was too much, too soon, and she didn't need more oral. She wanted him inside her, but he was gentle as he worked her, never pushing her quite to that place. He eased off to let her catch her breath, then swooped back in when she began to gather her wits.

Each moment became a rolling orgasm of yes. Of Hank. Of pleasure so intense she wanted it to end as much as she hoped it went on forever. Until she couldn't catch her breath and her belly hurt from the tension. She pulled upward, grabbing his head and forcing him to look at her.

"Enough," she gasped. "Enough."

He nodded, his eyes dazed, but he didn't move.

She levered herself downward. She tugged on his arms, she twisted beneath him. She did everything she could to get him on top of her so he could finally fill her like she wanted.

He refused to budge. He pushed himself upright. She managed to tug on his chest and press a kiss to his nose and eventually his mouth, but he would not go further.

"Hank!" she cried. "Please!"

His face was pulled tight with strain and his grip on her hips held at the edge of pain.

"Hank?"

"Do you remember when Peter kissed Abby?" he asked.

What? She didn't want to think about anyone but him right then, but he persisted.

"She'd gone back to being human and he could see her. He knew what she was. She was afraid of how he would react, but all I saw was love in his eyes. Love as he kissed her. Love as he held his wife and his child."

Cecilia nodded. Of course, she remembered. The scene had been so beautiful it had hurt deep inside in a good way. The place where all her cynicism rested had cracked, and the effect had been so powerful that she'd pretended to look away. She'd ducked her head to her tablet when her gaze had really been on them.

"I want that, Cecilia. I want to love my wife like that, to cherish my child no matter what."

"Of course, you will."

He shook his head. "I'm not saying this right." He took a breath, his chest expanding even as his hands left her body to curl tight to his chest. "She loved him, too, Cecilia. All three of them, together. Such love. A real family."

She nodded. "I know."

"I want that, Cecilia. With everything I am, I want that."

There was hunger in his eyes. A need that pervaded every cell in his body. And she felt his hunger echo inside her, an ache for a love that made three people stand strong in the face of staggering change.

"I want that, too," she echoed. Then she tried to lift his face to hers so she could kiss him. So she could offer him everything they both wanted, but he shook his head.

"I want that, Cecilia, but I won't ever have it unless you choose me. You have to choose me freely."

She straightened. "I do choose you."

He sucked in a breath, the gasp loud and harsh. "I'm trying to think rationally here. Is this normal for you? To feel this way after a day? A half hour ago, you thought you had a brain tumor."

"You said I'm not magical. You said I have a choice."

"You do." He rocked back on his heels. "But you're exhausted and the entire world has changed for you. Maybe this is a stress reaction."

Now she was getting angry. Yeah, sure, she'd been thinking all those things as well. Every single one had filtered through her thoughts on the drive over here. But damn it, she knew all those possibilities and she was choosing him anyway. She wanted this. Right now. No regret.

"I want you," she said firmly, and she watched his entire body ripple in reaction. Like he needed to go to her right then, but his mind was keeping him back. "You don't believe me. Why don't you think I could choose you?"

She watched him react to her words. The motions were subtle, but she was watching him closely. His eyes widened, and his breath held for a moment before he released it slowly. And when he spoke, it was with a quiet pain.

"How can I be what you want? I'm not educated, not like you. You probably make ten times the money I do. And I'm half animal."

"And you think that's how I chose a man? By his academic credentials? His bank account? And as for being an animal, you can change into a bear, but you're ten times the man of anyone I've ever met. You're patient, you're smart."

"You can't know that."

She stopped long enough to really think about that. They'd been together for one day and it had been an eventful twenty-four hours. "I've seen you under pressure. That's when the real man comes out." She touched his forearm, stroking his smooth skin. "I do know. And I do choose you."

"You need time," he pressed. "To be sure it's not a brain tumor."

She grimaced, knowing that he was right. Everything was happening so fast. If she were honest, she'd admit that even though body felt sure, her mind wasn't completely convinced. And then he had to hammer the last nail in her sex-fest fantasy.

"You won't get that time if you're pregnant."

Gut punch. Sure, she was choosing him now, but she wasn't calculating on a baby. The idea was ridiculous, except he clearly believed in the possibility. "A condom—"

"Will break."

"You don't know that."

"What are the odds that all of Brittany's records would corrupt like that?"

A trillion to one.

"Do not underestimate magic."

She sighed. "I want a child."

"I'm glad. Do you want to get pregnant right now, this very moment?"

Yes. No. Maybe. Hell, her rational mind said that was too big a decision to make so casually.

"Then help me give you the time to fall in love. Because if you're pregnant with my child, I won't leave your side. Ever." He exhaled. "And we'll never be a happy family like the Randolphs.

We'll never be like that because you never had the time to resolve all your doubts."

She dropped backward, her gaze on the ceiling. Her body was sated and exhausted. Her mind even more so, yet she recognized an underlying emptiness in her womb. She wanted him inside her. She wanted his child.

Was that magic? Brain tumor? Or just plain biology?

"I want that kind of love, Cecilia. I want a family like theirs."

"So do I." She looked at him. "Maybe I want it with you."

They both heard the "maybe" like it was uttered in an echo chamber. It repeated between them, exactly proving his point. She hadn't committed to him yet. Not fully. And if she got pregnant, then that whole decision became more complicated.

She sighed and closed her eyes. Life was so strange. Twenty-four hours ago, none of this was even on the horizon.

"Are you still wondering if you have a brain tumor?" he asked.

Damn it, he was relentless! "I get it," she huffed. "I haven't locked in. Twenty-four hours is not enough time to make a lifelong commitment." She opened her eyes to pin him with a frustrated glare. "Have you? Are you sure I'm the one?"

She watched him nod. No doubt. No hesitation.

"I'm sure," he said.

She could see that he believed it. He had absolutely no doubts as to what he thought or wanted.

"You can't know me that well yet."

He didn't argue. And when she looked at his expression, there was a Zen kind of acceptance there. For him, it was a fact.

"So…you love me?"

"Yes."

She shook her head. "What does that mean to you? That you want to have sex with me? That you want me to bear your children? That you'll—"

"Care for you every second of your life. That I'll spend every breath and every dime I have to make sure you are protected and happy. That you can make whatever choices you want, whenever you want. That you are free to be amazing while I cheer for you from the sidelines. I want the best for you, Cecilia. And I'm going to make sure you get it. As much as I possibly can. You are the center of my balance."

He said it so earnestly. And even if she doubted the certainty in his voice, she felt it in his body. There was passion in his words and determination in his body. So solid. So clear. As he declared without regret or fear that he was devoted to her happiness.

"So you won't make love to me because that might create a baby—"

"Which makes everything more complicated."

"And you want to give me the time to settle my doubts. And possibly get a CT scan."

His lips quirked up at that, but his nod was solemn. And then his eyes got a kind of twinkle. "But there might be other things we can do. If you want."

Oh, she wanted. She 100 percent wanted. But now she understood his restraint when she had literally begged him to penetrate her. And damn, her heart melted all over again. He was holding back for her sake.

She flashed him a coy smile as she pushed up on her elbows. And then she maneuvered a bit more, sitting up in front of him. "Lie down," she ordered. "It's your turn."

His eyes blazed, but he didn't move. "No penetrative sex. You promise?"

God, when had that ever happened? The guy making her promise there would be no penetration. No babies. "I promise."

He shifted around on the bed and she moved to accommodate him. And because she had already burned off a lot of her tension, she was able to take her time with him. She stroked his body with tender caresses while his breath grew short and tight. She kissed his nipples and teased his belly. She wasn't as thorough as he had been, but he didn't seem to mind. When she grasped his penis, his hips surged upward. When she sucked him into her mouth, he whispered her name.

He was going to come too soon, so she pinched the top and pressed deep into the space behind his balls. She was a doctor and some things had been fun to learn in biology class. But even with all her training, he would not be held back. He gripped her leg and looked at her with such burning need. So she squeezed his stalk and pulled down while he thrust.

Once. Twice. By the third, he had arched up on the bed and his cum shot from him in an impressive display. She never thought it would be fascinating to see, but she was wrong. Turns out, she was fascinated by all of him. Every single moment.

"Yabba dabba do," she murmured when he finally regained his breath.

He gaze locked on hers in surprise, and then he burst out laughing.

"Yabba dabba do," he echoed breathlessly.

She chuckled and together they cleaned him up. Then he lay back down and spread open his arms, inviting her to cuddle up beside him. She went willingly, tucking herself as tightly as possible against him.

Could she do this? Could she settle right here happily for the rest of their lives? Was she ready to make that decision right now?

Maybe. Her body said yes. Her mind was so busy running in a dozen different directions that she ignored it.

"Just sleep, Cecilia," he said as he pressed his lips to her forehead. "We'll figure out the rest in the morning."

"Okay," she agreed, and she shut her eyes. She let her mind spin away until she couldn't hear it anymore. She was drifting on the sweetness of his breath, of his heartbeat, and just being with him right here, right n—

Her phone rang with an annoying chime. It was the standard iPhone ring, and yet it had never bothered her more. She wanted to ignore it. Hell, she desperately wanted to throw the damn thing out the window, but she knew that was irresponsible. What if it was Dennis calling with a breakthrough? What if it was another patient like Brittany? One who would survive but only if she and Hank were there to help?

She jerked herself upright and thumped angrily across the room. Her phone was at the bottom of her tote, so she had to pull out her tablet and computer before she could read the phone's screen. And when she did, she let out a blistering curse.

Hank was by her in a second, his body taut, his expression fierce. "What is it?"

"My boyfriend," she spat. Then she thumbed on the phone.

Chapter 19

Hank felt his entire body strain with violence. His bear wanted to kill the rival now. His mind strained to hold the animal back. Of course, she had a boyfriend. She'd told him so.

Meanwhile, she brought the phone to her ear. He wanted to snatch it away and roar into the phone. He controlled himself only by clenching his hands into fists and grabbing onto a Zen mantra in his mind.

The greatest worth is self-mastery. The greatest worth is self-mastery.

He would not kill her boyfriend. But he would listen in to her conversation without apology. Fortunately, his ears were good enough to hear it all.

"Hello, Yu. I'm so sorry—"

"You got caught up in your work. So what else is new? Hey, I sent over an email. I've got a theory of what the Detroit Flu does to the neural system as it pairs with the endocrine—"

"Yes, I saw." Her voice was impatient, and she rolled her eyes as she spoke. "It's an interesting thought, but I haven't got the resources to investigate it. Listen, Yu—"

"I know, I know," he said still laughing. "I thought we could work on it when you get back. Before the next outbreak—"

She snorted. "There's always an outbreak, but Yu—"

"Not if you put in for a transfer. Not if we get a grant, and with my credentials, we could get a big one—"

"Yu, stop!"

He did. A long pause as she took a breath.

"Look, I'm sorry to do this over the phone, but we're over. Please understand that I think you're an incredible guy, but we're just not compatible. I'm so sorry."

Silence again, and then rustling as the man shifted his grip on the phone. "Cecilia? What are you talking about?"

"Look, I could give you reasons and explanations, but they won't help. You know there's never been any real passion between us. You forget me as often as I forget you. I can't even remember the last time we kissed."

"What?" He didn't sound angry, just really confused. "Cecilia, when was the last time you slept?"

"About two seconds ago. I was asleep when you called."

"So this is a dream? Or because of a dream? You know you don't think clearly on a case. And this Flu is a nasty one. You've been going nonstop—"

"Do you remember our last kiss? Have we ever held hands?" She looked down at where her fingers were entwined with his.

Yu's answer came out slow. "We're intellectuals. We don't need that kind of display."

"Well," she said with a smile, "I guess I'm not as intellectual as we thought. I'm sorry Yu, but we're done. Good-bye."

She thumbed off her phone and set it down. Then she looked straight into Hank's eyes, touching his face with a slow caress that he felt in every cell in his body. "I never put it together before now. With Yu, it's just…thinking. With you, I feel so much. More than I ever thought possible."

He felt his center warm at that. She was coming around to him. Or maybe he was starting to believe she could love him. But it wasn't enough. "We need to get to know each other better."

She squared off with him, her expression shifting into challenge. "Okay. Let's start with what we do know. What do you know and like about me?"

He couldn't begin to name them all, but he started rattling off generalities. "You don't freeze in a crisis, you think and think well. You make me laugh when I feel at my worst. And you have this way of talking doctor that gets me hard."

"What?"

He tried to mimic her. He lifted his chin and stared down his nose at her. "This is Hank. He's here to help. If you question me, I'll cut off your balls."

She laughed. "I did not say that."

This time he was the one who touched her. "Of course, you did. With your body and your tone. And I loved it." He pressed a quick kiss to her lips. "It's part of being an alpha female."

She blinked. "I'm not an—I mean, I…" She frowned. "Am I?"

He grinned. "Oh yeah."

"Huh. Go figure." Then she wrapped her arms around him and dropped a kiss on his nose. "Want to hear what I like about you?" she asked.

More than he wanted his next breath.

"The guys I know are all really smart, but give them a hangnail and they fall apart. Brilliant in their own field of study, but anything outside of their expertise, and they're a mess. They're so threatened whenever they don't know the answer, but you just roll with it. You let others have the answers if you don't, and you pitch in without ego when you do. It's wonderful."

He lowered his forehead to hers. "I have an ego."

"But it doesn't get in the way." She wrinkled her nose. "And by the way, I'm talking about myself, too. If I don't solve this Flu, I'm going to fall apart. Fair warning."

He smiled. "I know. Don't worry. I'll be there to pick you up."

She pulled back. "You're supposed to say that I will figure out it. That you have faith in me, and I'll get a promotion because of my brilliance. All the normal boyfriend bullshit."

He shrugged. "This is a shifter poison. Even if you do figure it out, you won't be able to tell. At least not the normal people." He tried to put an apology in his tone, but she had to know the truth. Even if she got a magic formula that solved all their problems, she wouldn't be able to share it with anyone but the shifter community. That would be very hard for her. For anyone in her position.

Her mouth opened in shock and stayed that way for at least three breaths. He could see her mind working the angles, trying for a solution that would satisfy everybody. "But this is important research. It's a medical problem. People are dying!"

He nodded. He knew. "Tell the shifters. We'll tell our kind."

"But it's not just your kind who are dying. And what about Brittany? She didn't even know she was part shifter. What about all those hybrids out there?"

"We have people in every part of the world. We'll get the information out to those who need it."

She shook her head. "That's bullshit, and you know it. Brittany's one in a hundred. That means for every Brittany, there are ninety-nine people who start to become hybrids but don't make it. Their higher cortex dies, and they turn aggressive and angry."

He winced. He hadn't realized stable hybrids were that rare.

"If I find a solution, we can't keep this secret."

He didn't argue with her. They weren't going to agree. Sure, it would be wonderful if they could spread the information to the World Health Organization or whatever national and international scientific body needed to know, but that's not how the shifter world worked. It sucked, but it was a fact.

She swallowed and looked away. "See? That's what I like about you, even when I hate it."

He frowned. "Come again?"

"You respect me enough to tell me what you see as the truth. And you let me disagree with you." She leaned forward. "And for the record, I do disagree. If I figure out a cure, I'm publicizing it. I'll try to keep the magic out of it." She rolled her eyes. "I'll have to if I want anyone to read it, but I'm giving it to whomever will take it."

He took a deep breath. "We'll find a compromise. When you figure this out—and for the record, I do think you will solve it—then we'll work out a solution together."

She tilted her head. "You believe that? Really?"

He wasn't sure what she referred to. Did he believe she would solve the medical problem? If anyone could, it would be her. Did he think they'd reach a compromise? He hoped so. He really did.

She snorted. "I also like that you don't lie to me. You think this is going to be a problem."

He shrugged. "I think that this is a future fight. Right now, we need all your energy on solving the problem."

She nodded her head. "Agreed." She brought her hands up to his shoulders and used her thumb to tease the hair at the base of his neck. "You talked about seeing the Randolphs in the hospital room. About the love they shared."

He nodded, the memory still having the power to make his gut clench in yearning.

"I remember the moment a little differently. I saw the happy family pulling together..."

"Yes—"

"Because of you."

He pulled back. "No—"

"Yes. All day, you stood there. You never even sat down. You stood there watching, helping where you could, and most of all...you listened. I never felt threatened in that room. Not even when Abby went all big and bear."

"You should have been frightened. That situation could have gone bad any number of ways."

"I know, but that's the thing. You were there and you're so solid..." She slid her hand down his shoulder then across his chest. "You don't fall apart ever. You're not hampered by ego. You don't falter when we're attacked by rabid wolves. You listen with respect to whatever anyone says. And you care." She spread her fingers open, her eyes going down to where she pressed against his heart. "You know who you are, you listen, and you care. That's what I saw in that room. That because you were so solid, the rest of us could find our strength. You gave us space to be as we wanted because none of it threatened you, and that kept everybody calm. Even in the midst of chaos, you gave us all strength."

So many words, such precision in phrasing. God, he loved this woman. What she said may or may not be bullshit. He honestly didn't know. He felt the resonance in his core, though. And he loved that she saw his strength. But as for quiet…He shook his head.

"I'm terrified all the time now," he said softly. "Since the moment I met you, I'm terrified you'll get hurt. That you'll run from me. That I won't be able to protect you, help you…" Love you.

She grinned. "Well, I'm not running now, am I? And you're right here with me."

Yes, he was. And that meant that right now, he was content. More than content, he was blissfully happy. He was about to kiss her. She was angling her head for just that, and he was leaning in for a taste. Or a lot more than a taste.

But then her stomach rumbled, loud and empty. A sure sound to any shifter that he had neglected his mate. She was hungry. He pulled back and asked a very serious question.

"Will you let me feed you? Cook for you?"

She blinked, obviously startled. Then she burst out in laughter. "That's like asking me if I want a Nobel prize. Of course, I want that!"

He grinned. "How much food do you have here?"

She blinked. "Um, tap water?"

"Poisoned."

"Right. So I think I have…um…let me think. Absolutely nothing."

"Let's go to the grocery store. There are a few that still have something on the shelves. And then I will make you a feast."

She laughed. "I don't care if it's an expired hot dog. I'm starving."

He took her to a grocery store. He didn't let her eat any hot dogs, expired or otherwise. The place was indeed stripped of all the easy foods, but they had Spam left and soups that had been canned outside of Detroit. Bottled water, too, mostly because no one outside of the shifter community believed that the water was tainted. He grabbed a couple jars of spices and some fresh fruit while she snatched up the last granola bars left on the shelf.

They talked the whole time. At the grocery store, while he cooked, and while they ate. He rubbed her feet while she read the data Dennis had sent via email. And then he rubbed her all over, spending extra time on the breasts he had so ignored earlier.

They had intended to watch a movie together, but she was the only thing that interested him. And it turned out that sixty-nine wasn't the only fun way to experience oral. There were advantages to having a doctor as a lover.

All in all, it was the best night of his life. She was with him, she saw him, and she listened. Not just to his funny stories, but to his tales of the army and of his dead brother. He hadn't spoken about these things to anyone, but they came out with her. And it felt so good to share them, even as she spoke of her life in school and of being overshadowed by a brilliant father and a domineering mother.

They would have talked all night, but he knew she needed to rest. She needed to tackle the Detroit Flu with fresh eyes tomorrow. So well after midnight, he tucked her against his side and held her quiet until she slept. He drifted off, too, dropping into a deeply relaxed state, one that nourished him far beyond what he was used to. It was because of her. Because she held him as she rested and that made him content at his core.

Bliss.

Which is why he was caught off guard when the werewolves woke them at dawn.

Chapter 20

Cecilia knew something was wrong the moment she was covered by a heavy blanket while Hank leapt from the bed. She'd barely gasped when she heard the door open and him growl, "Step one foot inside and you're dead."

She pushed her head out from under the cover to see Hank fully naked facing off with three men in loose sweats. She recognized two of them from the werewolf contingent who'd come to Mother's house.

"We've come to speak with Dr. Lu," the one she didn't recognize said. His hands were held up in placating gesture and he appeared to be the leader.

"Polite people knock. They don't pick the lock," Hank said.

Meanwhile, one of the men behind the leader sniffed loudly and his lips curled in disgust. "He's going to be a problem."

Then the leader turned to her. "Dr. Lu, I'm Derek Sims, beta of the Detroit Wolves. We need to have a civil conversation. I apologize for how abrupt this seems, but we feel you're in danger. There is urgency and it's best if you come with us now."

"She's safe with me," Hank growled.

"Dr. Lu—"

Cecilia sat up, holding the covers to her chest. "Dr. Lu needs to get dressed."

"I'm afraid there's too much danger—"

"Bullshit. Step outside, guard the door." She held up her phone. "I've got police and bears on speed dial." Then she rubbed her eyes. "And if you want a civil conversation, you can get me a large mocha at the Starbucks next door."

Hank stiffened. "They use water—"

"I've been drinking it every day since I got here. I'm pretty sure I lack any shifter DNA, so I'm not at risk." She turned back to the wolves. "Grab a couple water bottles, too. Thanks."

The cranky werewolf bared his teeth. "We are not lapdogs, little girl. We do not—"

"You said civil conversation, right?" Cecilia interrupted. Her gaze hard on the leader. "Or was that a lie?"

"No lie," he said with a slight dip to his head, though she could tell he was forcing himself to say it. "We will get the coffee—"

Hank interrupted. "Get Frappuccinos instead. The bottled ones with the seals intact."

Cecilia looked at him. "You think they'd drug me?"

"They picked the lock here to surprise you."

The leader growled. "Bears are overly suspicious. And we're wasting time."

Cecilia gestured them back. "Then go get the Fappuccinos and let me get dressed!"

The three werewolves backed away, their expressions showing varying degrees of anger. But they did as she ordered probably because Hank was there looking like he was about to go grizzly on them. Hank shut the door in their faces, then stood there vibrating tension while she scrambled out of bed.

She dressed quickly and cleaned up. She waited for Hank to do the same, but he remained at the door, standing tall in all his naked glory.

"You really think they're the danger."

He shrugged. "Wolves and bears in this city haven't gotten along for generations. I don't trust them."

"I got that. But…um…don't you want to get dressed?"

He shook his head. "Wolves are faster than bears, but in close quarters like this, I can do some pretty major damage."

"I don't want any damage to anyone."

"I don't want to either. But—"

"You don't trust them. Great." She sighed and pulled out her phone. "Give me five minutes to check my email and then…" Her voice trailed away as she thumbed into the data that she'd received last night. "Wow," she breathed.

"What?" Anxiety burst through the word, but she waved at him to show that it was okay.

She kept reading. There was too much to process in five minutes, but the summary was pretty succinct.

"Cecilia—" he began, and she waved at him again, answering without looking up.

"The data that you guys sent earlier? A bunch of it came from a lab in Ann Arbor run by Dr. Sherilyn."

"Yeah. Shifter lab at the University of Michigan. She's an ocelot."

"I sent her our data yesterday while we were waiting on Abby to…" Cecilia looked up. "An ocelot? Seriously?"

He shrugged. "We aren't all dogs and bears."

"Right." Damn, there was so much to learn. The excitement of that nearly buried her annoyance at being woken up too damn early by rude werewolves. Then she was back in the data Dr. Sherilyn had sent. "She's done some great work. Pretty clear how the body is effected by this Flu."

Hank shifted, his body relaxing slightly in hope. "Can you stop it?"

"Too early to say—"

Heavy pounding on the door interrupted her words. She had to force herself to close up her phone and pay attention to the situation at hand. Hank looked at her, and she nodded. He pulled open the door, then jumped back quickly as he took up a protective stance in front of her.

The wolves sauntered in, their leader empty-handed but the other two carried hot coffee, Frappuccinos, and an assortment of muffins. Impressive. She hadn't thought Starbucks had any bakery items left.

"How'd you get those?" she asked as her nose twitched. She might not be a shifter, but she sure as hell could smell baked goods.

"We have a wolf who bakes. These are hers."

Wonderful! Except she now realized that Hank wouldn't want her to eat them. Possible poison or whatever. So with a sigh, she gestured to the table. Everyone gathered and sat, except for Hank. He stood beside her bristling and naked. It was actually pretty sexy, but she didn't let herself focus on that.

Instead, she grabbed a bottled Frappuccino and twisted it open, feeling for the pop to prove it hadn't been tampered with. It popped, she drank, and it tasted wonderful. She leaned back in her chair.

"Okay. Civilized conversation. What's going on?"

"Good morning, Dr. Lu. Our alpha promised that we would answer your questions. We are here to do that."

She frowned. "I thought the meeting was tonight."

"It is. We are here to take you to where we gather so you can—"

She held up her hand. "Stop. I'm not going anywhere with you right now. There's too much going on."

The werewolf arched a brow. "You are in significant danger."

That phrase ought to terrify her, but honestly, she'd been too amped up from adrenaline these last days to get worked up. "Really? From what?"

"Hybrids are everywhere, the water is tainted, and as a scientist who knows about shifters, you are a valuable person."

She nodded and looked at each of the werewolves in turn. "Sounds really scary," she deadpanned. "That's why I've got a guard with me here." She glanced at Hank. "And I spend the rest of my time at the hospital." She took another sip of her drink. Damn it was good. "But you're here now, I've got some questions—"

"We want to offer you a job, Dr. Lu."

She blinked and stared at her drink. Had they drugged her? They couldn't possibly be offering her a job. "I work for the CDC."

"But you're aware of shifters now. Surely, you realize that there is a limit to the type of research you can do—and report—to the ignorant."

He meant to the world at large, to all those people who are not in on the secret. "Yeah, well, that's a discussion for another day. Right now, I have a flu to stop and—"

"We can help you with that. We have a lab with scientists who are in the know."

"Like Dr. Sherilyn?"

All three werewolves curled their lip in disgust, but it was the beta who spoke. "Cats are notoriously isolationist. They don't share, and she is outside the city right now. We have a lab inside. Surely you want to meet the scientist who has already isolated—"

"It's the twenty-first century, guys. Give me their email addresses. We don't need to communicate in person."

Mr. Sims's expression flattened out. "This information is highly sensitive. We value our people's safety above all things. We do not share—"

"Then I think you're the ones being isolationist. Scientists share data. It's what we do." Truthfully, that was a bit of a lie. Researchers could be as territorial as anyone, but she wasn't going to go to some secret lab with these people. Not even with Hank tagging along for protection. She didn't know if it was his paranoia creeping into her or the fact that she had juicy data sitting on her phone from the supposedly territorial Dr. Sherilyn. Either way she had plenty to work on without visiting some secret lab with guys who picked her lock while she was sleeping. Which meant she was done with this conversation.

"Look guys, this has been fun and all—"

The werewolves attacked.

The speed of it was so startling that Cecilia kept talking while it was going on. "—but I've got a ton of work—Eep!"

One werewolf jumped across the table, wrapped an arm around her chest, and hauled her backward. The other two shifted in the blink of an eye. Suddenly wolves were leaping out of their clothing, and as they jumped forward, Hank tripled in size.

The table was knocked aside, banging hard into her knees. She was already screaming, but the bastard's meaty fist was on her mouth, muffling everything she did. She tried to bite down. She tried to kick and claw, but she hadn't the strength or the leverage. And pretty soon she was pinned against a muscular human chest.

Meanwhile in front of her was a battle too dizzying for her to follow. She saw Hank, big and black in the center of the room. His claws were huge and he fought with precision as wolves came at him from every side. He'd told her wolves were fast, but she hadn't processed what that meant. They were constantly in motion, leaping at him, taking a swipe or a bite, then landing out of his reach. Two of them worked together to keep Hank from doing anything but defending himself.

Or so she thought. Until he connected one of his razor-sharp claws with a wolf. She heard the canine yelp and blood spurted in the air, but she couldn't see more. The other one was still coming at him, and there was definitely blood on Hank's face and torso. His? Theirs?

All the while, she was being carried steadily toward the door. The only reason she wasn't there already was that her captor had to avoid the battle.

Panic clawed at her throat. Not just for her, but Hank, too. The terror of being dragged away against her will and the rapid violence in front of her. Too fast to process except for panic. Too much to see except chaos and blood.

And Hank. In the center with flashing teeth and claws.

Then something flew at her. Something large and furry. She barely saw it coming when she felt the impact. A wolf, heavy and squirming. It knocked her off her feet. More important, he slammed her captor backward as well.

She felt the impact as the bastard holding her crunched against the kitchen counter. She was breathless and squished, but also suddenly free. While the huge werewolf scrambled away, she fell forward onto her knees. She started moving as fast as she could. Away from the assholes. And screaming loudly.

Someone had to help them. Someone—

Something touched her foot and she kicked out, snapping a wolf head back. Take that, beta big shot. Take this as my rejection of your job offer. Then she heard a roar, and this time it was low and very bearlike.

Hank!

She looked up to see blood burst from his neck and shoulder. Oh damn, damn, damn. One of the wolves had opened up his neck. That was bad. His entire left arm was dangling useless, though he still swung viciously arcs with his right.

Who was left standing? Who was still moving?

She did a quick scan. Her captor was on the floor, his spine possibly broken given the way he was clawing with his upper body. But then she saw him shimmer and change. The man became a wolf with fully functioning legs.

Fuck.

The one who had been thrown into her was still on his feet, too. He was spinning around to get a bead on Hank, though he seemed slower than he'd been before. And the one who had tried to bite her? He was recovering as well, though she could see a pool of blood spilling out of his belly. And maybe intestines, too. Could wolves recover from being disemboweled?

She had to do something so she grabbed the first thing she could. Her desk chair. A metal thing on wheels. She slammed it into the one still on the floor and gleefully watched as it also fouled the footing of the guy who'd just shifted into a wolf.

And then there was another yelp and more blood. She didn't need to look because the third werewolf landed with his throat slit on top of the chair before flopping down on the gutted wolf.

Which left the last one standing on shaking legs. The one who should have had his spine broken. He looked at his bleeding companions, then back at Hank. Then he dashed for the door. Except the door was shut, and wolves can't open them. His front paws scrambled at the knob to no avail.

Hank advanced, lumbering steadily forward while blood poured from his neck. Not spurting, she realized. Not arterial, but it was still bad.

"You want out?" she screamed at the wolf. "Back up!"

She pushed onto shaky legs. Hank roared out a bellow, but she wanted the wolves out. Not dead. Just gone.

The bastard dog backed up, his claws digging into the thin carpet while Hank dropped from his upright position to all fours. Cecilia half crawled, half walked to the door and hauled it open. She barely jumped back in time to avoid being clipped by the last wolf as he ran free.

She wanted to scream something vicious after him. Something mean and cutting, but she hadn't the breath. Only weakness in her legs as she turned back to Hank. She had to stop the bleeding. She had to stitch…

He was shimmering bright gold as he turned back to human. Where before there'd been a blood-covered bear unsteady on his feet as he lumbered toward her. Now there was a naked Hank, his body twitching, his shoulder…neat and perfect.

Healed.

"Thank God!" she gasped as she closed the distance between them. Her arms were around him in a second, and he lifted her up to complete the embrace with one arm. But even as she held him tight, he maneuvered her to be on the far side from the remaining wolves. From the…bodies.

She didn't have to look to know that the one who'd been disemboweled was probably dead by now. It wouldn't have taken long. And God, the stench in the room was overwhelming. Blood and bile, not to mention spilled Frappuccinos.

"Hank," she said against his neck. "Hank." That was it. She just kept repeating his name while he buried his face in her neck.

Eventually he spoke to her. Or maybe he'd been speaking all along, but she hadn't heard him. Anyway, she did now.

"…hurt? Cecilia?"

"What? No, I'm fine."

And she was. He still set her gently away from him as he looked her up and down. She took the time to inspect him as well. He was perfect. Not even mussed, the hair and the blood all gone. She, on the other hand, had bloodstains everywhere, but no damage. No pain. Just really shaky as the adrenaline burned out of her body.

"Pack up," he said to her softly. "I'm taking you away from here."

No argument from her.

She accomplished it quickly with his help. She didn't even want to study the bodies. It was too…She couldn't even think of it. Violence wasn't a part of her life. Not like this. And while she kept touching Hank to make sure he was here, to make sure he was safe, too, the rest of her was recoiling from the entire event. What had just happened? The wolves had tried to abduct her? Why?

She stripped out of her clothes and changed into something that wasn't bloody. A shower would have to wait until the hospital. Her electronics appeared to be fine, so that was all quickly packed up and put away. Hank called someone to report the attack. She didn't care who so long as she didn't have to handle it.

Then she was seated in Hank's car, no longer busy with packing up. In the silence, the questions came back louder until finally she started asking them out loud. And even then, they didn't come out how she intended.

"This world of yours is terrifying. You know that, right?"

He squeezed her hand. "It's your world, too. You just didn't see it before."

"Why would they attack like that?"

"For the exact reason they told you. You're a brilliant scientist who knows about shifters. Do you know how rare you are? We need scientists. Doctors, researchers, the whole gamut. We need them to solve shifter problems."

"Then why not just tell the world about you? Then every-body can—"

He shook his head. "You know why."

"Magic again."

"Do you think you're the only one who's tried? In thousands of years, lots of people have tried to tell."

"And?"

"And nothing. Atlantis dropped into the ocean. Pompeii buried under lava."

She let her head fall back against the seat. "That's ancient history."

"Electrical outages, a couple tornadoes, but it doesn't even have to be that big. The magic will give you a heart attack or food poisoning.

And even if you do manage to get the words out, they won't be able to hear you. And if you print it, they won't read it."

She looked at him, her mind whirling. There was something his words sparked. Something important that she couldn't quite remember.

It didn't take him long to notice. She was staring at him while she grasped at his words. What had he said?

"Cecilia?"

"Say that again."

"What?"

"What happens when people try to talk."

He looked at her oddly but complied. "Heart attack. Food poisoning. Electrical problems—"

"Food poisoning! That's it. Someone I know had food poisoning. Someone…"

She grabbed her phone and dialed. Dennis answered immediately. "Yeah?"

"Who was it at that last conference we went to? The one in New York. Someone had food poisoning."

"What?" Dennis had obviously been deep in something else.

"Just answer the question. Who had food poisoning?" She started to remember. "He was a speaker. Presenting some paper about junk DNA turning people into wolves." Oh my God. How they'd laughed about that. The wolf part hadn't been in the title. It had been something about DNA adaptation in previously blah, blah, blah. She couldn't remember. But when the speaker had started talking, he'd definitely been talking about werewolves. She was sure of it now.

"Oh yeah," Dennis said, his voice getting lighter. "Poor bastard was hallucinating on stage, remember? Kept throwing up and yet still trying to talk. Had a bucket and everything, but—"

"What was his name?"

"What?"

"Dennis, it's important. What was his name? Where is his lab?"

A pause. "You're losing it big time."

She sighed. "Just look it up for me. Please?"

"I am." There was clicking in the background as he typed. "FYI, no more bodies last night. I think it's slowing down. We've gone eighteen hours without a new case."

She nodded, waiting impatiently. She could have looked it up on her own phone, but she didn't remember as much as Dennis did. He'd attended the guy's lecture and had been laughing about it for weeks afterward. She'd just about given up when Dennis abruptly laughed.

"Got it! The guy's name is Dr. Oltheten of the Gunnolf Lab in... Well, look at that. It's right here in Detroit."

Of course, it was. "Text me the address, will you?"

"Sure. Are you going to tell me why?"

"I think he's got data that can help us."

"Werewolf guy? Please."

"He was sick, Dennis. I'm sure you say all sorts of crazy things when you're feverish."

Dennis snorted. "Yeah, but the poor bastard is always going to be known as werewolf guy. His career is finished."

"Yeah, maybe. Thanks."

Her phone dinged, telling her the text had arrived. She ended the call with Dennis and showed the address to Hank. "Take me here."

He frowned as he scanned her face. "You sure you're up for another confrontation?"

"He's a scientist and he's been trying to get the word out. There isn't going to be any confrontation. He'll likely kiss my feet in gratitude."

Hank didn't respond, but she could see the skepticism in his eyes.

"Look, I'll never doubt your paranoia again. You were right about the wolves from the first moment. But this guy…he's a scientist. These are my people and we don't…" This morning's violence reared up in her head, and she choked the words and the images down. She wasn't going to think about that yet. Maybe not ever.

"Shifters aren't generally violent, Cecilia. Not more than normal people, except maybe at puberty. But this stuff in the water and the quarantine…" He shook his head. "We're all going a little crazy."

She believed him. Which made it all the more important for her to talk to this guy and put an end to the madness.

"Dr. Oltheten will have our answers. I'm sure of it." And that's what she needed. The security of one scientist talking to another about measurable data. It was the world she knew, and it didn't include people changing into werewolves and trying to drag her out of her hotel room. Data didn't spurt blood or get disemboweled right in front of her.

Science was sane, and she desperately needed some sanity right then because she was still shaking. It helped that Hank was right here beside her. His presence was the only thing that was keeping her from running screaming to the nearest airport. She didn't want to leave him. She wanted to stay by his side and really work on their relationship. But she couldn't do that in the middle of all this Detroit Flu chaos.

"The hospital is safer," Hank began.

"The answers aren't there. If they were, I'd have already found them. I need to talk to a scientist who knows about shifters. That's Dr. Oltheten." He would help her make sense of this. He would put everything into a data-driven box, and together they'd solve the problem of the Detroit Flu. Then all this madness would end, people would stop trying to abduct her, and she could focus on being with Hank.

That was her plan, and nothing was going to stop her from executing it.

Chapter 21

"Let's talk this through," Hank said, gripping the steering wheel of his car as he tried to remain calm. He was driving slowly, heading in the general direction of the hospital, but he could just as easily hit the freeway and take her straight to the Griz home base where he could protect her.

"Okay," she said. "I want to talk to Dr. Oltheten. I'm sure he has data that we need."

He saw the hard jut of her chin and knew she was going to be stubborn. But even as he looked at her sitting in his car completely safe, his mind kept replaying the sight of her being dragged away.

It amped up his adrenaline and made it hard to focus. But Cecilia was a woman of logic. She wasn't going to stay hidden away without a good reason, so he fought down his terror for her safety and worked with his brain instead of his brawn.

"The wolves wanted to take you to some supersecret lab of theirs."

"Yes."

"And you just learned of a shifter lab in Detroit. That has to be the same place."

She shook her head. "Dr. Oltheten has been trying to get the word out about shifters. Why would the wolves take me to him? They already know."

He didn't have an answer. Just a lot of worry. "Let me take you to the hospital. I'll get Simon to check it out and then get you and this Dr. Oltheten together in a safe—"

"Aren't you tired of this?" she interrupted. "Don't you want this to end now? He's got information, I'm sure of it." Her voice was tight and anger radiated out in waves from her body. It hadn't been an hour since they were attacked and here she was pushing for something he knew wasn't safe.

It didn't take him long to figure out what was going on. She was feeling trapped and vulnerable, and for a woman like her, science data was the way out. Right now, she would take any risk to get it.

But that didn't mean it was smart. Or that part of him wasn't cut deeply by her words. Because she didn't just want out of the Detroit Flu problem. She wanted out of the shifter world entirely. She hadn't said it, but he knew that's what she was feeling. And if he had any doubts, then the way she curled away from him was answer enough. She even drew away when he reached out to touch her. And rather than talk, her nose was buried in her cell phone as she studied whatever data had come in this morning.

"Cecilia, we need to think about this."

She looked up and shot him a hard glare. "Either take me to this lab or I'll jump out and call a cab. But either way I'm going."

He believed her. And yes, he could tie her up in some hotel room to keep her safe, but that was the surest way to end any hope of a relationship between them.

"Okay," he said softly. "I'll drive us there, but I'm going to take some precautions, too."

She shrugged. "Do whatever you need to, but get me there."

Fair enough. He turned the car toward the freeway and the Griz home base. Sure, he'd take Cecilia to the very suspicious Gunnolf Lab, but he wasn't doing it alone. And he sure as hell wasn't going there without backup.

* * *

"Hello, Dr. Oltheten? I'm Dr. Cecilia Lu with the CDC." Cecilia gripped the edges of her phone and tried not to see the gun that Hank tucked into his jacket. They were at the Griz home base and everyone was suiting up as if they were going to storm Fort Knox. And while they'd been doing that, she and Alyssa had found a phone number for the Gunnolf Lab. It had taken forever, but they'd managed it. The place had to be doing secret government research. No one else was that paranoid about keeping off the Internet.

Cecilia had called, talked to a receptionist who connected her with receptionist who then handed her over to a lab assistant, and then finally, hallelujah, they had called over Dr. Oltheten himself. Or so she hoped.

"Yes, hello? This is Dr. Oltheten."

Cecilia looked straight into Hank's dark eyes and grinned. She'd finally gotten through! She didn't waste time and got straight to the point. "I know about shifters. I know you tried to tell the world about it and no one believed you. I believe you, Dr. Oltheten. And I want to talk."

There was a long silence on the other end, and for a moment she wondered if they'd been cut off. Then she heard a gasp that might have been a choked off sob. It was hard to tell. But a moment later, he spoke, his voice quavering with his enthusiasm. "The CDC, you say? You know about shifters? Werewolves and cats. Bears, too. Do you know about the bears?"

She released a low chuckle. "Yes, I know about bears. I'm working on the Detroit Flu. I think it's a poison—"

"Yes, yes. In the water."

He already knew. She was getting more hopeful by the second. "I'm working for the cure. Can you help me?"

"I can! Oh, I have been praying for someone such as you. You must come here. I can show you what I've figured out. It's been hard, you know, after I tried to speak in New York. Everyone has been laughing at me. I have been trying and trying to make them see that shifters are real."

The pain in his voice was authentic, and she sympathized. To know something so significant and yet be publicly humiliated for it. It was horrible! "I know they're real, Dr. Oltheten. I'm so sorry that we laughed at you."

"So you will come here? We will solve this problem together, yes?"

She nodded even though he couldn't see it. "Can you email me the data—"

"No, no." The words came out more like a moan. "You don't understand. After New York, no one would hire me. I had to come here. They were the only ones who offered me a job, and the work requires security. Do you have a security clearance?"

She grimaced. "No, I don't."

"Doesn't matter. They monitor all my email, I wouldn't be allowed to send it. But you can come here. You're from the CDC. They know about the crisis. So many people sick with the Flu. That's why you can come now because so many are home sick. Otherwise, I couldn't get you inside."

"Can you just tell me what you've found out?"

"I have to show you the samples. You have to see it for yourself."

At another time, she would have laughed at that suggestion. Data was data. She would see when the science showed it to her. But she wouldn't have believed in shifters if she hadn't seen Hank turn into a bear with her own eyes. She absolutely believed there were shifter issues that had to be seen to be understood.

"What are your samples?" she pressed.

"Shifter blood and tissue. Exact slides of how the water affects the neurons. I think I know how to stop it, but I'm not sure. I need someone else to check my work."

She nodded, her hands actually itching to see what he had. "I need that data, Dr. Oltheten. Can I talk to your boss? What are you researching there?"

"You know I can't say. And my boss is not here right now. It's the only reason I think I can get you inside. He doesn't know I do shifter research. I hide it from him. So long as I do their work, he lets me be." Then there was a muffled sound on the other end of the line. Another person speaking? The noise of a fume hood kicking on? She could only guess. Then he was back, his words rushed. "Can you come soon? It must be soon."

"Dr. Oltheten—"

"I'll tell them at reception. I'll tell them you're bringing me data I need. Show them your credentials. They can't turn away the CDC, right?"

"But Dr. Oltheten—"

"Come soon!" Then he hung up.

She stared at her phone and then looked up at the room at large. Every eye was on her, but she focused on Hank. With short, clear sentences, she repeated her entire conversation. She could see Hank's mouth tighten with every word, but to his credit he didn't interrupt. He waited until she was finished and then shook his head.

"Sounds fishy."

She shrugged, acknowledging his point without agreeing. "Lots of government labs are like that, and we know he's been doing shifter research on the side. It's his passion." When no one argued that, she pressed her point. "The risk is worth it. I need to see his data, and this is the only way."

Everyone looked at Simon who didn't look any happier than Hank did, but in the end he nodded. "We go," he said. "But we do it smart."

No argument from her. She didn't care what precautions they took so long as they left soon. Thankfully, it didn't take them long. Less than ten minutes before Hank turned to her.

"Ready?"

"You have no idea how much," she answered.

She looked around him at a circle of normal-looking guys, if "normal" meant ripped abs, loose clothing, and an animal stillness that was almost creepy. Simon and Alyssa were the leaders. Both looked calm, focused, and in Alyssa's case, heavily armed. Then there was Vic, Simon's beta, and Detective Kennedy. And damn that guy sure looked exhausted, but he appeared grimly official with his detective's badge on a chain around his neck.

There were others, too, but they were assigned to stay behind. It was just the six of them with Cecilia being the only one who refused to acknowledge the danger of the situation. They were all walking to their cars when Cecilia's phone dinged. A quick glance told her it was more information from Dr. Sherilyn, the only shifter scientist on the case. Unlike Dr. Oltheten, she refused a face-to-face and wouldn't talk on the phone unless it was an emergency. It was all emailed info and texts, but this last one was a doozy. She read it the moment she got into Hank's car. There was lots of data, but thankfully Dr. Sherilyn was efficient. She'd put in a summary at the top.

1. The poison worked to activate latent shifter DNA.
2. It was water soluble and would never be picked up by any water filtration system.
3. It stayed in the body far longer than expected. Two to three days before the body was able to clear it from its tissues.
4. It had massive effect on existing shifters. It made them more aggressive, yes. But also more emotional all the way around. It was subtle, but it absolutely colored everything a shifter did for days.

Cecilia had already guessed the first three conclusions, but she stared at the fourth for a long, long time. Shifters who drank the water had heightened emotions and made decisions under the influence of those emotions. Things like passion and love were artificially increased. She looked at Hank while her mind tallied up data points.

Would a man like Hank really fall in love with her in the space of twenty-four hours? Was that logical?

No. It was much more likely that he was showing symptoms of the poison. What he called bonding magic was more likely the influence of the Detroit Flu.

Cecilia stared out the window, not seeing the buildings outside. He'd said he loved her, and she'd believed him. She'd ignored logic and gone with what she'd been feeling. What they'd both felt. But what if all of it was a lie because of the tainted water? What if she'd allowed herself to dream about children and a home in the suburbs when everything would disappear after the poison left his system?

Pain cut deep, shredding dreams she hadn't even realized she wanted so desperately. A family with Hank. A life with a man who calmed her, understood her, and was devoted to her happiness. But his feelings weren't real, and the pain of that realization nearly cut her in two. But she wasn't going to cry. There wasn't time for it. What she was going to do is end the Detroit Flu forever and then she and Hank could sit down and figure things out. Or maybe she'd just go back to Atlanta and pretend that this whole magical nightmare had never happened. Because it was just too much to process.

Hank noticed her distress. He even tried to touch her, but she pulled back. She couldn't allow herself to respond now that she knew his affection was the lingering effects of the poison. She wasn't going to expose herself to feeling anything with him until this was over. Then they'd see where they were. Until that moment, she would just hold herself together by focusing on the problem at hand.

Eventually, they pulled up to Dr. Oltheten's lab. She climbed out and headed straight for the front door. The others parked at different locations, hidden somewhere doing supersecret spy soldier stuff in case there was a problem. They hadn't shared the details with her, and she was hoping that none of it was necessary.

She walked in and met the front desk security guy. He was an older man with dark eyes and a bored expression, but his expression narrowed when he noticed Hank standing a step behind Cecilia. Hank hadn't said a word, but she'd known he would follow her inside. And despite her revelations of the last hour, she was grateful to have him beside her.

His emotions for her might not be real, but hers had solidified the moment she'd seen the wolves attack him. She loved him and wanted to build a life with him. And even if he turned from her tomorrow, at least he was with her now, supporting her as she faced down this damned Flu.

"Hello," she said firmly, drawing the guard's eyes to her. "I'm Dr. Cecilia Lu with the CDC. I'm here to see Dr. Oltheten."

The guard's expression cleared. "Dr. Oltheten is excited to meet you. He's been waiting."

She nodded. "That's excellent. If you'll point the way?"

"Sign here," the man said. He spun a clipboard around, and then he looked at Hank.

"He's with me," she said quickly, hoping to forestall a problem.

"No problem," the guard said. "Always happy to include our ursine friends…assuming he leaves his weapon here."

Cecilia's head snapped up. *Oh hell.* Hank confirmed her thoughts before she could even phrase the question.

"He's a werewolf. This is the wolves' lab."

"Don't get your panties in a twist," the guard said. And yes, there was something definitely wolfish about his expression. "We want to solve this Flu as much as you do."

That sounded reasonable, except now Dr. Oltheten's words didn't add up. Why would he hide shifter research from the werewolves?

"I think Dr. Oltheten needs to come down here to me," she said, but it was too late. Two more guards came out from a back room and though neither of them looked particularly threatening, she knew they weren't about to let her leave. Well, not her, but maybe Hank could escape. She touched his arm. "Maybe you should wait outside—"

"Not a chance."

He wasn't leaving, so they went through the rigmarole of being patted down. Hank gave up two pistols and a knife. How had he hidden those? And she let the guard inspect the briefcase Alyssa had given her, which had nothing but her electronics inside.

"Second floor," the guard said, motioning them to go on through a door set behind the security station. "Right through here."

He wasn't following them and being threatening? Cecilia took that as a good sign. Even better was that it was relatively mundane housing for a high-tech lab: a two-story office building with security and offices on the first floor and the lab on the second.

Hank didn't let her go first up the stairs. He pushed her behind him as he slowly opened the door to the second floor and then stepped inside before her. She watched from the stairwell as his body visibly tensed. She saw his shoulders shoot backward and his hands curl into claws. But he didn't shift. He couldn't since he'd gone bear this morning and had to wait another two days before doing it again. And then he grimly gestured her inside.

She went nervously, but she was determined. She stepped out into a cluttered, messy lab, allowing the heavy fireproof door to thunk closed behind her. She looked around her, mentally sorting through the equipment scattered about. She noted immediately that it was all secondhand, of the ancient model variety. For all that beta Sims had claimed a beautiful lab, this was not what she was used to even at the cash-strapped CDC.

The second thing she noticed was the smell. Hybrid stench, pure and simple. It made Cecilia's eyes burn and her gag reflex kick in. Fortunately, it wasn't bad enough that Cecilia doubled over, but damn, that would take some getting used to. And some industrial-grade ventilation.

And then there were the people. Five plus her and Hank. All men, probably all wolves, and all of them grinning.

That did not bode well, especially since she now recognized one of them as the werewolf alpha Emory Wolf. But closest to her was a middle-aged man with a balding pate and a feverish look in his eyes. He turned to her with the widest grin and approached her quickly.

"Dr. Cecilia Lu. I'm very excited to meet you. Were you at my presentation? I was so sick, but I prayed—literally prayed—that my message would get across. Have you seen my paper? I couldn't get it to upload onto my website, and of course no one would publish it, but you know about shifters."

His words came manically fast, but she followed them. Hell, she'd probably sounded like that a few times in her life. So she shook his hand but she kept her expression cold. "Why did you lie to me, Dr. Oltheten?"

"What? Oh, yes! Sorry." He rubbed a hand over his forehead and across the top of his head. It was like he was smoothing down hair that had long since disappeared. "Emory said you wouldn't come if you knew I was working for him. But I didn't lie about the rest. I have data on the Flu. I know all about it. And he's an excellent employer, I can tell you that for certain. I'm sure we'll get along famously."

She held up her hand to stop him from speaking, and her eyes went to the werewolf alpha. "I don't accept jobs from people who try to abduct me. Or kill people."

He arched a brow. "I don't believe I was the one who killed anyone." His voice trailed suggestively away and his eyes went to Hank. Which was bullshit, and they all knew it. The werewolves had attacked them first. But now that she was here, she might as well make the best of it. If she could get any information out of Dr. Oltheten, then this would be worth it. She hoped. And in the meantime, she'd lead with false bravado before she hightailed it out.

"Whatever," she said with a sigh. "Consider this my official refusal of your job offer." Then her gaze went to Dr. Oltheten. "But I need to see your data. People are dying."

Dr. Oltheten nodded. "You know it's not a virus. It's—"

"Privileged data," the alpha interrupted. He gestured to two of the other men in the room. They nodded, each picked up a cardboard box, and disappeared out a far side door. Meanwhile, the alpha strode forward, his expression congenial. "Come work for me, Dr. Lu. I'm confident that you and Dr. Oltheten will figure out how to stabilize the hybrids. We need them functional, not crazy."

It took her a moment, but she figured it out. "You're creating hybrids on purpose." Not a question, and he didn't deny it.

"I'll admit that this has gotten away from me. I didn't expect so much damage."

"Damage? You mean the dead people?"

He sighed. "That's why you're here. Work with him. Find a way to stabilize the hybrids. It's what we all want."

Cecilia glared at him. "And if I say no?"

He smiled as he headed toward the same distant door. "Don't. People are dying, and he can't figure it out alone." Then he pushed his way through the far door.

"You can't do this," Cecilia cried. "You can't—" Her words abruptly stopped when she heard a heavy thunk. She didn't at first know what the sound was, but Hank did. He spun around and tried to open the near door, but it didn't budge.

He spun immediately to search for the other doors, but Dr. Oltheten held up both his hands. "Don't bother. We're locked in." He exhaled loudly. "I'm sorry it had to come to this, Dr. Lu. The alpha means it quite literally that you'll work for him."

"Bullshit," she snapped. "He can't make me do anything."

"No, he can't. But Travis over there can make life very unpleasant for your friend."

Travis grinned at her. Which is when she noticed he was armed with a pistol and a Taser.

"He can try," Hank growled in response.

"Yes, but I have chemicals everywhere. Including the serum in its original form. It's quite potent." He pointed to a refrigerator filled with vials and bottles where it stood between Travis and Hank. "Nobody would like what happens to them if the shifters get exposed." He looked expectantly up at Hank. "You are a full shifter, right? They get very aggressive. I'm a hybrid now, but I lose control sometimes. It's very scary. In fact," he said with a sigh, "as the only normal human here, Dr. Lu, you'll be in significant danger. And then all the good things we can do together will be lost. You don't want that, do you? I've gone to a significant amount of trouble to wake people up to shifters. I've sacrificed my entire career, you see. My wife, too. She never accepted. Refused to believe and it destroyed our marriage. I had no hope until my sister developed this serum and the alpha funded my research. It's important. You see that right? People need to know about shifters."

Once again, it was hard following all his rapid-fire words, and then when she did, she felt her hands tighten at her sides. "You're saying you're the one who created the Detroit Flu? You're the one—"

"Oh no!" he said, though his expression was more like a man pretending to be humble. "Like I said, my sister and her friend developed it. But she sent me the data and I refined it." His expression tightened. "Or I thought I did. Apparently not everyone handles becoming a hybrid as well as I do."

She gasped as she jerked forward. "Doesn't handle it as well? People are dying! We've had one case—one!—in all of Detroit that wasn't lethal. Most of them lose their higher cortex. They're aggressive, dangerous, and dying!"

His eyes widened. "Oh no. I'm sure that's not true. I mean, the alpha told me there were a few who didn't manage well. That's what he wants us to work on. A way to stabilize the degradation in the frontal cortex, but it's only in a few cases. Look, I changed just fine."

Then he did it with a snap of his fingers. Snap, and he suddenly sprouted fur on his face and body. Tufted ears, cat features, and fur on every exposed piece of skin.

"I even have a tail!" he said as he twisted to show the bulge in his abruptly less-loose pants. His words were slightly garbled thanks to his feline mouth, but she could still understand him. "And smell that?" He inhaled sharply. "I can control the scent now, too! That took some practice, I can tell you, but the alpha helped me learn how. It was easy, don't you see?"

Another snap of his fingers and abruptly he was back to normal. Cecilia couldn't resist a surge of scientific interest. The idea that she could study him closely, his DNA and his shifting abilities. And yes, even the degradation of his frontal cortex, because she sure didn't believe he had his full functioning brain. At least the moral centers had to be deficient. Good God, to infect an entire city was monstrous even if he didn't understand the extent of the damage.

Meanwhile, Hank was less distracted. Though his eyes were on the other shifter, he spoke directly to Dr. Oltheten. "So you did this. You brought the Flu to Detroit." Though he spoke calmly, she could feel the fury radiating out from his body.

"It's not a flu," he corrected with exaggerated patience. "And I simply refined it as a drink instead of an injection. I also helped stabilize it, you know. Otherwise, how could I change so easily—"

"How did you get it into the water system?" Hank interrupted, his tone harsh and judgmental.

Bad idea. Cecilia had worked with countless scientists, and not a one liked being interrupted or judged by someone they considered less educated.

"I did not," the man sniffed as he turned to look at Cecilia. He was close enough now to touch her arm as he pleaded with her. "You understand, don't you? How important it is for shifters to be known. Think of the diseases they can cure. Think of what we can learn from just this—" He snapped his fingers again, and bam, back to a fur face.

She recoiled in a slight cry, in part from the sudden wash of cold that came with the shift. She'd never noticed it before, but then again, she'd never been this close to someone as they changed. And so interesting to see it in action.

Her thoughts stuttered to a halt when she saw a dark blur of movement out of the corner of her eye. She'd been focused on Dr. Oltheten, so she missed Hank leaping to attack Travis. Just like her, the man had been watching Dr. Oltheten and hadn't even realized what was happening until he was flying into the back wall.

The crash was loud as they banged into a worktable. Test tubes jiggled, a couple beakers crashed, but all was a flurry of motion and muscle power. Travis shifted into a wolf the same way as all the others. One second human, the next beast, and a large one at that. He snapped at Hank's neck and scrabbled with paws and claws.

Dr. Oltheten spun around, his voice loud though garbled in his distorted mouth. "Stop this! Do you hear me? You'll get us all killed!"

But all Cecilia could think was, not again. Not this again.

She grabbed Dr. Oltheten's arm because he was gesturing and nearly clocked her with an elbow. It was pure adrenaline reaction that made her duck, then grab. But once she had a hold of him, she gripped the man hard. She didn't want him interfering with Hank.

It happened so fast. She heard the awful sounds of a struggle. Bangs and growls. She'd just grabbed on to Dr. Oltheten when Hank threw the wolf to the side. The wolf was caught in his clothes, she saw, and fumbled to fight and get out of his shirt at the same time. Plus, it was hard to grapple hand to hand when all you had were paws.

But the beast wouldn't stay down long. He was shedding clothes, and his mouth was open, baring long deadly teeth. A man couldn't fight that and win. Not without getting hurt, not without getting—

Hank dove forward into the pile of clothing. Cecilia screamed. She didn't want him going closer to the animal. Not now that the wolf had sprung up onto all four paws. Hank hit the floor, sliding slightly as he dug into the clothes. And then he twisted.

Bang! Bang! Bang!

Sharp reports that had Cecilia dropping to her knees, bringing Dr. Oltheten with her. Gunshots, deafening in her ears. The smell of sulfur and bile, then the copper of blood. She had to see. She had to know if Hank was okay. Was he okay?

She pushed upright on shaky legs to see Hank coming to a stand as well. He had a pistol in his hand as he stared at the floor. "Rookie mistake," he said to no one in particular. "They always shift first. Never think about the weapons at hand."

Then he pushed the pistol into the back of his jeans.

"Why did you do that?" Dr. Oltheten screeched. "Why? We're stuck in here! He's the only one who gets us food. He tells them to open the door to our bedrooms."

"Calm down, Doctor," Hank said, his gaze going to her. "Cecilia? You okay?"

No. No, she wasn't okay. Her heart was hammering in her throat and the smell was bad. Growing worse and worse, in fact. She started gagging. It was Dr. Oltheten.

Hell. He was upset and letting off the hybrid stench. She couldn't breathe.

Hank's eyes snapped into focus. "Calm down!" he bellowed at the doctor as he leapt around a lab table to get to her side. She had a hand pressed to her mouth and was reeling on her feet, but she was able to turn to the doctor.

"Get. Control," she gasped.

His gaze swung to hers, and for the first time she saw how frightened he was. His eyes bulged white and his hand went to hers.

No claws for him. Just a furry hand where he gripped her wrist. The other went to his chest, digging there in panic.

In panic, she realized. The scent came from panic.

"Breathe!" she ordered, but it was too late.

He collapsed down onto one knee, then two. Then his body went rigid and he dropped.

Heart attack. She was sure of it.

She tried to catch him, but he was too heavy. Hank was there, too, flipping the man creature over so that he lay slightly twisted on his back. Cecilia felt for his pulse.

None.

She pushed forward to start chest compressions.

"One, two, three..." she counted as she pushed on the man's chest. But when the time came to give him breath, she didn't know how to get her mouth in the right position. He still had a cat face and the smell this close made her light-headed.

Oh shit. It was worse than that. She reeled off sideways, scrambling for a waste can before she retched. Hank helped her, supporting her body as she heaved in choking gasps and convulsions.

Initially her mind remained on Dr. Oltheten. He was dying and without CPR there was no hope. But once her convulsions started in earnest, she lost track of the dying hybrid. Every part of her was consumed with the ravage of expelling everything inside her. And gratitude that Hank stood with her. That he helped her when her mind was whited out and her body was rejecting the very air she breathed.

Until it was over. Until her body quieted, and she sagged against Hank. She clutched his hand where it wrapped around her torso and she dropped her head against his chest.

"You. Hurt?" she asked.

"Bruises only. I'm sorry you had to see that."

She closed her eyes. What was one more fight in a day that started with violence? "Dr. Oltheten?"

"Gone."

"You should have helped him."

"It was too late. Ever try to give CPR to a cat? It's impossible to get a seal on their face. Not when it's that size."

She didn't want to think about it.

"And with the smell, I probably would have ended up vomiting all over him."

Like she had. Or had been about to until Hank helped her.

"This is insane. It's all…insane."

He didn't argue with her. He just held her. And what could he say? In two days she'd been introduced to shifters, attacked multiple times, and witnessed more violence than in the average Bond film. Well, that last part wasn't true, now that she thought about it. But she'd been up close and personal with it, and she was shaken to her core.

"We should get out of here," she murmured. Escape. That's all she wanted right then. To just escape.

"We will. Travis didn't have any keys on him, but we should be rescued soon."

She frowned as she looked up at him. "Rescued? How—"

The doors released with a loud *thunk*, cutting off her words. A second later, Alyssa poked her head inside. "You okaaay?" The last word slowed down as she took in the scene. "Ambulance?"

Hank shook his head.

"Dr. Lu?" she said, her expression excruciatingly sympathetic. "I know this is a lot—"

Her words cut off as Simon came striding in.

"We breached the minute the doors locked," he said. Then his gaze cut to her. "How are you doing, Dr. Lu?"

Why did everybody keep asking her that? She was fine. Though she'd just emptied her stomach and couldn't put enough strength into her body to stand. "Dr. Oltheten..." She took a steadying breath. "He created the serum. Him and his sister."

Simon nodded as if he'd already figured that out. "Any idea what was in those cardboard boxes they took out?"

Hank shook his head, while Cecilia started thinking well enough to ask questions. "How do you know about the boxes? How did you know when the doors locked?"

Hank touched her briefcase. "Your tablet and phone have been broadcasting this whole time. And mine."

She blinked. Right. That was a sensible precaution. Then Hank turned to Simon.

"Did you catch anyone?"

"We've taken control of the building, but Wolf never showed. We covered all the exits but—"

Alyssa cursed as she poked at her tablet. "Got the building specs. There's a basement. I'll bet my next paycheck there's a tunnel out from there and a secret exit."

"No bet," Simon growled. Then he focused back on Cecilia. "Can you figure this science out? From his notes?"

Hank turned to her, his voice soft. "You don't have to," he said gently. "You don't—"

She stared at him. "Are you kidding?" She was finally able to grab at a normal touchstone again. Science. The solution to the Detroit Flu. All right here. "Anyone see a laptop anywhere?"

"Over there," Simon said pointing to a work area hidden from her view by a cheap microwave.

She stood on shaky legs and started walking. Hank hovered beside her, a hand outstretched just in case. She didn't need it, and he didn't force the issue by touching her anyway, which actually made her sad. She really wanted him to hold her, but she was afraid that if she crumpled now, she'd never stop screaming.

So she sat down in front of Dr. Oltheten's computer and started typing. Lucky her, the guy didn't have password protection. What he did have was layers and layers of data that she could sink into until she forgot absolutely everything else.

"Don't look at it now," Simon interrupted. "Just point at what you want to keep. I want us out of here in twenty minutes."

"Yeah," agreed Hank. Then he looked at Cecilia and added an explanation. "We didn't get the wolf alpha, just some of his men." She stared at him, the message still not computing so he tried again. "They could come back at any moment."

The wolves back here. She swallowed and closed up the laptop.

"Get a box. I'll show you what we need to take."

Chapter 22

Don't give me that bullshit, Dennis. Tell me what happened."

Hank watched Cecilia, his body tight, his senses on alert. There was no reason for it. They were in the Griz headquarters and perfectly safe. Simon had installed sentries, video cameras, and God only knew what kinds of more subtle security in this converted Ace Hardware store. Since Alyssa's home had burned to the ground, they had moved in upstairs and Simon was taking no chances with his mate. Fort Knox probably had less security.

That made this the safest place to come with all of Dr. Oltheten's science shit. Cecilia had set up in a back corner and had been poring over them most of the night. Around midnight, she'd called Dr. Sherilyn and started talking data blots and adrenal compounds. Together they'd come up with a solution or so they hoped. A triple cocktail of existing medicines that would suppress the conversion to hybrid, assuming the victim got it in time.

Then they had to wait for a victim while convincing Dennis to try the treatment. A young woman had come in to the ER around two a.m. Dennis had administered the medication and now two hours later, everybody tried to listen in as Cecilia got an update.

"What does it matter where I got the idea?" Cecilia huffed into her phone. "It was magic."

Hank flashed her a warm smile, but she didn't see it. She was too deep in her argument with Dennis. Part of him was grateful. She'd been terrified not once, but twice today and the violence of it had shaken her to her core.

He'd watched her draw into herself, her eyes becoming haunted and her body strung tight. But ever since they'd grabbed Dr. Oltheten's data, her confidence had come back. She was firmly ensconced in the one area she ruled supreme: science. And as more and more of the pieces had fallen into place, she'd come alive in a way he'd never seen before.

This was her life's calling. She solved medical mysteries, and she would never be happy doing anything else. That was fine with him. He had no desire to stop her and would, in fact, follow her to whatever city she landed in. But what if she didn't want him around? What if she buried herself so deeply into science that she rejected all things magic?

She wouldn't be the first person to choose to go blind again. And the happier she got talking about chemical compounds, the more Hank felt her slipping away from him. He was already hovering too close, standing too much in her line of sight, just in the hopes that she wouldn't forget him.

But that hadn't helped. It had been over an hour since she'd even looked at him.

"Fine," she all but bellowed into the phone. "I prayed, Dennis. Happy? I prayed for a miracle, and I got one. Now for the love of

God—" Her words cut off as she shot to her feet. Across the room, Simon looked up. Alyssa was already halfway across the room, not even trying to hide that she was eavesdropping. "Are you sure? What about the blood work? Yes, yes, that weird enzyme I sent you." She dropped her head back as she glared at the ceiling. "Prayer. God. Miracle. That's how. Now is there any trace…?"

She abruptly crowed. A full-throated cry of exultation. She even did a few dance steps while she clutched her phone.

"Keep checking. I want updates every hour." She listened for a few more moments. Made a half-dozen illegible notations on a pad of paper, then she thumbed off her phone and turned to the room at large.

"It works," she said before anyone could ask. "At least that's the preliminary results. If we catch a Flu victim early enough, the cocktail halts the conversion. They don't become hybrids and…" She held up her hands during her dramatic pause. "There are no signs of brain deterioration." She grinned. "They don't go crazy."

The room erupted in cheers. Not just Hank who had been grinning from the moment she started dancing, but everyone in the room.

"You did it!" he said as he hugged her. She squealed in delight as he swung her around. But the moment he set her down again, other people were there. Simon clasped her hand and gave her one of his very rare smiles. Then Alyssa pulled her into an impromptu dance that had everyone laughing.

Cheers and congratulations all around, and though Hank was as happy as anyone here, he couldn't help but feel like the end was on the horizon. She'd solved the mystery of the Detroit Flu. She'd found a way to stop the poison's effect on a body, and so her task here was done. The quarantine would be lifted, she'd be off to the next challenge, and where would he be? Trailing along behind her like a lost puppy? Would she even want him there? Science was her life. It was hard to believe she had any room left for him.

The celebration continued for a few more minutes, but eventually Simon held up his hand. One by one, people went back to their tasks, which left the alpha looking at Cecilia with serious eyes.

"I need to talk with you, Dr. Lu."

She nodded, her expression sobering. "I know what you're going to ask."

Really? Because Hank had no idea.

"You're wondering if I'm going to publish the results. If the cure we've found can be distributed without exposing shifters."

Simon leaned against the table, his arms crossed as he looked hard at her. Then he turned to his mate. "Alyssa, can you summarize what you and Hank figured out about Dr. Oltheten?"

The woman nodded, her expression grave as she tapped on her tablet. "Hank and I went through all the personal stuff that we could find. It was pretty disorganized, but it goes like this. Dr. O and his sister were both cougar shifters, but he never manifested. Both were pretty gifted science-wise, but the family was a bit loony tunes. Anyway, after the wolf-cat war, their numbers were low, so sis and a psycho friend developed the serum that activated latent shifter DNA."

Cecilia frowned. "When did that happen?"

"Last spring. The Gladwin bears were on the front line for that one. We should have figured out the last name connection—Oltheten isn't a common name—but we're new to being in charge here. I'm still sifting through the old alpha's files."

"What happened to the sister?"

"She's gone, too. What we didn't realize is that before being captured, sis sent all her stuff to her brother. He never manifested as a shifter and always wanted to. Worse, his wife never believed, so he got it in his head to…"

Cecilia exhaled loudly. "To tell everyone. Get as many people as he could to believe so that she would finally see." It wasn't phrased as a question, but Alyssa answered it anyway.

"Yeah. That conference in New York wasn't his only attempt at getting the word out. He tried multiple times to tell his boss at Pfizer with the usual minor disasters: flu bug, electrical outage, lost data. Then he printed everything on paper, called a meeting of all the higher-ups, and got hit by a car on the way to the meeting."

Hank winced even though he knew all this information already. Still, it sucked to know the truth and despite every attempt to get the information out, magic made sure he was treated as a fool.

"He ended up fired when he distributed copies of his paper anyway. From there, he tried teaching high school science, but he kept trying to talk to the kids about werewolves."

Now Cecilia was cringing. "That couldn't have gone well."

"It didn't. He was fired, which is when Emory Wolf got his paws into him. He had his sister's notes by then and was getting ready to present his paper at the big conference in New York."

"Where he got food poisoning."

"And his wife left him. That was when he went completely bonkers."

Double whammy. Lost his career and his family in the same week.

"So he decided to infect the entire city?" Cecilia asked. "Why?"

"Near as we can tell, he hoped to make enough shifters that it couldn't be kept secret anymore."

Then Simon pressed the point. "It destroyed him, killed a ton of people, and all because he thought he was smarter than magic." He stopped speaking then, but his gaze was heavy on Cecilia.

Hank wanted to cross to her, to wrap his arm around her in support. He wanted her to know that he would care for her no matter what, but she had to see the example in Dr. Oltheten. He didn't want to distract her from the lesson. Brainiacs always thought they could outsmart everything. People, acts of nature, and magic. It had destroyed the Oltheten siblings, and he desperately hoped she would learn from their disaster.

He watched her closely, hoping for a clue as to which way she would jump. And in the end, she set down her tablet.

"This goes against everything I've ever believed. You know that, right?"

Simon nodded. "We know."

Cecilia didn't answer, and as the seconds ticked away, Hank felt his gut clench and his blood pressure rise. She was playing with her life. Dr. Oltheten had ultimately died from a heart attack because he couldn't live with the world's blindness. He didn't want that for her. He needed her to be alive and safe. So when the silence stretched too long, he stepped forward.

At first, he didn't think she'd accept his touch, but she didn't draw away. Their fingers entwined, and she gripped him with bruising force, but she kept her eyes and her body away from him.

"Dr. Lu…" Simon began, a warning in his voice.

"I won't publish, but I don't have to like it."

Hank spoke for the first time. "What if you could publish? To a shifter journal. I know it won't win you the Nobel prize—"

"Or any career recognition," Alyssa added.

"But it would get the information out to shifters everywhere. And they're the ones who need it."

Cecilia didn't answer, but she did lift her head. In that moment, Simon pushed the advantage. "I've been thinking about that exact thing, Dr. Lu. Shifters need a clearinghouse for scientific information. Dr. Sherilyn does what she can, but she's only one person and she has responsibilities to the university. But what about you?"

Cecilia frowned. "What about me?"

"Would you like a job running a shifter CDC? All the clans would pay to cover your costs. You could sort through the data we gather, pick projects to fund or even research yourself. You want to dig into our biology, don't you? And we need someone to help with shifter specific problems. You might not win a Nobel prize, but you would—"

"Save all of us," Hank said, when he really meant, save him. Because the idea that she might live and work here gave him hope that they could build a great life together. Here in Detroit.

He searched her face, praying that she was reaching for the same solution he saw. The exact job Simon was offering. He could see that she was thinking about it. She got a softness in her mouth as her brows narrowed over her eyes. But just when he thought she'd say yes, she pulled her fingers away from his.

"Two job offers in one day," she said. "I don't know what to think."

The first job offer hadn't been an offer at all, but a kidnapping by the wolves. That she equated the two set Hank's teeth on edge. Simon's, too, but neither pressed it. It was nearly dawn and they'd all been running full tilt for much too long.

"Well," Simon finally said, "let us know—"

Alyssa's curse interrupted his words and the alpha's head snapped over to study his mate.

"What is it?"

Alyssa looked up, dread in her expression. "I just noticed the time. Detective Kennedy hasn't checked in. He's forty-three minutes late."

Simon's expression flattened. "Call him."

She held up her phone. "Just did. Voice mail. He's probably off on one of his hunches again." She didn't look like she fully believed it, but then again, she didn't know Ryan like Hank did. The man only loosely followed any type of authority and had paid the price for that more than once. But that was before Simon took over. Except the new alpha didn't seem to like the detective's independent streak any more than Nanook had.

"Doesn't anyone follow orders around here?" Simon groused.

Alyssa arched a skeptical brow. "The minute there's a US military sign above our door, then you can expect standard protocol. Otherwise, as far as I'm concerned, you're all a bunch of cats and just as impossible to herd."

"We're bears," Simon grumbled, though there was humor in his tone.

"That only makes you bigger and more surly."

It was the normal banter between those two. Grumpy on one end, snarky on the other. Personally, Hank liked it, but it wasn't his place to comment especially when his alpha gave him a direct order.

"Hank, get home, get some rest. I'm going to need you full strength very soon. There's a war coming with wolves and you're my only medic."

Hank nodded and was about to salute when Cecilia started. "A war? What do you mean?"

Simon turned to her. "Your part is done, Dr. Lu. You've solved the medical crisis, but the wolves still have boxes of that poison. Dr. Oltheten merely created the serum. Emory Wolf is the one dumping it into the water supply. We've got to stop him."

"But the police—"

"Detective Kennedy is the police, and one of us. But I don't want to send normals against a pack of crazed werewolves who are trying to poison the city. Do you?"

Cecilia's cheeks colored, and she shook her head. "No, of course not. I just thought…"

"You thought it was over, and it is for you, but it isn't for us." His tone dropped to a serious note. "And it isn't for Hank, either. I'm going to need him."

She paled and again, Hank wanted to wrap her in his arms. Hell, he needed the comfort, too. The last thing he wanted was to step into another war. He left the military because he was sick of the violence. But Simon was right, there was no one in the city except the Griz who could take on a pack of psycho werewolves.

He opened his mouth to say something, but Cecilia held up her hand. "I get it," she said, her voice tight. "I don't like it, but I get it."

And she wanted no part of it. She didn't say that last sentence, but Hank heard it loud and clear. And wasn't that the last nail in his coffin? Because they might have found a way through if she could still have her science. But now she was looking at staying with a man who was steeped in violence. He wouldn't blame her one bit for blocking him entirely out of her life.

Meanwhile, Simon had no more time for them. He turned to

Alyssa and the tablet she held up to him. "Who have we got who can give back up? Where's Vic?"

Hank turned his back on the conversation, more interested in what Cecilia wanted to do. She'd dropped her hand but her back was rigidly tight.

"You don't have to make a decision tonight…" he started, but the words froze when she shot him a look.

"Ever try not thinking about something, Hank?"

He had. He was. He was trying to *not* think about her leaving for the CDC in Atlanta. So he tried a different tack. "Will you let me take you to my home? Will you let me protect you while you sleep?"

Her lips twisted into a pale shadow of a smile. "And when will you sleep? Who will protect you?"

Not a real question, except apparently in her mind. "I'll be fine," he said, "as long as you're safe." It wasn't a lie. A very deep part of him knew that to be the absolute truth.

"And if you're dead in a war? Then who will keep me safe?"

He flashed her a weak smile. "I'm trying not to think about that."

She chuckled. A sweet, mellow sound completely at odds with her words. "Let's go. I don't want to talk about us here anyway."

Talk about us? Words that struck terror in every man's heart.

Chapter 23

Cecilia didn't question Hank's assumption that she'd go home with him. Where else would she go? Her hotel room was wrecked, and the idea of finding another one just left her cold. She didn't want to be alone; she wanted to be with him. And the minute she stepped into his apartment, she knew this was the place for her.

Zen peace, plants everywhere, and the scent of him clean and strong. His personality and his quiet pervaded everything and that was just what she wanted right then. Well, that plus him with her. Safe, not in a war, and holding her through the night.

Her breath caught at the thought of that, of living here with him. She'd need an office for her work, but his quiet presence would be everywhere and that would fill a well inside her that she hadn't even known was empty until a couple days ago. Eventually they'd have a nursery for their child, probably at a new place. Somewhere near a park where a little girl could run wild or a boy could jump from trees into his father's arms.

The image ached in her heart. She wanted it so desperately that her eyes searched out the window for the nearest patch of green. Hank was setting her luggage down next to his bed, but he heard her breath catch. He turned to her, a question in his dark eyes, and she swallowed.

She had to talk to him. She had to tell him the truth about their bonding, but she didn't want to risk losing him. What if he found out that their bond was fake? That it would disappear in a couple days? Would he wait out the time and then set her free? On paper they had nothing in common, but she couldn't believe how well she fit with him. When she got intense, he kept her centered. When she was attacked, he kept her safe. When she was afraid, he was there, even in her thoughts. And when magic happened anywhere in her life, it was because he was with her.

What if he took that magic away? What would she do then? Her life before meeting him seemed so empty and dull. She was still fighting her fears when he stepped right in front of her. He entwined his fingers with hers and pressed a kiss to her forehead.

"It's okay, Cecilia. You're safe here."

"I know." He always kept her safe.

"Whatever you have to say, I can take it. It'll be okay. We'll figure it out."

Would they? Together? God, she hoped so.

He pulled her to sit on the bed. It was so tempting to just lay down. She'd sink into the mattress, he'd wrap his arms around her, and she'd have him for a little bit longer. But when she started leaning toward the pillow, he touched her chin.

"We can sleep now. God knows you need it. But will you sleep well? Can you tell me—"

"The poison in the water lasts about two days in the body."

He stared at her, and no wonder. She'd just blurted out a random fact like it was the end of the world. It was, but he'd need to understand the rest. "This crap they put in the water…it doesn't just make shifters aggressive. It heightens all their emotions. Anger becomes fury. Joy become ecstasy." She swallowed and forced the next words out. "Attraction becomes bonding." She touched his face. "Your connection to me, this deep need…it's not magic. It's biochemical. And it'll go away…" She shrugged. "Pretty soon now, I think. I know you haven't had any city water since we met, but you drank it before, right? Before you knew about the taint."

Her words came out very fast. It was the only way she could tell him that he wasn't in love with her. That what he felt wasn't real. Because, damn it, what *she* felt was vividly real. She wanted to spend her life in his arms. She wanted to have his babies. And she wanted to sleep beside him every night and wake to his smile every morning.

And why the hell was he just sitting there staring at her when her world was ending?

"Hank?"

He touched a finger to her forehead, spinning it in circles at her temple. "Your brain is working very fast right now, isn't it?"

"What?"

"You're thinking all sorts of things."

She nodded. Of course, she was. She'd just told the love of her life that his feelings weren't real.

"Cecilia, I need you to listen to me very carefully, okay?"

She nodded.

"I haven't had Detroit water for years. I hate the taste of it in anything. I use bottled water for everything except the shower." He touched her chin, tilting her head up to meet his gaze. "The poison doesn't go in through the skin, does it?"

"No. You have to drink it, and not just a little bit."

"I guess I'm in love with you for real then." He stroked his thumb across her lips, making them plump with a tingling fire. "I love you, Cecilia. It's not biochemistry. I don't even think it's the magic. It's real love because you're the most amazing woman I've ever met."

"I am?"

He chuckled. "You make me smile."

She reared back. "That's it? You're in love because I make you smile? Why aren't you married to Comedy Central, then?"

He grinned. "Because I want you. I want your brilliance and your intensity in my life. I want you to tease me when I'm too serious and let me feed you when you forget. I want to protect you, and hold you, and do lots of other wonderful things with you." He waggled his eyebrows, and his eyes seemed to glow in the early morning light. "I love you."

"I love you, too," she whispered.

Then it was time for him to start thinking. She could see it in his eyes. The way his gaze seemed to rove over her face as if he were looking for the answer there when she'd just said it out loud.

"Are…are you sure?" he asked. "I'm…my life right now is pretty scary."

She nodded. "I'm terrified for you, but that doesn't change how I feel. I need you in my life. I need your calm center and your magical smile. There it is!"

His lips had curved, and she loved it so much she traced it with her fingers.

"I know it doesn't make sense. We just met a couple days ago when you kidnapped me." She frowned. "You kidnapped me!"

"It was the only way," he said, an apology in his eyes. "And I was under orders."

"I know." She pressed her lips to his. He clung to her mouth as she teased across his. And when she pulled back, she stroked his face. "I can't make sense of it, but I know it's true. I love you. Will you… Can we…" Hell, what exactly was she trying to ask? "I want to stay in Detroit for a while. I want to stay with you and make this work."

"Yes," he said, almost before she stopped asking. "Yes, yes."

"Then you can't die in this war with the werewolves."

He didn't laugh off her words but took them seriously. "I'm very careful," he said softly. "And I'm very good."

Yeah, she knew that. She'd seen that every minute they'd been together. But suddenly, she wasn't so interested in discussing this anymore. He loved her, and it wasn't because of some poison in the water. She loved him, and it wasn't because of some magical bond. It was because he was magical, and they fit together perfectly.

So she kissed him again, this time using her tongue to tease at the edges of his lips. He responded with a low growl. He clutched her head as he thrust into her mouth. What started as a tease became a hot invasion. Their tongues dueled, and her body heated to inferno.

She let herself fall backward onto the bed, bringing him with her. He never left her mouth, but his hands no longer needed to hold her in place. They started to rove down her sides and underneath her tunic. She tugged at his tee, trying to drag it off him without breaking their kiss.

In the end, they had to split apart. He rolled to his side, his breath fast and tight. "I know you're tired, but—"

"Get naked now."

He arched a brow at her order, but didn't argue. While she stripped, he shucked his clothing. And then they just looked at each other. She was seated naked on the bed as she admired him in the early light. Sculpted muscles, sleek and dark, and touched with rose from the dawn. His penis thrust forward, large and proud, but it was his eyes that drew her the most. She saw steadiness there, even in the grip of passion. And she saw magic in him. The animal that prowled closer to her, setting one hand and then a knee on the bed and the man in him who touched her with gentleness and understood her in a way no one ever had.

How could she not love him?

"Get a condom," she said.

He froze, his weight barely on the bed. "What if it breaks?"

She smiled. "What if this thing between us is love, not magic? What if you're not bonded to me, you're just really good at being in love?"

"Maybe," he said, though he didn't seem like he meant it. "But what if you're wrong and you get pregnant anyway?"

"Then I'll love our child with all my heart." She arched a brow. "And Simon will be pleased to have a new employee studying shifter medicine."

His eyes flashed bright at that, but his words were low and predatory. "I don't want to talk about Simon."

She slowly arched her back, bringing her breasts into prominent view. "Me neither."

He was on her before she could do more. His hands on her

breasts, his mouth on hers. It felt like she was being completely surrounded by him, caressed everywhere, and all she could do was cling to him as she rode out the tide. He obliterated her thoughts, dropped her straight into an ocean of sensuous attention, and had her arching and moaning like a wild animal in heat.

It was wonderful. He sucked on her breasts, he stroked her clit, and made her cry out whenever he moved from one part of her body to another. So thorough. So perfect.

And when he spread her thighs, he remembered the condom though she'd long since forgotten about it. And while she lay there open and panting, he hooked his arms under her knees.

"Are you sure?" he asked, his body gloriously tight and hard as he waited at her entrance.

In response, she tightened her legs and pulled herself forward onto him. She didn't move that far, but it was enough. She saw his nostrils flare and his abdominals tense, and then he thrust hard.

Impaled.

Filled.

She never thought she'd love those words, but at this moment, he was everything to her. His body moved like poetry above her. The stretch of him inside her was like bursting into something new. As if she needed him inside her to become more than she'd been before.

She gripped him everywhere she could. She held him inside as he thrust against her. And she clung to his broad shoulders and caught his gaze with her own.

His tempo increased, every impact ratcheting her higher, hotter, hungrier.

She needed him now. She needed whatever it was she was becoming. And she needed this.

Him.

Now.

Her orgasm burst through her. Like her entire body compressed then vaulted forward.

Again and again. To the stars.

He slammed into her one last time then joined her. His body shook, and his eyes took on the light of a thousand suns.

Beauty. Wonder. Together.

They soared in a timeless bliss. And when it ended, the descent came by degrees.

Her body relaxed, languid and weak. He fell forward onto her, covering her with tiny kisses wherever he could touch. Her knees spread, and he let them fall to the mattress. And still he kissed her, adding tiny licks with his tongue.

Her neck. Her face. The curve of her ear. Even into her hair. He pressed his lips to hers over and over while she rested in the bliss of his attention.

Until her mind came back online. It was an easy shift, like stepping onto a moving walkway. But once there, she realized there was a special intensity to his kisses. A joy and a desperation she didn't understand.

"Hank?" she asked as she stroked her hand across his head. "Hank, what is it?"

"I love you," he said.

"I love you, too," she answered, knowing that there was more he wanted to say. But he didn't speak until she pulled his head up so they could look eye to eye.

"What's going on?"

"The condom broke."

She stared at him, the moving walkway in her mind shuddering to a halt.

"Cecilia? Are you okay?"

It took her a moment to decide. She had to mentally tally every part of her mind, body, and soul. Was she okay with loving a magical man? Was she okay with having his magical children? Was she okay with experiencing this kind of bliss every night and day for the rest of her life?

"Yeah," she said as her smile grew. "I'm wonderful. How about you?"

"I've never experienced joy this perfect before."

She touched his face, teased his furrowed brow, then tapped him playfully on the nose. "Silly," she said. "It's not joy. It's magic."

"Nah," he said as he pressed a kiss to her nose. "It's love. Perfect, awesome, amazing love."

When an alpha meets his match…

Don't miss *TAMING HER MATE*, the next book in the Grizzlies Gone Wild series, by *USA Today* bestselling author Kathy Lyons, available Spring 2019.

A preview follows.

Chapter 1

Duty or survival?

Detective Ryan Kennedy grimaced as he considered his options. He was soaking wet and stank as he crept through the Detroit sewer system. He had a hunch that the asshole wolves who had poisoned the city water were down here somewhere. All the cops who weren't at home puking were scouring the water supply for where the crap was being poured in. Ryan was the only idiot looking at sewage because he guessed the damned dogs were using this system to get around.

He was right.

Two werewolves trudged just ahead of him. They were men dressed in hip waders and tees, their scruffy jaws working as they groused about carrying boxes of something through the sewer system. Ryan would bet his grizzly hump that the boxes contained jugs of the poison that had been dumped in Detroit's water system over the last couple weeks. More than half of the city was at home sick, many hallucinating. A bunch more were outside rioting thanks to the aggression the poison caused. But that was nothing compared to what it did to shifters.

Regular shifters became like the Hulk with aggression and strength to match. Then there were the unlucky few who became hybrids, neither animal nor man but some hideous combination of both. Most went insane within a couple days. And these two bastards were perpetrators who had brought Detroit to the edge of destruction.

He had to stop them. The only problem was that he was alone down here, his phone didn't work through all the concrete, and the passageway narrowed ahead. No way could he follow the werewolves without being spotted.

He'd wanted to see where they were taking the poison. His only hope now was to arrest them and get them to explain the entire operation so he could stop it.

Which meant he had a choice. Attack them here, without backup, and hope to get answers. Or head back to safety and a cell signal to report what he'd found. Regulations and survival said to head back. There was no guarantee he'd win against the wolves. It was two to one and being able to shift into a grizzly bear wasn't helpful in the narrow spaces of the sewer system. But if he let them go, he'd lose the chance to arrest them and get information on where and why they were poisoning all of Detroit.

Duty or survival.

Duty always won. And right now, his primary duty was to the people of Detroit and preventing more of the poison from getting into the water supply. That meant grabbing those boxes and arresting at least one of the bastards carrying them.

He pulled out his gun and tried to judge angles. A miss in these tunnels could mean death on a ricochet, but he'd have to risk it. Or maybe the wolves would be smart and just surrender.

Yeah, right.

"Police. You're under arrest. Stop right there!"

His voice boomed over the sound of the water and echoed impressively. The wolves didn't care. One took off, box in hand. The other pulled out a gun.

Shit. Ryan ducked back. But then instead of shooting at him, the werewolf shot through the cardboard box.

WTF?

Pale green liquid gushed from the hole in the box. The serum. And the guy held up the box enough to guzzle some of it.

Oh hell. Ryan had never seen what the undiluted stuff did to shifters. The guy had no sooner swallowed twice than suddenly he was busting out of his waders in full wolf mode. The thing let out a roar and launched himself into an attack. Ryan got off a few shots—only way to handle a hopped-up werewolf—but then he was out of time.

His human skin couldn't take the attack, so he shifted straight into bear mode. He was in grizzly form by the time the werewolf hit him square in the chest. Or what would have been his chest if he'd remained human.

The werewolf had enough size and speed that Ryan slammed against the curved tunnel wall. His head was forced down, right onto the bastard's neck, and he bit down with all his grizzly strength.

The wolf howled and scrabbled with his feet against Ryan's belly, claws raking through the fur. Damn it, he was about to be disemboweled. So he threw the wolf off him, making sure to slam him as hard as he could against the wall. If Ryan was lucky, the creature's neck would break.

He wasn't lucky, but Ryan was free. The wolf spun around, teeth bared as blood dripped from his neck. Ryan's belly burned, but he wasn't ripped open, so he faced off as best he could in the narrow space. He tried to think of a better way to do this. He was excruciatingly aware that the first wolf was long gone, and the jug of poison was still pouring into the water. But his biggest problem was the super-crazed wolf that wasted no time in attacking again.

The creature was strong for a wolf, thanks to the poison, and Ryan struggled to grapple with him. The creature launched straight at his face, mouth open, claws extended. Ryan kept himself steady, never breaking eye contact. He needed to see if the wolf was rational. The snarls suggested no, but the relentless attack said yes. He could handle a rational werewolf, fight and not kill it so he could question the guy later. But if the creature was all animal, then there would be no end except in death.

On and on, the wolf kept coming while Ryan grew tired slamming the thing aside and hoping for a lucky blow. The creature was expending ten times more energy than Ryan, and yet still seemed as ferocious as at the beginning.

Ryan was already gasping for breath as he kept batting the wolf aside. Eventually, the creature would be too beaten up to rise again, at least that was the hope. But so far, the wolf wasn't slowing down. And it was lightning fast while Ryan struggled to keep up. Worse, his arms ached from the steady impact. His bear claws had scored a half-dozen hits, there was blood splatter all over the walls, but the werewolf would not stop.

Damn it, why wouldn't the thing tire?

Ryan caught the wolf hard under the jaw, slamming him to the side. The impact reverberated in the space as the creature slid to the floor, legs twitching. Was he down? The creature's eyes opened to slits, and Ryan saw madness there. Damn it, there was no man left. Only an insane determination to keep fighting. That meant—

Two shots exploded nearby, the echo deafening. Ryan flinched while the wolf's head exploded in a gory mess.

Hell. No way to interrogate the guy now, though he was grateful for the reprieve.

Ryan's arms dropped to his sides while his lungs worked like bellows for breath. The fight had taken a lot out of him, and he needed a moment to recover. Eventually, his breath eased enough for him to face his rescuer. So he turned only to see a man aim his gun straight at Ryan.

No!

He started to shift back to human. He needed to show that he was sane and not a shifter hopped up on the poison, but he didn't get the chance.

Two impacts like sledgehammers, straight to the torso.

He went down.

About the Author

Kathy Lyons is the wild, adventurous half of *USA Today* bestselling author Jade Lee. A lover of all things fantastical, Kathy spent much of her childhood in Narnia, Middle Earth, Amber, and Earthsea, just to name a few. There is nothing she adores more than turning an ordinary day into something magical, which is what happens all the time in her books. Winner of several industry awards, including the Prism Best of the Best Award, a *Romantic Times* Reviewers' Choice Award, and Fresh Fiction's Steamiest Read, Kathy has published more than fifty romance novels, and she's just getting started.

Check out her latest news at:

KathyLyons.com

Facebook.com/KathyLyonsBooks

Twitter: @KathyLyonsAuth

Instagram: @KathyLyonsAuthor

You Might Also Like...

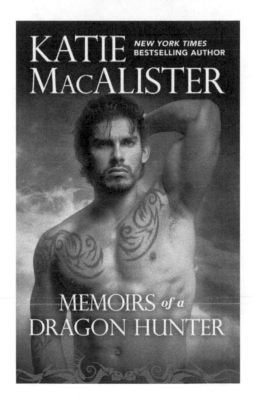

USA TODAY BESTSELLING AUTHOR

MEGAN ERICKSON

FINAL DAY

A WIRED & DANGEROUS NOVELLA

CELIA

New York Times Bestselling Author

KYLE

Tiger's Claim

A Shifter
Rogues Novel

TWISTED TRUTHS

NEW YORK TIMES BESTSELLING AUTHOR

REBECCA
ZANETTI

CPSIA information can be obtained
at www.ICGtesting.com
Printed in the USA
LVHW02s1644020918
588936LV00001B/54/P